Everything
ABOUT
YOU

USA TODAY BESTSELLING AUTHOR
LEA COLL

D1073275

EVERYTHING ABOUT YOU

Copyright © 2023 by Lea Meyer

All Rights Reserved.

This book contains material protected under International and Federal Copyright Laws and Treaties. Any unauthorized reprint or use of this material is prohibited. No part of this book may be reproduced or transmitted in any form or by any means, electronic or mechanical, including photocopying, recording, or by an information and retrieval system without express written permission from the author.

All characters and storylines are the property of the author and your support and respect is greatly appreciated.

This is a work of fiction. Names, characters, places and incidents either are the product of the author's imagination or are used fictitiously, and any resemblance to actual persons, living or dead, business establishments, events, or locales is entirely coincidental.

Get the Free Novella

When you sign up for Lea's Newsletter.

One

SILAS

"If you'll excuse me, I'm here to enjoy the wedding."

Her hair was pulled back in some complicated knot that bared her neck and shoulders. Her dress wrapped around her body in a way that made me want to unravel and discover her secrets.

Gia brushed past me, her floral scent lingering in the air as she strode with purpose down the aisle toward my hotel.

Irritation burned in my gut as I followed her. I hadn't known *she'd* be here. Gia Giovanni was my best friends' younger sister and the woman who never failed to spark every one of my competitive instincts.

I couldn't believe she'd shown up at one of my weddings. As the owner of a wedding planning service, Happily Ever Afters, she was my primary competitor when it came to weddings.

I kept a wedding planner on staff, Hannah, and didn't allow couples to use any other planner. A few years ago, Gia came to me with her offer to plan weddings for her brides at my resort. I could torture myself by working with the woman who drove me crazy, or I could distance myself from her. I didn't need the temptation.

I loved the Giovanni family, and the last thing I'd ever do was mess around with their youngest daughter and sister, no matter how much I wanted to usher her into the nearest closet and have my way with her. She was off-limits. Forbidden. And it only made her more attractive.

Gia opened the door to head inside the hotel. I grabbed it just in time, and she looked back at me in surprise.

"What are you really doing here?" I hissed into her ear.

I stood so close to her that I felt the ever-so-slight tremble in her body.

She pulled away from me, but I followed her, looking for somewhere I could talk to her alone. When I spotted a corner covered by a large potted plant, I grabbed her elbow and guided her there.

She looked up at me with a challenge in her eyes. "Why do you think I'm here?"

I braced my hand above her head. "To check me out."

I'd clearly lost my mind because I was fairly sure she was here to scope out my five-star resort, not get in my pants, but I loved the way her eyes flashed with red-hot anger. Getting a rise out of Gia had always been easy and unbelievably satisfying.

She placed the palm of her hand on my chest, right above my pounding heart, as if to push me away. Instead, her fingers curled around the material of my shirt, making my heart race. "You wish."

I smirked. "I wouldn't touch my friends' younger sister."

She tipped her head to the side. "Then why did you drag me into this corner?"

"I won't let you get away with whatever you're up to," I growled, a little distracted by her proximity.

She crossed her arms over her chest, pushing the globes of her breasts higher. "*I'm* not up to anything."

One blonde strand of hair fell from her updo and curled over her forehead. I wondered if the dyed-blonde hair was an act of rebellion from her Italian family. I swept it aside, loving the flash of awareness in her eyes as my fingertips brushed over her forehead. She wasn't immune to me. "You're always up to something."

She cocked her head. "Wouldn't you love to know what it is?"

"That's why I'm standing here." I moved closer to her, wanting to press my body against hers. I wanted to trace a trail of kisses down her neck, over her collarbone, and lower. I wanted to tug down the bodice of her gown so that her breasts spilled over. I bet Gia wore sexy-as-hell lingerie.

I'd gathered important details about her over the years. She was feisty, quick to start a fight, and highly effective at ending one with her sharp tongue. She always rose to a challenge, and I seemed to be the ultimate one.

I lowered my head, breathing in her scent, floral with a hint of something spicy, and her breath hitched. I let my breath trail over the shell of her ear.

"What are you doing?" Her voice was shaky.

"You've never been seduced?" I taunted as my pulse kicked into overdrive. There was a roaring in my ears that drowned out my good reason and any sense of self-preservation.

"Is that what this is? A seduction?" Her voice was light as air. She tipped her head slightly so I had more access to her neck.

I cupped the back of her head, giving in to my desires, and sucked hard on her neck. She moaned softly into my ear, and it was the most beautiful sound I'd ever heard. I would enjoy making this woman come apart. It would be the greatest challenge of my life.

I lifted my lips slightly and said, "We could be so good together."

Her fingers tangled in the hair at the back of my neck, and she pressed her tits against my chest. "That's a bad idea."

Her words said one thing, but her body was saying another.

"But so good," I said as I kissed her neck and then her shoulder, not remembering any reason why I shouldn't be touching and kissing her. I couldn't remember anything except for the hum of desire beneath my skin and the throbbing of my cock. I wanted her in a way I hadn't wanted anyone before.

Then she nipped the underside of my jaw, and everything inside me ran molten hot.

"Fuck. I want you."

She pulled away, her eyes flashing with irritation. "You can't have me. I'm not some prize to be won."

"I never said you were." I pulled back, a little confused about her reaction but knowing I shouldn't be touching her. Not with her brother, Leo, nearby.

I felt sluggish as she ducked under my arm and walked away. I let her go because I shouldn't have touched her at all. I straightened, running a hand through my hair. I'd seriously screwed up.

I prided myself on always being in control. I'd imagined myself making a move on her and kissing her a million times, but I never thought I'd lose my mind when I did.

I didn't need to watch the wedding because Hannah was excellent at her job. I only hired the best. But I couldn't stay away. When the ceremony started, I stood outside to keep an eye on Gia.

When the ceremony was over, the bride and groom walked down the aisle with their joined hands raised to cheers and a standing ovation.

I should have walked away. There was no need for me to ensure a smooth transition from the ceremony to the cocktail hour and then to the reception. But I couldn't move.

I was rooted to the spot as Gia walked down the aisle on Leo's arm. Her best friend, Harper, was on his other side, but I only had eyes for Gia.

She was gorgeous in anything, but there was something about that dress. The tease of that ribbon was fucking with my head.

Gia's gaze flashed to mine as if she remembered the way she'd pressed her body against mine only a few minutes earlier. I couldn't forget her breathy moans in my ear and the insistent way she tugged on my hair.

I had a fleeting thought that Gia would be wild in bed, but then Leo nodded in my direction, and my throat tightened. I shouldn't be lusting after his younger sister. I shouldn't be thinking about her at all. As far as Leo knew, we hated each other. Everyone knew it was difficult for us to be in the same room together without fighting. But when we were alone, that fire turned into desire.

I headed inside, knowing I should be doing anything but watching Gia Giovanni. If she'd stayed in Annapolis, I would never know what she tasted like.

To get back on track, I checked in with Brad, the chef in charge of the food for Naomi and Chris's wedding. Then I completed a quick tour of the hotel grounds, ensuring everything was running smoothly. I did this route several times a day to clear my mind, and it gave me the opportunity to check in with the various managers of each department.

I believed in hiring the best, but that didn't mean I wasn't closely involved in the running of my hotel. I'd bought the resort and renovated it into something beautiful, a five-star resort that was booked months ahead of time. I also wanted to be known as the premier wedding destination in the area, but Gia's business threatened that.

Early on, I set the standard that couples booking a wedding at my resort had to work with my wedding planner. They had to choose between Gia and me. Some dropped Gia and agreed to my terms. But others wanted her. It made me respect her even more.

She was good at her job. Now she represented a challenge not only to my business but to my body.

I wanted what I couldn't have.

What if we took out our frustrations in the bedroom, and to hell with everything else? It didn't have to mean anything. Her brothers would be pissed, but remembering that kiss, I was willing to risk it.

My footsteps faltered in the hallway of the hotel when I came around a corner and saw the flash of blue and heard the click of heels on the floor. Gia.

I quickened my strides until I was even with her. "What are you doing?"

Her expression was smooth, her tone dismissive. "I rented a room for the evening."

My jaw tightened. "I didn't authorize that."

Gia stopped moving and smirked. "You approve all your guests?"

"I should," I said, grinding my teeth together. I wasn't sure why she got to me.

Gia had stopped in front of a utility closet. Without thinking about what I was doing, I opened it with one hand and snagged her slender wrist with the other. I tugged her inside and shut the door behind us. I turned the lock and walked toward her until she was pressed against the door. She hit it with a thud and a release of her breath.

She looked up at me, her expression a mixture of wonder and heat. "What are you doing?"

"This," I said, just as my mouth descended on hers. Her hands grabbed at the back of my suit jacket as her lips moved under mine. I cupped her face, angling her so that I could dive inside that smart mouth.

I'd do anything to shut her up, to get her to think of me as someone other than her brothers' best friend and her competition. I wanted her to see me as a man she desired.

We volleyed for control.

She moaned into my mouth as I moved one thigh between her legs.

She lifted her leg and hooked it around mine so that I could press against her center.

"You feel like heaven, sweetheart."

"Don't call me that," she said as she claimed my mouth again. Her hands pulled me closer as she pressed herself against my cock.

I pulled away slightly and said, "I call it like I see it."

"Shut up and kiss me."

Kiss her. Touch her. Fuck her. I needed to be inside her. I needed her. I couldn't describe this out-of-control feeling. I was desperate for her. It was like we'd held ourselves back for so long that as soon as we unleashed this desire, we were unstoppable.

I pulled back, making sure the heat in her eyes matched mine before tugging on the bow at her waist. "I want to see you."

Her dress gaped open, her breasts spilled over a strapless bra, and a tiny strip of flesh-colored lace covered her pussy. I dropped to my knees, needing to smell her, taste her. "Fuck, Gia. You're so gorgeous."

Her chest heaved in time with the rise and fall of her breath.

"Are you wet for me?" I asked, looking up at her but not touching her to confirm.

She tipped her hips in my direction.

"You want my mouth, baby girl?"

Her jaw tightened. "I'm not your baby girl."

"Sure, you are, sweetheart," I insisted, loving how I riled her up, physically and mentally. "If you want my mouth on you, you're going to have to tell me." I wanted her to be honest with me. I wanted to hear that she desired me. That this wasn't a power play. I needed to know she wanted me as a man.

Gia narrowed her eyes on me. "Silas, touch me—"

I raised a brow, needing to hear the dirty words.

Her hand rested lightly on my hair. "I want your mouth on my pussy."

"Fuck. That word on your lips." Heat rushed to my cock as I hooked my hands in the band of her lace panties and tugged them over her hips. The sweet smell of her arousal spurred me on as I spread her legs with my shoulders.

Her fingers tightened in my hair as I breathed her in.

"I like you on your knees for me."

Without responding, because I loved it too, I dove in, licking and sucking, devouring her sweet taste. She relaxed against the door, her hands an anchor in my hair as she tipped her hips toward me, and I added a finger.

I looked up at her, wishing I'd taken the time to remove her bra. "I want to see you. Feel you."

Gia got the hint because she reached behind her back and unhooked her bra, allowing it to fall to the floor. Her hard nipples and pert breasts had me harder than a rock.

She was gorgeous. The hottest woman I'd ever had the pleasure of being with. In my lust-filled haze, I had a feeling it was because there was something else between us. Not just desire but mutual respect, an attraction that went beyond the physical, but I wouldn't explore that. This was a release of tension. An unraveling of pent-up desire. I wouldn't let it be anything else.

I wouldn't let the tenderness swirling in my chest soften my touch. In my wildest dreams, I never thought I'd be pleasuring Gia Giovanni in the closet of my hotel. Knowing this might be my only chance with her, I wanted to make it good. I wanted her to think of me long after her orgasm had faded. I wanted to ruin her for all other men.

I wanted her to light up only for me. A sense of possessiveness struck me while I added a second finger, mimicking how I'd fuck her with my cock. I sucked her clit and reached up to cup her breasts, rolling her nipples with my fingers.

She bit her lip and arched into me, whimpering with desire and need.

I wanted to make her feel good. I wanted her to call out my name. I found that spongy spot deep inside her and curled my fingers.

Her nails scraped my scalp as her muscles tightened, and she cried out. Her walls spasmed around me, and I held her up as she came down.

Her eyes were a little unfocused as she looked down at me.

"Next time you come for me, say my name," I growled.

The fog in her eyes lifted. "There won't be a next time."

She snatched up her bra and hooked it, covering her breasts

and pulling her dress around her, not bothering with her panties. She tied the ribbon with jerky hands and straightened her hair. Then she turned away from me, her hand on the doorknob.

"You don't want to return the favor?" I asked, unable to resist taunting her.

There was something hard and uncomfortable in my chest I couldn't seem to dislodge. I didn't want her to leave.

"I have no words except this"—she gestured in my direction —"was a mistake."

She turned the knob and was gone, leaving me in the dusty storage room that was filled with spare towels and cleaning supplies. I stuffed her panties into my pocket, pleased to have a memento from our time together. I had a feeling it wouldn't be happening again.

Two

GIA

I swiped my room card over the keypad, and when the light flashed green, I pushed the door open. Shutting it, I leaned against the solid surface, not quite believing Silas expected me to blow him in that closet, and that I'd wanted to. I wanted to get down on my knees like he had for me. I wanted to make him lose control.

I must have lost my mind because I didn't kiss guys in closets, and I never lost control. Not ever.

I felt this weird vortex of energy when I was around Silas. My friends had teased me, saying that it was attraction, but I hadn't believed it.

There was something about the way he'd pulled me into the closet and maneuvered me against the wall. I always felt in control when I was with a man. Like I couldn't let go. But with Silas, I forgot about everything, that he was my brothers' best friend, my competition. I was supposed to be checking out his hotel, not allowing Silas to feel me up.

I'd lost all sense of reason.

I wanted to be irritated at the way he'd commanded me to call out his name the next time he made me come, but I wasn't. I was hot all over, wishing he could fill me up, knowing it would be like nothing I'd ever experienced with any other man.

Silas had played my body, driving me higher, only to ease me down before doing it all over again. He was skilled with his fingers and his tongue, but I wanted more. I wanted to taste him. I wanted my mouth stretched around his cock. I wanted to see if he'd lose control the way I had.

I wanted to shock him, challenge him.

Disgusted with my reaction, I moved into the bathroom. My cheeks were flushed, my lips were swollen, and my hair was a mess. I looked like I'd been freshly fucked, and I wish I had been. I had a feeling if I'd asked, Silas would have lifted me and fucked me against the wall.

My nipples pebbled all over again at the image. He'd be strong and commanding, skilled and tender.

I loved the way he'd seemingly checked in with me, his gaze assessing, his fingers questioning, and when I'd given him the answer he wanted with my body, he'd taken control, allowing me to let go. It was an intoxicating feeling. One I wanted to feel again.

I was used to being the boss in my business, and I liked being in control of relationships. Not that I engaged in them often. Other men bored me. They didn't challenge me, not like Silas had.

I let my hair down, finger-combing it as best I could, before twisting it up again. My bag was in my car, so I didn't have a brush or makeup. I'd only intended to check in and see the room.

I hadn't even decided to stay, but there was something about being in Silas's hotel room that had me hot all over, despite the earth-shattering orgasm I'd just experienced on Silas's skilled fingers and tongue.

It was so wrong to want more with Silas. Not only was he my biggest competitor, but my brother was at cocktail hour, probably wondering where I was. Leo was overprotective by nature. He'd eased up over the years, realizing I could handle myself, but it wouldn't stop him from searching me out if I stayed away for too long.

I used the lipstick in my tiny silver purse. Satisfied I didn't look as disheveled as I had when I came into the room, I took one last sweep of the room. It had a king bed with a view of the water. It was a gorgeous room with upscale décor and luxe linens. I expected the best from Silas when it came to the resort's accommodations, but I couldn't help but wonder if I'd get the same treatment if he was in my bed.

Would he be a tender lover or a passionate one? I had a feeling I'd only seen a glimpse of his potential in that closet. He'd held himself back, as if he needed to be in control to give me pleasure.

My pussy clenched at the memory of his fingers inside me. I wanted more. So much more. But first, I had to get back to the reception before Harper or Leo came looking for me.

I took a deep breath and opened the door, finding the hall empty. A strange emptiness filled my chest. Was I expecting Silas to be waiting for me?

It was his hotel. I was positive he could easily figure out which room I'd been given since I'd used my legal name. Would he get a key and let himself in in the middle of the night?

A thrill shot through me at the idea. Could I handle one night with Silas and then go back to the way things were? I was positive I could separate sex from emotions, especially with Silas. I didn't have any tender feelings toward him.

My heart hadn't skipped a beat when his strong hand had encircled my wrist and tugged me into the closet. My breath hadn't whooshed from my lungs when he'd backed me up against the door. His scent, musky with a hint of aftershave, hadn't invaded my senses, stealing all sense of reason.

Nope. I wouldn't acknowledge that Silas Sharpe had gotten to me. He'd bared more than my body inside that closet. It wouldn't be smart to get any more involved with him.

It was a mistake.

I strode toward the reception, my head held high. If Silas was watching me on camera, I wanted to show him I hadn't been affected by what happened between us. It didn't change anything. He was still my biggest competitor, and I had no business seeking pleasure in his arms.

I took slow, deep breaths, urging my heart to slow as I calmly made my way to the table where Leo and Harper were sitting. I hoped it wasn't obvious I'd just had the best orgasm of my life with my enemy in a broom closet. Not that anyone would believe it.

I slipped into the seat next to Harper. "What did I miss?"

The waitstaff set bowls of salad in front of us.

"Just the rest of cocktail hour," Harper said.

"You get any good intel?" Leo asked as he removed his hand from Harper's chair.

"I took a walk to see the grounds. The property is gorgeous." I hadn't seen much of the property beyond the inside of the closet. I hoped they wouldn't ask any follow-up questions.

Leo's eyes widened. "You've never been here?"

I rolled my eyes. "If it wasn't obvious, Silas doesn't want me here."

Leo shifted in his chair. "He'll come around. You're my sister."

"And his number-one enemy." Guilt pricked my conscience because I didn't feel great about keeping things from him. I picked up my fork to eat the salad. Part of being here was scoping out the food. "From what I can tell, he runs a beautiful resort. The accommodations are luxurious, and the waitstaff is professional and accommodating."

"Are you staying overnight?" Leo asked me.

"I want to get a better feel for the hotel." I had visions of showing up at the bar tonight and Silas buying me a drink. It was stupid, but I craved him.

"I want to get back to Evie," Harper said.

"I'll take you," Leo offered, and I breathed a sigh of relief. I didn't know what I planned on happening tonight, but I didn't want my brother or best friend anywhere nearby.

"Don't you need to spend time with Silas?" Harper asked Leo, and I tensed, hoping he'd say no.

"I can grab a drink with him anytime, and if you need to be home, I'll get you there."

Harper's expression softened. "Thank you."

"Anytime."

I'd never been so grateful that my brother was a genuinely nice guy. Even if he had plans with Silas, he'd change them to ensure Harper made it home okay. I felt a little bad that I was lying to them. As much as I wanted to get a feel for Silas's resort, I was more interested in scoping out his body.

In an attempt to pretend this entire fiasco was business-related, I said, "Their wedding planner is organized and well-prepared. The wedding and ceremony went smoothly."

"You thought it wouldn't?" Leo asked.

I knew Leo respected Silas's business decisions. "I was hoping there would be something I could exploit."

Leo leaned back in his chair. "You aren't in direct competition, you know. If a couple wants a resort, they come here; if they want a venue in Annapolis, they go to you."

I sighed, hating to admit this to my brother but needing to hear his thoughts. "I've been losing more clients lately. When I ask why, they say they prefer the all-inclusive offerings of Silas's resort."

Harper shook her head. "Can you blame them? I can't imagine planning my own wedding. There are so many details."

"Yet you don't mind doing it for other people," Leo said.

"I'm not a wedding planner. I'm the manager," Harper said.

"That's right," Leo said as I sipped my champagne.

Dinner came, and we dug into our respective entrees, chicken or steak, while speaking to the other couples at the table.

Finn played his guitar for the couple's first dance, and when guests filled the dance floor, I said, "You two should dance. We need to blend in and look natural."

"Not like we're on a supersecret spy mission?" Leo teased.

I waved a hand at him. "Just go dance."

I needed a minute to process what transpired between me and Silas. The time I spent in the hotel room wasn't enough to clear it from my memory. I wasn't sure I'd ever forget it.

That's when I spotted Silas in the rear of the tent, his gaze on me. I checked to ensure that Harper was dancing with Leo. Those two seemed engrossed in each other, so I grabbed my purse and headed in his direction.

His gaze stayed on me as I made my way through the maze of tables to stop in front of him. He arched a brow. "You need something?"

His words, combined with the heat in his eyes, were like a bomb detonating inside my body. I was hot all over and desperate for another round. Instead of answering him, I asked, "Are you planning on spying on us all night?"

"Isn't that what you're doing?" His stance was deceptively relaxed, but I knew he was hyperaware of me.

I smiled, feeling cooler when I thought about business and not Silas Sharpe seeing me naked and writhing under him. "Your resort isn't competition for the high-level service my wedding planners provide."

Silas flicked his gaze over my head, then back to my face. "Are you looking for something else, then?"

Without waiting for a response, he touched my elbow and guided me around the corner. I heard the music drifting from the tent, but we were out of sight of the party itself.

"What are you doing?" I hissed.

"Giving you want you want." Then his hands cupped my face, making me feel both cherished and adored before he kissed me. His hard body pressed against mine, and I arched toward him, needing and wanting more. He made me ache for him.

I lost all sense of space and time, forgetting about the reception, my brother, and my best friend until there was nothing except Silas's mouth on mine.

"You staying the night?" Silas asked as he eased back.

My lips felt swollen, my cheeks hot. "You know I am."

"Good." Then he walked away, leaving me wanting more.

It was so irritating that he had this effect on me. It was like a switch had been flipped, and now, we couldn't contain our desire for each other. Desire we'd been perfectly able to ignore for years.

I smoothed my dress and touched my swollen lips. How long had I been gone? Would Harper and Leo notice that I'd just been kissed? I didn't think I had time to duck inside the restroom, so I hoped I'd make it back to the table before Harper and Leo so I could use the compact in my purse to fix any damage.

I hated that Silas made me lose control like this. I was acting so out of character. I was here for business, not to fuck Silas Sharpe, even though I wanted to. I really wanted to know what it was like to get the full Silas experience.

Could I justify it to myself that it was purely for business? That I was testing the bed for bridal couples? I stepped away from the planter and into the tent. My heart sank when I saw Harper and Leo alone at our table, watching me walk toward them.

"Where were you?" Leo asked, his gaze steady on me.

I smoothed my dress for a second time. "I was just checking on things."

"Anything we can use?" Harper asked as I sat.

After a quick glance at Leo, I said, "We can talk about it later."

Leo's lips twitched. "So, I can't know about the secret workings of Happily Ever Afters?"

"It's on a need-to-know basis, and you're friends with the enemy," I teased.

"You really want to know?" Harper asked Leo.

"Not unless you have late-night sleepovers and throw pillows at each other." The table fell silent. "No, wait. This is my sister we're talking about."

I narrowed my eyes on him. "Is that what you think we do?"

"You drink champagne to celebrate a job well done, don't you?"

"Yes," I said, my throat feeling tight.

"Isn't that how the rules were created?" Harper asked, and my stomach dropped.

Leo turned his attention to me. "What are these rules?"

I waved a hand at him. "No sleeping with coworkers. That kind of thing."

"Is that all?" Leo asked.

Harper grinned, tapping a finger on her chin, and that's when I realized that her eyes were glossy. "Oh, there's more. Let's see if I can remember correctly... There's no sleeping with coworkers or members of the wedding party—oh, and Gia's brothers."

It was bad enough that I'd created those rules and then wrote them down, but to have Harper repeat them in front of my brother? I was never going to live this down.

"Wait. What?" Leo leaned in to ask Harper. "Did you say there's an office rule about not sleeping with Gia's brothers?"

"Yeees. Everyone knows you're off-limits."

"I didn't realize we were ever an option," Leo asked, his tone a little lighter.

Hopefully, he thought it was all a joke. In reality, I'd created those rules to exert some control over my friends and employees. I'd been burned too many times in the past.

"You know all my friends liked you, even in high school. I just like to keep things clear."

Leo's expression smoothed over. "Is that true, Harper? Did you like me in high school?"

"Not Harper. She'd never betray me that way." I shook my head, implicitly trusting my best friend since childhood. I'd had issues with other girls befriending me to get closer to my brothers. I'd even walked in on one of my best friends at the time, making out with Matteo. But Harper had been by my side through everything.

Needing to talk about something else, I scanned the room,

and seeing the wedding planner next to the bride and groom at the cake table, I said, "Oh look, it's time to cut the cake."

"Let's get a closer look, shall we?" Harper asked as she stood and moved toward the four-tier white cake with cascading flowers. "Did you learn anything useful?"

I rolled my eyes. "Just that Silas runs a tight ship."

"We suspected that."

"I can't believe he drew Harrison away from me," I said, attempting to draw on the anger I'd felt when I'd heard he'd poached my supplier and forget about how good he'd made me feel afterward.

Harper frowned. "But he didn't. Not really. Harrison's in the business of renting wedding supplies, and he's the only one in the area who designs and builds arbors."

I was used to my friend trying to get me to see things a different way, but I was stubborn and desperate to put Silas back into the box I'd labeled *Enemy*. "He did it on purpose to piss me off. I bet he offered him an incentive."

"Harrison is building a business, just like you are. He's not going to turn down paying customers," Harper insisted.

I sighed. "I'm not mad at Harrison."

"You came to this wedding to get some insight into Silas. We didn't find anything, so maybe there isn't anything to find. He runs a good business, just like you do. You can coexist. You aren't offering the same things."

I'd gotten insight into how skilled Silas was with his fingers and tongue. I wasn't nearly done exploring that side of him, but I refocused on our conversation. "I don't like that he poached my vendor."

"He didn't, though. He works for both of you," Harper said, familiar with the way my mind worked. It took time for me to see things differently, if ever.

"I'll never forgive him for it." I wouldn't forgive him for how my body reacted to him.

Harper laughed. "You didn't exactly like him before you learned about Harrison."

I smiled, wondering if hate sex was a thing. "True."

"Your brothers are friends with him. Maybe he's not that bad."

I was sure my brothers didn't see the side of him that I had today. "Silas has taken some of the biggest clients from me recently. I can't let it continue. I need to figure out a way to handle this. I'm trying to get the Christmas Tree Farm on board. It's something we could offer that's different."

"Have they changed their mind about working with us?" Harper asked.

"They won't give me a definitive answer." My stomach tightened. The Monroes' farm was an amazing possibility. It would increase our weddings during the winter. I wanted to be able to offer it as an option, since so many brides were interested in holiday and winter-themed weddings.

"Is it the son—Emmett—that's the issue?

Lori, the woman who owned the farm, was interested, but her grumpy son, Emmett, wasn't. I couldn't blame him for being worried about the effect it would have on his Christmas tree customers, but I was used to getting what I wanted. There was an angle to pursue there. I just hadn't figured out what it was. "I think so. I'm going to send Ireland to talk to him. Maybe she can talk some sense into him." Ireland had a knack for dealing with difficult brides, and grumpy men shouldn't be any different.

"You're successful because you're hardworking and the brides know you'd do anything for them."

It felt good to hear someone else say I was successful, but I felt like a fraud, especially when the business wasn't as profitable as I'd like. "I have to figure this out."

Harper leaned in closer and lowered her voice. "Don't look now, but he's watching us."

"I won't give him the satisfaction of knowing he gets to me."

Although it was probably too late for that. Silas had the ability to read me like no one else. That's what made me think he'd be great in bed, and I really wanted to give in to the temptation and find out.

"Are you still planning on staying the night?" Harper asked.

I nodded as a man in a suit approached me. "Would you like to dance?

He looked handsome, but he didn't spark anything inside me.

I glanced over at Silas to make sure he was watching, then placed my hand in his. "I'd love to."

"I'm going to head out. I need to get Evie," Harper said.

Knowing Leo would take care of her, I said, "Have a good night."

The man pulled me into his arms. "I'm Deacon."

"Gia." I smiled tightly, wanting to put on a good show for Silas but not feeling comfortable in this man's arms. Not like I had in Silas's.

Out of the corner of my eye, I saw Silas stalking toward us. My heart galloped in my chest for what I hoped would be a confrontation.

Three

SILAS

There was a roaring in my ears as I crossed the room. I had no idea what had gotten into me. I didn't like the idea of another man dancing with Gia. Logically, I knew she wasn't mine, but my body wasn't listening.

I paused next to them, knowing better than to ask. "I'd like this dance."

"She's with me," the other man protested.

I knew exactly how to exert my energy so he'd back off without even consciously thinking about it. I moved toward Gia, and the man naturally stepped back, dropping her hand.

"What if I don't want to dance with you?" Gia gazed up at me with a slightly amused expression.

"You do."

She tipped her head to the side, considering me. "How can you be so sure?"

"You weren't dancing like this with him." She'd immediately taken my hand and pressed her body against mine.

"I don't know him."

How could I explain that reason wasn't coming into this conversation? I saw her, and my caveman brain took over. There was no place for logic when it came to Gia Giovanni.

She shook her head. "You're impossible to figure out."

"Is that necessary when we can just enjoy tonight instead?" I had visions of her on my bed, her legs spread wide, her pussy glistening. I couldn't stop thinking about what I wanted to do to her.

Her cheeks turned pink. "Is that what you want?"

"I want you."

Her brow furrowed. "What about—"

My jaw tightened. "Stop."

"We're ignoring all the possible consequences?"

"Nothing else matters." Everything in my body was telling me that this was the right move. Even if it made no sense. Even if I betrayed my friends and her brothers. I wanted her, and I was going to have her.

"You're very sure of yourself."

I chuckled. "Like you'd be with a man who wasn't confident."

She gave me a look. "You're bordering on cocky."

I brushed a thumb over her cheek. "You like that too."

Gia frowned as if I confused her. "I don't think I do."

I moved her in a circle, expertly avoiding the other couples, and then leaned in to whisper in her ear. "Oh you do. You loved it when my hands were on you. You especially enjoyed my tongue."

The flush on her cheeks deepened. "You're trouble."

"And you love it." She needed a man who challenged her both in the bedroom and out.

"Why now?" she finally asked after we'd danced without speaking for a few seconds.

"I promise, I haven't thought of you naked—much." That was a lie because I'd thought of her naked ever since her family invited me along on one of their vacations to Deep Creek, and Gia wore that red string bikini. I thought she'd done it on purpose to drive me crazy. She was young and seemingly innocent.

I'd wanted to pull the string on her top and suck on her tits. I'd wanted to spread her legs and fuck her. But she was my best friends' little sister, and her family trusted me. So I'd pushed those desires down deep.

Maybe it had come out in the form of barbs and taunts, but I had to do something with all this pent-up desire. I needed to release it on the woman who tied me up in knots.

Gia shook her head. "I don't believe you."

"You have no idea what you do to me." My voice was rough.

Her gaze met mine, and whatever she saw in my eyes must have told her I was telling the truth.

"One night. No strings. No one needs to know."

Something flashed in her eyes. She wanted me too. "I don't normally sleep with my competitor."

"Is that what I am to you?" I was supposed to look out for her, like her brothers did. But I wasn't ever in the position to do so. We'd kept our distance over the years. And in my case, it was necessary. As soon as we got close, I proved that I couldn't control myself.

"I don't do relationships. I don't have the time or patience for them."

I chuckled. "It's a good thing I'm not looking for one."

She gave me a slight nod of her head.

"You want to get out of here?" I asked, needing to make sure I read her signals correctly.

Gia shrugged. "I don't need to say good-bye. Leo and Harper already left, and—"

I grabbed her hand and started walking. "You don't know the bride or groom."

Gia jogged in her heels to keep up. "My room or yours?"

"Mine." I curled my fingers tighter around hers as I led the way through the dance floor and out of the tent.

Despite her bravado, I sensed that Gia didn't pick up men. That meant she was selective with whom she slept with.

I should have been contemplating the repercussions, but instead, I was planning every way I could have her in the next few hours. I'd do everything I could to get her to stay the night. I knew she'd want to bolt as soon as it was over, but I didn't want that. I wanted to see her come apart, and I wanted to be there to put her back together again.

She wasn't a one-night stand or a conquest. She was everything I'd ever wanted. I didn't have any plans beyond tonight. I refused to let myself think that way.

One night. No strings. That's what I'd promised her, and that's what I'd deliver. But I didn't promise to leave her the same when I was done. I wanted to ruin her for all other men, and I would. She'd be begging for more in the morning. I was positive about that.

I didn't stop until I stood in front of my penthouse on the top floor.

"Is this where you live?" Gia asked, taking in the large suite and the floor-to-ceiling windows that faced the bay.

"I own a house too."

"Of course, you do," she muttered as she moved around the room, seemingly drawn to the balcony. I opened the slider, and she stepped through. She stood at the railing, her hair blowing in the breeze.

I stepped behind her, sweeping her hair off her shoulders to place a kiss on her bare skin. "I could have you here. Bend you over and spread those gorgeous legs. No one would see us."

Her breath hitched.

"You want that." My body tensed, wanting more, but I waited.

She turned, looping her hands around my neck. "I want you."

My hands gripped her hips. We hadn't kissed in the closet, and I made up for lost time now. I explored her mouth, my tongue tangling with hers, as I pressed ever closer to her body.

She broke away. "I want to taste you."

"I want to fuck you." I expected her to flinch or step back, telling me I wasn't what she wanted. But instead, her eyes flared with desire.

"You want that too. I can make you feel so good."

"It doesn't mean anything," she said with a defiant tilt to her chin.

"Of course it will, sweetheart. I want to conquer this sweet body. This time, you'll scream out my name."

She swallowed as I tugged on the same ribbon I'd untied earlier.

"Tsk. Tsk. No panties. You're a naughty girl." Her panties were burning a hole in my pocket.

Her lips twitched. "It's all your fault."

"It's your last chance to leave." I'd been going slow ever since I let her into my place, but I wouldn't be able to hold back. I'd been primed for her ever since I tasted her.

She arched her brow in challenge and then let her dress fall to the floor. She reached behind her and unhooked her bra, baring herself to me. She stood, confident, not worried about who might see her or that I was fully dressed.

"You're beautiful." All pretenses fell away. I didn't need to throw barbs at her to keep her at bay. She was mine for the night, and I didn't want to waste any time.

I touched her breasts, rolling her nipples and breathing in her soft gasps of pleasure. "So beautiful. So confident. So strong."

She arched into my hands and spread her legs slightly.

I needed to drive her wild. I dipped my head, taking her nipple into my mouth. Her hands tangled in the hair at the nape of my neck, holding me to her.

I couldn't believe she was here, naked on my balcony. It was like a dream come true, and I didn't want it to end. I laved first one nipple, then the second. I reached between her legs, sliding my fingers between her folds. She was wet.

"You want my cock?" I asked her, lifting my head to see her reaction.

She nodded shakily, her body flush and her muscles tight.

"You need me to make you feel better?" I paused the motion of my fingers.

Gia tipped her hips forward, riding my fingers. "Silas, please."

"I love the sound of my name on your lips." Especially when it was needy and breathy, as if she couldn't get enough. I kissed her, knowing I'd never get enough of her. One night wouldn't satisfy me.

When she was on the edge, I turned her, helping her brace her hands on the railing. The lights on the balcony were off, and no one walked along the shoreline below. No one could see us. She was safe.

I quickly shucked my clothes and grabbed a condom from my wallet, wanting to feel her.

She looked over her shoulder at me. "Silas."

"I'll never get enough of you saying my name." I smoothed the condom down my cock, lining up at her entrance. She was needy and wet, and I slid inside her, inch by glorious inch. The only thing that would have felt better was if there was nothing between us.

I gripped her hips hard enough to leave marks. I pulled out to the tip and slammed inside her, giving in to a rhythm that left us both panting for more.

She arched her back, looking gorgeous in the moonlight. I almost wished we'd chosen a different position so I could feast on her as she lay spread out on my bed. But we had time for more. This wasn't it. It couldn't be.

I reached around to cup her breast, tweaking her nipple, and then lower to circle her clit. She pushed back on my cock, making me lose my mind.

As soon as she spasmed around my cock, I went over, thrusting deep. I curled myself over her back before finally pulling out and disposing of the condom. I pulled her to me.

"Hot tub?" I finally asked her, nodding to the one in the corner.

"Yeah, that sounds good," she said, her voice soft.

"You didn't scream my name," I reminded her.

She smirked. "The night is still young."

"Is that a challenge?" I removed the cover, checked the temperature, and turned on the jets and lights.

"Is everything with you a competition?" she asked as I held my hand out to her to help her inside.

"With you." I sat next to her, the warm water feeling good on my skin.

It felt like she was too far away, so I pulled her closer. I had a feeling Gia was used to pushing people away. Either men were naturally intimidated by her, and she was protecting herself, or she avoided intimacy.

Whatever the reason, I wouldn't let her pull away from me. Not tonight.

"What are you doing?" she asked when I set her in my lap.

"Holding you."

She looked at me with uncertainty before finally asking, "Why?"

"Because I want to." That was a little surprising for me. I enjoyed sex, but I never cared about the aftermath. I didn't need to cuddle with a woman or keep her close. But I wanted to with her.

She settled on my leg, in the circle of my arms. "You're different than I expected."

I loved the feel of her naked body. She was so free and confident. She didn't have any insecurities. "How so?"

She laughed, but it sounded a little insecure. "I thought you'd kick me out afterward."

"Why would you have sex with someone like that?" I asked, turning her so I could see her face.

"I prefer that, actually. I don't do relationships, remember?"

"Just because you aren't interested in a relationship doesn't mean sex has to be cold and unfeeling."

She didn't have a response to that.

I suspected I'd thrown her off again. I loved doing that to her.

"Do you live here full time?" Gia finally asked, and I

suspected this was her way to move on from a vulnerable topic, and I let it go for now.

"This is just easier when I'm working."

"I can see that. No commute. Beautiful accommodations."

"Who wouldn't want to live in a five-star resort?" I murmured into her hair, breathing her in.

"I wouldn't." Her shoulders stiffened.

"You seem like a woman who enjoys luxury." She wore designer purses and shoes. Her brothers teased her about it over the years, but she said they were her symbols of success.

"Mmm. I do."

"But not a penthouse?" I turned her slightly so that she was facing me yet still able to enjoy the view of the water.

She pursed her lips. "I prefer a home. I don't think I'd want to live in a hotel."

"I feel as if I'm alone. The staff doesn't intrude when I'm here."

Gia's gaze narrowed on me. "I would have expected that you'd have them wait on you hand and foot."

"I like my privacy. Downstairs, they're all Mr. Sharpe this and Mr. Sharpe that. Up here, I can just be myself."

Gia nodded. "That makes sense."

I traced a path on her arm, content to just be with her. To get to know her better. I knew what her brothers said about her, that she was driven and hardworking.

"Why don't you work with your family?" I asked, genuinely curious.

Gia stiffened and tried to move away, but I held on tight. "I wanted to run my own business."

"I can understand that. But your father—"

Gia huffed out a breath. "My father wants me to work for him. He doesn't allow much room for innovation or other ideas. I want to be my own boss. I don't want to answer to my father and three older brothers."

I hadn't thought of it that way. "My brothers and I all do something different."

"You come from money. There's freedom to that."

"Don't you? Your father's business is successful."

Gia snorted. "I worked for him. He paid us less than the other workers, and he said he could because we were family. But he doesn't skimp on high-quality ingredients."

"Your brothers never complained."

"I suspect he paid them more. I think it had something to do with me being a female. He said I could make it up in tips."

"Did you?"

"I wasn't happy about working there, and it showed. I wanted to manage the place. I had so many ideas. I wanted to renovate and pay the employees more."

"He wouldn't listen to your ideas?" I knew what it was like to have ideas and need to act on them immediately.

"No. So I couldn't stay there."

"I get that." And I respected her more for it.

"Now I make all the decisions. I hire my employees and pay them what they're worth. Same with my independent contractors."

I suspected I paid Harrison more than she did. But I'd done that on purpose to draw him away from Gia. I could afford it, but I suspected Gia paid her employees more at the expense of her own business and her salary.

"Are you drawing a salary?" I asked, concerned that she wasn't taking care of herself.

She tensed. "I have to. You know that."

"But are you taking advantage of it, or are you paying yourself less than your employees?"

"I have a home, and I buy nice things. I'm fine."

"You have to take care of yourself."

"I didn't come here to talk about me." She turned to straddle my lap, her pussy sliding over my already-hardening cock.

"You wanted to forget everything."

She slid over my cock. "Uh-huh."

"I can help." I sucked on one nipple, wanting to slide inside her but knowing we needed a condom. She didn't trust me like that. Not yet. And since this was one night, it wouldn't be smart. She wasn't looking for a relationship, and neither was I.

I wanted her to ride my cock.

"I need to grab a condom."

She held tight to my shoulders. "I'm on birth control, and I'm clean."

"Are you sure?" I knew she wasn't reckless.

She nodded, and I said, "I'm clean too."

This time, when she rubbed over my dick, the tip slid inside. Her head tipped back, and her mouth opened with a gasp.

"You feel so good. Like heaven."

She sank down over my cock, inch by glorious inch, until I filled her.

I anchored her to me, helping her lift and lower herself over me. She rose up and down, her breasts bobbing in front of my face. I alternated between sucking on her nipples and kissing her.

She moaned, and I swallowed the sound, not wanting anyone to hear. The sounds of her pleasure were just for me.

When she went over, her head tipped back, her hair dipping into the water as she trembled and shook. I gripped her hips tighter, thrusting once, twice, and then I let go.

The thing that had lodged in my chest earlier dissipated. Gia standing naked in my hot tub and in my home seemed right. I didn't want the night to be over.

Four

GIA

I gripped the towel tighter to my body as Silas turned off the jets and covered the hot tub. I was trembling. I told myself it was from the contrast between the hot water to the cool air, but I think it had everything to do with what we'd just shared in that hot tub. I'd completely let go, lost myself in the moment, and hadn't insisted on using a condom. I'd never done anything so risky. I was ashamed and freaked out.

"I'm going to use the restroom," I said to him, opening the door and slipping inside. I just needed a few minutes to pull myself back together.

I dried off with the towel, avoiding looking at myself in the mirror. When I'd thoroughly scrubbed my skin, I realized I'd forgotten my clothes.

I felt bare, not just physically but emotionally too. I'd felt something in that hot tub that was more than a physical release, and it was scary. I couldn't lose anything to Silas Sharpe, especially my heart.

This was supposed to be a onetime thing. A release of tension. Not the start of something more. The idea of a relationship with Silas was ludicrous. He didn't want one, and neither did I.

I didn't have the time or the interest, but my heart was pounding out of my chest.

I had a feeling Silas wanted me to stay the night, probably for another round, but I wasn't sure that was a good idea. I wouldn't survive sex in his bed. It was too intimate. Too involved for what we were.

People had one-night stands at weddings. It was normal. That's how Abby and Nick met. Unfortunately, I didn't sleep with a stranger.

I was such an idiot. I drew in a shaky breath and startled when there was a knock on the door. "Yes?"

"I have clothes for you."

I wrapped the damp towel around my body and knotted it before opening the door a few inches.

In his hands, Silas held a T-shirt and shorts.

"That's not my dress." My mind was racing with what it meant.

"I figured you'd want to be more comfortable." Then he arched a brow. "You are staying the night, aren't you?"

I chewed my lip. "I have a hotel room."

He shoved the stack of clothes into my hands. "You won't be needing it. Stay here."

There was a hint of a challenge in his eyes I couldn't ignore. "Fine."

He smiled cockily, then walked away to give me privacy. I let the towel fall to the floor and drew the shirt over my head and pulled on the shorts. Both were too big for me, but they were soft and comfortable. I had to admit it was better than putting on a fancy dress.

I combed my hair with my fingers and took a few deep breaths before opening the door.

Silas moved toward me and held out his hand. "I want to show you something."

I bit back a smart comment because he seemed genuine and placed my hand in his. He led me through the penthouse to the bedroom, where a fire burned in a fireplace. One wall had floor-to-ceiling windows. The moon reflected off the surface of the water.

"I wanted to show you the view."

"It's gorgeous. I've read that it's better for your health to be near the water every day."

"I can attest to that," Silas said as he drew down the covers and lay down. Then he patted the bed next to him. "Lie down."

I sat stiffly on the bed, noting my dress, shoes, and purse resting neatly on a chair by the door. Would it be awkward to leave now? Or should I sneak out in the middle of the night?

"Please," Silas said, and I couldn't deny him or the draw of the bed. I lay down next to him, and Silas rolled so that he was propped up on one elbow. "I can't believe you're here."

"I can't either."

"You look perfect in my bed. Like you were always meant to be here."

My skin heated. "Do you know how ridiculous you sound?"

"Shhh. Let me." He leaned down and touched his lips to mine, kissing me softly, his hand resting on my thigh.

Just as the threads of desire wrapped around me again, he withdrew. "Get some rest. You must be tired after your day of sleuthing."

My lips twitched as he settled next to me, his arm banded around my waist. I turned to face the windows, and Silas adjusted, spooning me. I should have pulled away. I should have gotten dressed and left.

The moment was too good for me to leave just yet. I closed my eyes, intending to get up soon, but drifted off.

When I woke later, Silas had rolled away from me, and the moon illuminated the room. Now was my chance. Silas was asleep and couldn't ask me to stay.

I couldn't stop thinking about how I hadn't used a condom with a man I shouldn't trust.

Was he getting close to me on purpose so that he could gather useful information to build a better business? Would he steal another vendor? My mind was racing with the possibilities.

I needed to be in my house. I needed to be alone. I'd let too many pieces of myself go today, first in that closet, on that balcony, and then in Silas's bed. Being with him was dangerous for my heart and my business.

I needed to be smart about this. There was no future with Silas Sharpe. Even if it was possible, my family would never accept him. My brothers trusted him as a friend but not with their sister.

I quickly put on my clothes, being quiet so I wouldn't wake Silas, and then I tiptoed out of the suite, shutting the door quietly behind me. I didn't want to chance him coming to see me in my room, so I headed toward my car.

My home was my safe place. I never let a man sleep overnight. It felt too intimate. But to be fair, it felt that way in Silas's bed as well.

When I finally parked in front of my house, I wondered if I was running from Silas or from myself. I didn't think I'd be able to sleep, so I showered, removing any trace of Silas from my body. I allowed myself a few minutes to remember how it felt to be with him, and then I pushed it down deep.

There wouldn't be a repeat. I got dressed, not sure what to do with Silas's clothes, but in the end, I threw them in the hamper. I'd have to get them back to him or throw them out. I couldn't keep them. I didn't want any memory of our night together.

But those thoughts felt like a lie because I'd never felt like that with anyone else. Not wanting to examine that too closely, I started the coffeepot and sat at my small table to drink my first cup of the day.

The sun was just rising, and I couldn't help but think what the view would have been like over the water from Silas's bedroom.

Had he already woken up and noticed I was gone? Should I have left a note?

I dismissed the idea because I didn't want to give Silas the impression we were a thing or that we had any potential.

My phone buzzed when I was well into my second cup.

Unknown:

Running?

I didn't have Silas's phone number. How had he gotten mine? There was no way it was anyone other than him.

Irritation burned through me. I bet my brothers had given it to him at some point so that he could keep a protective watch over me. Except that had never been Silas's role in my life.

Angry, I stood up and got ready for work. There was no escape except the one I always found when I was buried in work.

No one would show up to the office on a Sunday, so I'd have the place to myself. No one would pressure me to go home. I didn't even have to go to family dinner because no one expected me.

I tried after I first opened the business, but my father wanted me to give up on it and work for him. He didn't understand that there wasn't anything for me at the restaurant. He already had my three brothers working there. I wanted something that was my own creation, and we didn't agree on anything.

If I wanted to keep my business, I needed to figure out a way to keep mine profitable.

At work, I got lost in paperwork and spreadsheets, brainstorming possible marketing ideas to bring in more high-dollar clients. What did I have that Silas's resort didn't?

It was late before I finally locked up and headed home.

Now that I wasn't focused on work, that message from Silas taunted me. Was I running?

I was ashamed to admit that he was right. I usually met things or people head-on, but Silas had this way of convincing me to do things I wouldn't normally do. If I'd stayed, we would have had sex again. And I wouldn't survive another round with him. How many more rules would I break with him?

Silas Sharpe was dangerous to my equilibrium. I needed to avoid him. I needed to go back to how things were before he went down on me in that closet.

But I couldn't ignore his message.

At home, I drew a bath and contemplated my options. The obvious choice was to tell him we couldn't do it again. But my fingers hovered over the keys in indecision.

Why was I hesitant to tell Silas nothing could happen? It felt like a lie. Last night felt too real. As if it was the start of something huge, but there was this wall there, a barrier because nothing could happen between us.

We'd always be competitors. He'd always be my brothers' best friend. He came to family events and holidays.

We needed to pretend it didn't happen.

> I want to forget it ever happened.

Then I deleted it. It was too honest. Finally, I settled on:

> We both know it can't happen again. It was a one-night thing that my brothers can never find out about.

Then I turned my phone over so I couldn't see the screen, and I tried to distract myself with the bath. But it was no use. I turned it back over to see if a message had come through.

> Whatever you have to tell yourself.

I felt the loss of what might have happened if Silas wasn't my competitor and a friend of my brothers. But I wasn't open to relationships with anyone. It wasn't just him. I liked my life. I loved my business. I didn't need someone trying to steer my life like my father had.

This isn't over.

I had to resist immediately typing *oh yes it is*, like a child because that's the person that Silas brought out in me. I was bratty and out of control, but that stopped now. I would be cool when it came to Silas. Nothing he did or said would affect me.

Then I remembered how it felt to be completely at his mercy. Bent over with my hands on the railing while he fucked me. It was raw and real and the craziest thing I'd ever done. On some level, I must have trusted him to let go like that. But I pushed that idea away too.

Silas wasn't a nice guy. He didn't want me. I was someone he could manipulate to get what he wanted. I had to remember that. Any thoughts of tenderness were a lie.

But that didn't sit right with me either. I was a mess, and it was all Silas Sharpe's fault. Everything came down to him, and I was tired of it.

I vowed to put him and his text messages aside. I started by deleting his words and not saving his number as a contact. I didn't need him or his number. I was a strong, independent woman.

I never got caught up in having amazing sex with a hot guy. But if I was honest with myself, I'd never *had* amazing sex with a hot guy. Everything was different with Silas. It was as if he could see me, *all* of me, and it was addicting. It was like he knew who I was and what I needed on a visceral level. I needed control, but I needed to let go too.

Silas's words that *it wasn't over* rang through my consciousness the rest of the night. A small part of me wanted him to come to me, to pursue me. But the rational part of me knew he wasn't good for me.

He was a onetime indulgence. It would be gluttonous to go back for more.

Five

SILAS

When I woke up to an empty bed, I couldn't say I was surprised. Gia had this ethereal quality about her. Like I'd never be able to hold on to her. It only made me want to hold on tighter.

I had a feeling things got too intense for her, and she just couldn't deal. I hoped she couldn't resist coming back for more. But she'd have to overcome that rational side of her brain, which I knew was strong. I'd bide my time and see how she handled things going forward.

I wanted her to become addicted to me, to my touch, to everything I could offer her because I was positive she wouldn't get it from anyone else. There was something between us. Something I'd never experienced before, and I already wanted her again.

After my last text, I stayed up way too late waiting for her reply. When it never came, I decided to let her make the next move. I understood she was concerned about her brothers, but we were adults. I was positive we could have a physical relationship and keep her brothers out of it.

I loved the Giovannis and wouldn't want to alienate them. They'd always been good to me, including me in family gatherings, even when I was younger.

I was a patient man. I'd give Gia some time to come around to the realization that no one else was me. I was cocky enough to think that one night with me would have her coming back for more. That the memory of our evening would overcome all reason.

But as the weeks passed, my patience began to wane. I'd resisted showing up where I suspected she'd be or reaching out to her. But my ego had taken a hit.

I'd been in close contact with her brothers, giving business advice regarding their recent expansion to a second restaurant. I didn't ask how she was because she wasn't someone I usually discussed with her brothers. But it was hard.

I wanted to know if she was thinking about me. If she remembered our night. With every day that passed, I began to think she was either incredibly stubborn or she hadn't been affected like I had.

I refused to believe the latter, so when the Giovannis announced a private grand opening party at the newest Giovanni's Pizzeria, I said I'd go. It was assumed I would as a family friend, but I wanted to see her. I wanted to confirm that she was affected by my presence.

I timed my arrival so that I missed the ribbon-cutting ceremony. I didn't want to see Gia for the first time when she was busy. I wanted to catch her off guard.

I walked inside, unsure of what to expect. Gia was near the door, her mouth dropping open slightly before she recovered. "What are you doing here?"

I sensed Leo moving toward me, probably trying to diffuse an argument.

I nodded toward him. "Your brothers invited me."

Gia's hands moved to her hips, and I was drawn to the tight black dress she was wearing, with a belt at her waist with a gold symbol. It accentuated her small waist and curves. A vision of her naked and riding my cock in the hot tub popped into my head. I worked hard to clear it because I was in the same room as her brothers.

Gia's eyes flared with a mixture of irritation and something else—maybe desire. "You're not welcome here."

Leo stood by her side. "Gia, be nice. Whatever beef you have with him, can you let it go for one night? Can you just be happy for us?"

Evie ran up to Leo, holding a chain. "Can you put the necklace on me?"

Gia's face softened at the sweet interaction.

Leo squatted in front of her to put it on. "Of course."

Once it was on, Evie looked up at me, and my heart squeezed. "Do you like it?"

I cleared my throat. "It's beautiful, just like you."

Evie smiled. "Leo's marrying my mommy."

The admission made my heart thump a little harder. "Did I miss something?"

Leo grinned widely. "I just asked Harper to marry me."

Genuinely happy for my friend, I hugged him. "Congratulations. Although I didn't even realize you were dating."

"I've liked her forever, and when I finally realized she was the one for me, everything fell into place."

My mind flashed to all those moments on my balcony, and to the one I kept coming back to—Gia naked in my bed. The moon illuminating her skin as she closed her eyes and finally relaxed. I finally settled on, "That's great."

"What do you know about love?" Gia asked with a slight sneer.

I thought about it carefully, wondering why she was asking. If she thought I wasn't one for relationships, she'd be right. "I can like it for other people."

I wasn't sure if it was the right thing to say, but she nodded. I looked around at the dining room. "This place looks great."

Leo clasped my shoulder. "Thanks for helping us. We couldn't have done it without you."

"You asked Silas for business help? Why didn't you come to me?" Gia asked.

"You don't own a restaurant," Leo pointed out.

"I own a business."

I couldn't help sparring with Gia. "It's different."

Leo sighed heavily, clearly wanting to avoid a confrontation, and asked me, "Do you want a tour?"

I waved him off, needing time alone with Gia. "I can walk around while you enjoy time with your fiancée."

"Silas, it's so good to see you again." Harper appeared at Leo's side.

I was happy for my friend, but I didn't want the same thing. I was confident Gia and I could have something enjoyable while it lasted.

When Leo put his arm around Harper, murmuring in her ear, I asked Gia, "Are you my tour guide?"

Gia spun on her heel and moved away without waiting for me to follow.

"Where are you going so fast?" I asked her when I caught up.

"I'm trying to lose you."

I touched her elbow, spinning her around to face me. "Are you sure about that? I kind of want a repeat."

She crossed her arms over her chest. "Of course you do."

I decided to try a different tactic. "You look beautiful tonight, and the party is amazing."

She huffed. "You've been here for five minutes."

I grinned. "And someone's already gotten engaged. It has the making of an epic party."

Gia's lips twitched. "Are you always this charming?"

I nodded, confident that was the case. "Always. You've never given me a chance before."

"Mmm," she murmured, fighting the pull of her answering smile.

"How about that tour?" I asked, eager to get her alone.

"I would think you've already seen everything if you've been advising my brothers."

I shook my head. "It's mainly been phone calls and messages. I haven't seen the place in person."

"Fine." She sighed and led me around the dining room, pointing out the differences between this new restaurant and the original.

The furnishings were meant to be welcoming and comfortable. The colors chosen were classic pizzeria, yet tasteful. But it was the black-and-white photographs I couldn't help but notice. "Are these of your family?"

Gia moved closer so I could see them. "There are a few where we posed with customers at the other location."

I was fixated on a picture of Gia on a swing, one of her brothers next to her. "You were a cute kid."

Gia rolled her eyes. "I was really into pigtails back then."

I chucked her chin. "Adorable. Were you a princess or a tomboy?"

I remembered her being a tomboy, so it was interesting how into designer clothing she was now. I rarely saw her out of heels and a dress.

"Tomboy. That's what happens when you're the only girl."

"I have all brothers."

"Are they all as obnoxious as you are?" Gia teased.

I held my hand over my heart with mock shock. "I'm not obnoxious."

"Aren't you?" She moved on to the rest of the dining room.

There were pictures of the Giovannis at barbecues and holiday gatherings. In every one, Gia had a huge smile on her face. I wondered what happened to cause the rift with her family that I'd sensed the last few years.

She led me through the empty kitchen, which was usually Matteo's domain. There were stainless steel countertops and appliances. Everything was clean and shiny. "They've hired cooks, and Matteo will train and oversee them."

"But he'll still work at the Annapolis location?"

"That's right."

I'd advised Matteo to hire cooks at his restaurant so he could have some time off. I was pleased he'd listened.

"Matteo has some ideas for catering, to offer family-style meals. Large portions at an affordable price. The idea is, if you want a Giovanni-like gathering, we handle the food; you bring the family."

"I love that. They can use it in their marketing materials."

By the way Gia blushed, I had a feeling she'd coined it.

"But he didn't mention anything to me about wanting to cater."

Gia rested one hip against the counter, and all I could think about was gripping her hips when she was bent over my railing. "That's because he doesn't think Papà will agree to it."

I blinked to clear the vision from my mind. "Why not? I think it's clever."

"Papà doesn't like change. We need to ease him into things over time."

"Is that why there seems to be animosity between you and him?"

Gia stiffened. "You could say that."

I was getting a clear picture of what was going on. "He wants you to work in the restaurants."

Gia smiled stiffly. "Family sticks together. You know his motto."

I frowned, not liking what I was hearing. "Are you saying he disapproves of your business?"

"He thinks planning weddings is frivolous. Who would pay for that?" Gia made a move to slip past me, but I stopped her with a hand on her arm.

"Does he not realize how much people are willing to spend on weddings? And even with smaller budgets, brides and grooms want someone else to handle the details."

"Papà doesn't think like you."

From what I'd seen, Mr. Giovanni's business ideas were solid, but he tended to like to stick with what he'd always done. He wasn't continually coming up with new innovations like me or Leo. "He's old-school, but I don't understand why he's not proud of what you've accomplished. Your business is successful and thriving."

Gia cocked her head. "How do you know?"

"I'm aware of what's going on." I justified it to myself because she was a competitor, but that wasn't the whole truth.

"You're aware of business in general, or you've kept tabs on me and Happily ever Afters in particular?" Gia asked astutely.

I sensed this was a minefield, and I was going to misstep. "I'm aware of my competitors. I meet with couples after they've gone to you. Then they ask why they can't use the wedding planner of their choosing at my resort."

Gia tipped her head to the side. "And why can't they?"

"You know it's standard operating procedure at a resort," I said, trying to focus on business when I really wanted to pull her to me and kiss that cherry-red lipstick off her lips.

"And you know that only occurs at all-inclusive resorts. That's not what Chesapeake Resort offers. We work with several hotels in the area."

Gia had come to me early in my ownership of the resort and proposed being my exclusive planner. At the time, it was just her, and I doubted her ability to handle both Annapolis weddings and my resort. I also knew I couldn't be trusted around her. "Those hotels either don't have planners or they're substandard. They're all too happy to allow the bride and groom to pay for a service they should be providing."

"It's your business. You can do whatever you want," Gia insisted.

I shook my head, my stomach sinking. "I don't know how we got from me asking about the rift between you and your father to our businesses."

"It's intertwined."

"But it's not."

Gia considered me for a second before she said, "You drive me crazy."

I stepped into her body, heady with the scent of her. "I know one way we can get that out of your system."

She tipped her head back to meet my gaze. "What did you have in mind?"

"We continue what we started on my balcony." I was a little bitter that I never got an opportunity to take my time with her. "I want to taste you again."

"You want a repeat?" she asked breathlessly, her cheeks pink.

"I'm starved for you," I practically growled. I hadn't been this close to her in a long time, and it verified that nothing had changed.

Her eyes darkened with desire, and she swayed into my body.

I steadied her with a hand on her arm, then curled my fingers with hers. It felt intimate, the pang going straight through my heart.

Then she stepped back, tugging her hand from mine. "That's not a good idea."

"Oh I think it's a great idea. You need me to give you an earth-shattering orgasm."

"I have other things that help with that," she said, and I was dying to know what toys she had in her nightstand drawer.

"As hot as that is, you can't get that same feeling without me."

She rolled her eyes. "I doubt that."

I stepped closer, lowering my voice. "You don't remember how good we were that night? In the closet, bent over my railing, and you riding my cock in the hot tub."

Her cheeks flushed. "My family is here."

"Yet no one is in this kitchen." I wanted to lift her onto the pristine countertop, spread her legs, and verify she was wet from this conversation and from the memory of us, but I wouldn't expose her like that. Her father could walk in at any moment.

The thought was like cold water being poured over my head.

"I think you've seen everything," Gia said dismissively.

I grabbed her wrist. "Oh I haven't seen nearly enough."

She tugged away again. "And you won't."

"Why not?" My tone was tortured. I never begged a woman, but I felt desperate for her.

Her lips twisted. "It's a bad idea. You're friends with my brothers. We're enemies."

I scoffed. "We're only enemies because you treat me that way. We could have been business partners."

"I tried that, remember? You turned me down."

"You wanted to be my sole wedding planner. I didn't want to depend on someone whose business was elsewhere." I wasn't sure where I was going with this. I preferred making brides use my planner.

The majority of my brides wanted Gia, and I strong-armed them into using Hannah. I stood by my business practices because it was extra profit for me. I needed to get this conversation back on track because if she was able to keep her distance, she'd never give us another chance.

"What are you saying, Silas? Spell it out for me."

"I have a proposition for you."

Her eyes flared.

"You handle one bride. But it has to be you. Not one of your employees."

"Ireland and Aria are perfectly capable of handling a wedding," Gia said carefully.

"That may be so, but my couples want *you*."

Her eyes widened.

I stepped closer, my hand still encircling her wrist. I felt the flutter of her pulse and the delicate bones of her wrist. "When they come to me, they always ask if they can use *you*, not Ireland or Aria. You are the face of your company. You're the brand."

She studied my face. "You want to work with me?"

I grinned. "That's right. You'll come to my resort and work with one couple."

"How would we handle compensation?"

Gia was used to pocketing the entire fee, so this would be a challenge. "For every bride that is a referral from you, you'll get ten percent."

"Are these couples I'm working with?"

"The ones you're not. If you work directly with the bride, you'll get fifty."

She shook her head. "That's not enough."

"It's fair. I researched rates. And if you don't work with this one couple, then the deal is off." I was prepared to go a little higher. Gia wasn't the sort of woman who took anyone's first offer.

"We'd need to negotiate the rate. Do you have a couple in mind?"

"I'll find one and send you the information." My heart picked up that she was considering my proposal. I'd gotten Harrison to work with me on a similar angle. I liked to make them an offer they couldn't refuse. But Gia was different. I needed to secure her presence in my life. It was worth more than the perfect deal.

"Send me the information and let me think about it."

My jaw tightened. "This is a limited-time deal, Gia."

She gave me a look. "It sounds like you need me."

"Oh I do." In my bed and riding my cock. Maybe taking her from behind. But I didn't think that's what she was talking about.

"The couples want me, and you're manipulating them into an exclusive contract with the resort."

"It's a marketing tactic. One that's been highly effective because they want *you*." I knew if I wanted Gia in my bed, I'd have to make some concessions. It wasn't hard because I admired her and the reputation she'd built. I was confronted with it every time I sat down with a couple to seal a deal.

"This isn't some cheap tactic to get me into your bed, is it?"

I laughed. "It's not cheap. I'll do whatever it takes to get what I want."

Gia rolled her eyes. "You're impossible."

"I'm the only one that can handle you, and you don't like it. You don't like that you let go that night."

For the first time, she looked uneasy, and she shifted away from me. "I don't want a relationship."

"It's more than that. I made you lose control, and it scared you." Was it because we hadn't used a condom? "We can use protection if it makes you uneasy."

"It's not the condom. It's you. *You* make me uneasy."

I nodded, satisfied. "Now we're getting somewhere."

"Nothing's ever going to happen between us, Silas. The sooner you realize that, the easier this will be. I'll work with one couple, and we'll have a contract outlining the details."

I nodded. "I'll have my lawyers prepare one."

She arched a brow. "And my lawyers will review it."

I grinned. "I love a woman who can talk business."

"One couple. Then you're out of my life." She walked through the double doors into the dining room, leaving me alone.

"We'll see about that," I murmured to the empty room. The point of the arrangement was to see if we could work together. The truth was, I didn't feel right about telling couples they had to work with Hannah if they were set on Gia. It was a good marketing tactic, and it worked. But I wasn't sure the couples were happy with Hannah. I think they'd prefer Gia, and there was only one way to find out.

Six

GIA

I couldn't believe Silas dangled the one thing in front of me that I'd wanted for years. A chance to work with brides at his resort. Why had he changed his mind?

Was it because he wanted to get close to me? It was obvious he wanted to continue our physical relationship. But he hadn't said anything about liking me or wanting to date me. Not that it was a real possibility, but maybe I wanted to know that I got to him, and it wasn't just physical.

He might be trying to get close to me to use something against me. I couldn't trust him, even though I felt like I could when we were naked. Business was different, and I'd do well to remember that.

I'd help with one couple and prove that I could be around him and not lose my head again. Could I be around him and not give in to him? Did I want to?

Could we have a physical relationship that didn't go anywhere else? Just two successful people getting a release with each other? No strings and no promises?

I would have believed it if I hadn't already felt the way I did when we were together. The thing that held me back was that he hadn't felt the same way. It was purely physical for him.

I smiled and nodded the rest of the night and was disappointed when Silas didn't try to get me alone again. It was ridiculous, but I liked our banter and his references to our sexual encounters. He fired me up and got me thinking about something besides business.

I needed to prove to my father that opening a business was the right move and that I could be successful. For me, success was determined by the numbers, and Happily Ever Afters wasn't there yet.

I wouldn't admit defeat—not to my brothers or to my father. I needed to make my dream work. Harper had convinced me that if I wanted to expand, I needed to hire more people. I had moments when I thought I should let the employees go and handle everything myself. But that was my old way of doing business.

Now I was glad we'd hired more planners because it would allow me to concentrate on Silas's couple and give them my full attention. If it went well, and he allowed me to handle more brides at his resort, that would be good for my business. It would be worth it. If only I could resist him.

When everyone left the party, I volunteered to stay and clean up. I kicked off my heels, slid on flip-flops, and cleaned the tables. I was just taking out the garbage when a car pulled down the alley. I probably shouldn't have taken out the garbage while I was alone.

The window lowered. "What are you doing out here?"

I breathed a sigh of relief when I saw it was Silas and lifted the bag. "Taking out the garbage."

"Are you here alone?" he asked as he stepped out of his vehicle, which was a sleek black sports car.

I shrugged. "I had to clean up."

"Does your family know you're here by yourself?" Silas asked as he took the bag from me and threw it effortlessly into the large dumpster.

"Why does that matter?"

His jaw tightened. "They wouldn't like it."

"My family doesn't like a lot of what I do. I stopped caring a long time ago." I turned and went into the restaurant to wash my hands. That was a little harsher than reality.

When I was finished, Silas took off his suit jacket, laid it carefully on the counter, and took his time rolling up his shirt, revealing sinewy muscles and a dusting of hair. He washed his hands and dried them on the towel I offered him.

When he was done, he turned to face me. "You don't mean that."

"Don't mean what?" I asked, a little distracted by his exposed forearms.

He crossed his arms over his chest and cocked a hip against the counter. "That you don't care what your family thinks."

"I care too much." That's why I worked so hard. Not that my father ever noticed. He was all *Leo did this*, and *Carlo did that*. It was hard to be seen in a sea of men.

Silas considered me and then finally said, "You're trying to prove yourself to your father."

"Then the joke's on me because it's not possible to get his approval. At least not for me." I wasn't sure why I was being so honest with Silas. He was my enemy, not a confidant.

"He's proud of you," Silas said softly as he moved closer to me.

"How do you know? You might be friends with my brothers, but you don't know my father." I lifted my chin to maintain his gaze as he moved ever closer.

"How could he not be? You run a successful business. You're courageous." His voice was deep and smooth, lulling me into believing him.

I liked how he'd described me, but I never thought Silas would be complimenting me.

He stopped when he was inches from touching me, and I licked my lips in anticipation of him kissing me. "How could anyone not be impressed?"

"That's what I'd like to know," I said breathlessly.

He touched my chin, tipping it up farther. "I am."

Then he lowered his lips to mine. It was a confirmation of everything we'd already shared and a testament to everything we could be.

His hand cupped my jaw as he stepped into me, my body pressed against his, soft against hard. I melted into him, wanting to get lost in his words and his touch.

Silas Sharpe was addicting. I'd craved this since the last time we were together, and I had no plans to walk away from him this time.

He kissed me tentatively, as if it was our first kiss instead of one of many. One brush, then two. My entire body was warm all over, lit up for him. When he pulled back, I followed him, hoping to catch his lips again.

Silas stepped back. "Are you finished here?"

"I'll just do a quick run-through to make sure I didn't forget anything." I couldn't believe I'd been so lost in him.

I was thankful he'd put a stop to it. I left the kitchen, needing as much space as I could get. I shouldn't take him up on his offer to work with him. Unfortunately, I'd already agreed, and I didn't want him to think that I was worried I couldn't control myself around him, even if it was the truth. The very uncomfortable truth.

Silas followed me through the restaurant.

"Everything's in order. I'm going to head out," I said brightly.

Silas waited for me at the front door. "Why didn't you hire someone to clean up?"

"Because I can handle it," I said, wanting to unlock the door, but he was blocking my exit.

Silas crossed his arms. "I thought Harper convinced you to hire people to help?"

I tipped my head to consider him. "How do you know that?"

"Leo talks."

Irritation shot up my spine. "He has no business talking to you about me."

"I'm not your enemy."

"You are." But my insistence fell flat. He'd stopped because he was worried about me. He was willing to work with me despite my usual defensiveness when we were around each other.

"You came to me years ago asking for a partnership, and I'm willing to try it out. If we're going to do this, we need to call a truce."

I nodded stiffly. "I can be professional."

His lips twitched. "You can be with everyone but me."

"I'll do better."

His lips twitched. "So you'll give it a real chance?"

"Of course. It's what I want. What I've always wanted."

"To work with me?"

And apparently more. "Yes."

"Is that all you want?"

My mind flashed back to that tender kiss in the kitchen and the way he'd devoured me in the closet. "Absolutely."

His expression was dubious. He didn't believe me, but it didn't matter. I was going to lie to him and to myself. Nothing good could come from kissing him again.

When he'd kissed me so sweetly, I'd wanted more. Which was ridiculous. I didn't know any man capable of being tender. Sex was a physical release and nothing more. It didn't leave me wanting more. Not like it had when I was with Silas. Which was why I should be staying away from him. But business came first. "I'm looking forward to working with you."

He grinned. "I never thought I'd hear you say that."

I shook my head. "Were you driving by for a reason?"

"I wanted to see if you were still here."

That surprised me. "You were checking up on me?"

"I was worried about you."

To hear him clarify what I already sensed was interesting. It made me think there was more to him than his ruthless business side. Was there hope for something between us? I immediately dismissed it. Neither of us wanted a relationship.

Yet he hadn't pursued that kiss when I was more than willing to take it further. What was his end game?

He grabbed his suit jacket from the back, waited while I locked up, and walked me to my car.

I prided myself on being an independent woman, but I liked that he'd stopped by to check on me and waited to ensure I'd made it safely to my car. When we reached the driver's-side door, I turned to face him, unable to contain my curiosity. "What was that in the kitchen?"

His suit jacket was draped over his arm. "You mean when I kissed you?"

"Yes." My voice was gruffer than I'd intended. I didn't usually ask men what their intentions were, because mine were the only ones that mattered.

He considered me for a few seconds before he finally admitted, "I was in the moment." His expression was so genuine I believed him.

"Why did you stop?"

He brushed a hair out of my face, his soft touch sending tingles down my spine. "The next time we kiss, I want it to be because you initiated it. Because you made the conscious decision to be with me."

My skin tingled, and my insides felt fizzy with excitement even as I said, "That's not going to happen."

He cocked his head, and his lips twitched. "Are you sure about that?"

"Positive." I drew on my MO with guys. I was the one in control. I liked it better that way. I refused to give in to the idea that I enjoyed how he'd initiated our first kiss or when he'd pulled me into that closet to pleasure me.

Silas stepped closer so that we were touching from thighs to my chest and then dipped his head to murmur against my jaw. "You're a tough nut to crack, Gia Giovanni."

The scruff of his day-old beard scraped deliciously across my cheek. I wanted to feel it between my legs. I wanted him to make me come apart again. My core ached to feel him inside me.

"It will be challenging but worth it." Then he stepped back, the air between us cooling considerably now that he was standing a foot away from me and not touching me.

"We're supposed to be working together. We're professionals."

Silas rocked back on his heels. "Is that how you want to play this?"

How was he so cool and seemingly unaffected when I felt like a bomb ready to explode? Could I erase the distance between us and kiss him? Would I give in and make that first move?

He'd issued a challenge, and I'd meet it with one of my own.

I shoved the idea aside that I might like giving in to Silas Sharpe. That I would most likely enjoy every minute of his lips and hands on me. But clinging to my way of handling things was more important.

I needed to hold on to control in this situation. My business and my future depended on it. Letting go with Silas might feel good in the moment, but the repercussions would be catastrophic. I'd never allowed myself to completely let go with a man, except for the times I'd been with Silas, and the implications scared me.

Who was I without my carefully constructed habits? I'd gotten this far on them, and I wanted more gains before I could relax and declare my business a success.

Silas sighed. "I like you. I want to spend time with you. But you have to make the next move."

My jaw tightened under his scrutiny and his soft words. They were infiltrating my heart, curling around the frayed edges, and filling the empty chambers. "So you've said."

Silas looked down at the ground as if he was trying to find his next words, and then he lifted his gaze to mine. "You are stubborn."

"Everyone knows this about me," I said softly, keeping my eyes on him.

"I'm going to figure you out. What makes you tick, what gets you soft."

Something about the word *soft* broke through my hard shell, splintering my carefully constructed walls. My face heated, and my fingers curled into fists by my side. "Why?"

"Because I like you."

Tears sparked behind my lids because no one had ever made this much effort to pursue me. I was a shield, deflecting come-ons and requests for dates like I would change the channel on a TV. Men were usually easy to handle. Unfortunately, this one wasn't. He was infuriating and relentless. I knew this about him in business, but I never considered what it would be like for him in this situation. "Nothing can happen between us. Have you forgotten about my brothers?"

"I'd never do anything to mess things up with your brothers, your family, or our businesses."

"You can't guarantee that." Besides, he was worried about the external factors. He hadn't mentioned the possibility of getting hurt. It was the single thing I'd avoided my entire life. I broke things off with guys first. I'd only felt the sting of a breakup once, and I vowed never to put myself in that situation again. I never let it get that far. And I certainly never allowed myself to fall for a guy. If I allowed myself to be vulnerable with Silas, it would be a mistake. He had the power to get under my skin, to infiltrate my walls, to make me feel.

"Everything about you drives me crazy, and I'm relentless when I want something."

"I've noticed." I ignored the first part of his statement for my self-preservation and focused on the second. He'd wanted Harrison's arbors, and he'd gotten them. I didn't even want to think about the financial deal he gave Harrison to get him to work with him.

"This isn't over," he repeated the message he'd sent me over text after our first night together.

"I'm happy to work with one of your couples and to see if a business arrangement between us is possible, but that's all this is." I put on my business voice because I couldn't handle Silas when he was pursuing me on anything other than a surface level. He said he only wanted something physical, but that's not what we shared that one night. It was so much more, and either he didn't get that, or he didn't care. Which meant he was reckless.

I didn't do anything that wasn't carefully thought out, the risks and benefits analyzed and dissected. I didn't need to do an autopsy on Silas to know that he was dangerous to my equilibrium. He'd already demonstrated that with every touch and every kiss. I melted when he was near, and I couldn't afford to let go with him. No matter how persistent he was, I wouldn't give in.

I moved aside as he stepped close. I wondered for a second if he was going to give in and kiss me first. Triumph surged through my body and eased when he opened the door for me. "Have a good night, Gia. Get home safely."

Disappointment coursed through my body as I slid inside and set my purse on the passenger-side seat. He braced his arms on the doorframe and leaned inside, his cologne filling the interior of my small sports car.

"Do me a favor and text me when you get home."

He was so close I could tug on his tie and his mouth would lower to mine. It would be so easy, and it would feel so good. So why didn't I do it? Give in to the pleasure that I knew I'd experience in his arms and under his body?

I bit my lip as visions of his body pressing me into the mattress took hold, and I almost lost control.

He tapped the roof of the car and pushed away.

"Why?" I couldn't help but ask.

"So I know that you got home safely."

Because I was used to this with my brothers and respected his request, I nodded. "I will."

The resulting smile was so bright, I blinked in surprise. "It's only a matter of time."

Despite my irritation, I smiled. "You're dreaming, Silas. I'll never give in."

"Oh, you will," he said with a wink as I turned on the car and slammed my door shut. I didn't need Silas to taunt me, to remind me of how tenuous my control was when I was around him.

I backed out and avoided looking at him watching me drive away. I'd had a taste of him, and it would have to be enough to last a lifetime because I wasn't going back for more.

Seven

SILAS

I watched Gia drive away, desire humming under my skin. It wasn't in my nature to deny a woman who wanted me, but I'd restrained myself during that kiss. I could easily have given in to my baser instincts and lifted her onto that countertop, spread her out, and given us both the pleasure we wanted.

That would have been the easy thing to do. It was what I wanted to do. But I'd had a lot of time to think about what happened between us, and I didn't want to mess things up again. I had a feeling if Gia felt out of control of the situation again, she'd run even further.

I needed her to come to me, which was a gamble when I wasn't sure she would. She was stubborn and strong and unlike any woman I'd ever been with. I wanted to do this the right way.

I liked her more than I should, and more than was reasonable when we didn't have a future. I'd convinced myself I'd only wanted something physical, but it was more than that. I wanted to make her come undone, not just physically but emotionally. If I did that, it would be more than any relationship I'd attempted in the past.

But then, Gia already meant more to me. She wasn't just some woman I'd admired from afar. She was my best friends' sister. I'd avoided meeting up with her brothers since I'd been inside her, but I couldn't avoid them much longer. Our guys' weekend at the resort was coming up. We'd go out on my boat, drink, and catch up.

I wouldn't mention Gia, but it would be awkward as hell thinking of how I'd betrayed them. I wasn't certain I'd be able to keep it from them, but I didn't have a choice. Even if the guilt felt like this brick weighing down my chest.

I hadn't gotten much farther than getting Gia to give in to me. I didn't think about the repercussions or what it meant. Or anything other than getting her back in my bed, where she belonged.

I knew I wouldn't be able to resist her if I saw her again, and I was right. Now I'd orchestrated a situation where we'd be working together. It wasn't smart. But I was looking forward to seeing her every day. I just hoped I could hold out and keep my word.

I wanted to follow her home and tell her I'd lied. That I didn't care if she gave up control, as long as I could have her.

But I brushed that idea off because I knew Gia would push me away harder each time until she cut off all ties. I didn't want that.

I got into my car and drove home. I hadn't been able to stay in my penthouse suite since Gia had slept over. Everywhere I looked, there were memories of her and me, and I couldn't be there without seeing her in the hot tub or bent over the railing. And since I couldn't have her, it made everything worse.

Instead, I drove to my house. The two-story colonial was at the end of a long driveway hidden by trees. I'd fallen in love with the place as soon as I'd seen it. I loved the privacy and the view of the water from the back of the house.

It was why I'd bought the resort. I'd always wanted to live by the water. I grabbed a beer from the fridge and sat on the screened-in porch, enjoying the sounds of the night, the crickets, the occasional frog, and the lapping of the water. The moon shone over the water, reminding me of the night Gia was in my bed.

If only I could hold on to her. I told myself I wanted something physical, but it had always been deeper than that. I liked her. I respected her. I wanted to see her succeed.

My phone buzzed with a text. When I saw it was an image of Gia lying in bed with barely there lingerie, I fumbled the phone and almost dropped it.

Letting out a breath, I took a second look. The caption was: **Home safe and sound**. Gia wore a deep purple lace bra and panty set, her breasts spilling over the cups, and my fingers itched to tug them down. A second image came through with her rolled over and throwing a sultry look at the camera over her shoulder. In this one, her bra was removed, her back enticingly bare, and the lace of the thong disappeared between her ass cheeks.

When I recovered as best I could, I responded.

> You always send naked pics to guys?

I didn't think she was the kind of woman who did things like that, and it made me even harder.

> Just you.

I wasn't sure if that made me feel better.

> Why are you teasing me?

It was more like torture.

> Are you alone?

> Fuck, yes.

> What are you wearing?

61

Are you sure you want to do this?

Are you naked yet?

I fumbled the phone again as I stood and headed inside, locking the slider behind me and taking the steps two at a time to get to my bedroom. I toed off my shoes, unbuttoned my shirt, and flung it onto the armchair in the corner, then pushed down my pants and briefs, leaving them to pool on the floor.

I got set up on the bed and texted her again.

I am now.

Let me see.

I needed to regain control, so I video-called her.

Gia's face came on the screen. Her cheeks were flushed.

"Are you touching yourself?" I asked, fisting my cock.

"Wouldn't you like to know?" Gia said.

"Show me," I demanded. "I want to see your fingers inside you."

She tipped her head back as if my words made her hotter. "I'm not there yet."

"Get there," I growled.

She slowly lowered the camera, giving me a tantalizing shot of her full breasts, hard nipples, flat stomach, and bare pussy. Her perfectly manicured fingers were circling her clit.

"Spread your legs wider. I want to see if you're wet for me."

"I'm always wet for you, Silas."

I squeezed my cock, almost losing it. I loved how free she was over the phone. Was it the distance that made her let go? Or the fact that she'd initiated this, so she felt like she was in control? She was going to find out that control was an illusion. Relationships and sex were a give and take, not one person leading all the time.

"Can you set up the phone so I can see all of you?" I wanted to see her face.

The image dropped as she must have fumbled the phone, and then she finally got it set up so that the camera was between her legs, and I could see her breasts and face. "You're so sexy."

She bit her lip, one hand squeezing her breasts, tweaking her nipple as a finger dipped into her channel.

I used the pre-cum from the tip of my cock to lubricate the skin and pump. "That's it, baby. Pretend it's my fingers."

"Are you touching yourself? I want to see." Gia's voice was demanding, and I loved it.

I set up the phone so that my hands were free, and she had a good view. I fisted my cock and stroked. "You see how hard you make me?"

"That's so hot," she said breathlessly.

"Tweak those nipples. I want them hard and aching for me."

She whimpered as she followed my command.

"If I were with you, I'd suck on your clit. Hard."

"I want that."

I refrained from saying she could have had that tonight because I was patient and knew it wouldn't get me anywhere. I liked her like this, hot and aching for me.

"But I wouldn't let you come. I'd make you wait and come on my cock."

Her cheeks flushed a deeper pink. "I want that too."

"Use two fingers and pretend it's my cock filling you up."

She complied, but her eyes fell closed.

"Watch me," I said as I gripped my cock tighter, jerking myself off hard and fast.

Her lips parted as she opened her eyes and watched me. "I'm so close."

"I am too."

"I want to ram into you, filling you up. I'd suck on your nipples, then flip you over and take you from behind. I'd grip your hips so hard I'd leave bruises the next day. I'd pull out to the tip and ram back inside. Over and over again. Driving you wild with need, but I wouldn't let you come."

"Silas, please." Her voice was breathless, needy.

I wondered if she wanted my permission. "Come with me, Gia."

As soon as her body jerked, the orgasm I'd been holding at bay flew through my body, and cum spurted over my hand and onto the comforter. I grabbed my shirt and wiped up the excess.

When I was cleaned up, the camera wasn't between Gia's legs anymore. She'd moved it so that it was showing her face.

"Thank you for sending those pictures." She didn't strike me as someone who would do something like that, so I had a feeling it was something she did just for me. And what we'd just shared was intense.

She looked away from the camera. "I've never done that before."

"Neither have I."

"It was nice," she finally said.

"It was more than nice. It was phenomenal." I liked that she'd let go with me. She might have thought it was safe because we were in two different places, but it was still sex. We'd manage to connect without being close physically.

She laughed softly.

I loved her like this. Flushed from her orgasm and sated. I wanted to be with her so I could hold her. But I knew she needed space and time. But this was a great first step.

"I loved that you shared that with me. Sleep tight, Gia."

Her eyes widened slightly, as if she hadn't expected me to get off the phone so quickly, but I wanted to keep her wanting more. "Yeah, okay. Good night, Silas."

I ended the call. I hoped I did the right thing by engaging her. It allowed her to think she was in control when she was really letting go with me. She'd done something she never had before, and we'd shared that experience together. I could only hope that it was the right move.

I prided myself on always knowing the next right thing to do, but I'd never encountered anyone like Gia before. She was so tightly wound it was a challenge to get her to unravel. And I wanted to do it again and again and again.

I'd never been so challenged by a woman before, and I was enjoying every minute. It didn't take long for women to bore me. There was the anticipation when you first met the gaze of a gorgeous woman across the room, but it could fall through when she spoke. I liked any woman I spent time with to be intelligent and successful. But Gia took it to another level. I had a feeling it was because she wasn't attracted to my money or my success. If anything, it repelled her.

It wasn't just our mutual connection with her brothers that made her pause. It was the connection she felt when I was near. She was scared of the way I made her feel. I could sympathize because I felt the same way.

But I knew it would be worth it. I was confident I could keep things from her brothers and the rest of her family. No one had to know.

I took a shower to clean off, and the memory of Gia working over her clit and pumping her fingers inside her pussy had me hard.

I gripped my cock and replayed that vision in my mind, and in no time, I was spurting over the walls of the shower. I still wanted her, and I had a feeling I'd never get enough.

Eight

GIA

I felt a little shaky the next week, reliving that encounter with Silas. There was the kiss in the kitchen, his refusal to take things further, and then his challenge for me to come to him. On the drive home, I'd been confident I could resist him, but when I'd gotten undressed for bed, I was aroused and aching for him.

I had this impulse to send him a picture before I took care of things myself. It was naughty, and I was usually careful. I never took pictures and sent them to guys. Which meant, on some level, I trusted Silas.

It might have had something to do with the way he seemed to care for me. He'd stopped at the pizzeria to make sure I wasn't alone, and he didn't use the opportunity to take advantage of what I was eagerly offering him. He wanted me to come to him. It only made me want him more.

I was positive he knew exactly what he was doing to me, and I wanted to return the favor. I wanted to drive *him* crazy and show him what he was missing.

Unfortunately, it hadn't sated my desire; it had only made me burn hotter for him. I'd never seen anything sexier than a man stroking his cock. Now I couldn't get my mind off how many times he'd jerked off to the memory of our video call.

Was he as affected as I was? Did he want me as badly as I wanted him? I'd been hot and bothered all week.

I had to get myself together because we'd agreed to meet today to talk about the couple I'd be working with. I was both looking forward to it and dreading it. It was always interesting when we were in the same room. He challenged me and turned me on at the same time. And that was the problem. I had to resist him. I couldn't give in to his stupid ultimatum. That meant he won.

If I was honest with myself, it meant something a whole lot deeper. He wanted me to let go. To give him some of the control in our dynamic, and I wasn't prepared to do that. I'd never done that in any relationship, and I certainly wouldn't do it with him. I needed to keep the upper hand at all costs.

Although, I thought he'd flipped things on me over the phone, by video calling me and ordering me to touch my nipples and fuck myself with my fingers. I was completely helpless when it came to Silas, especially when it felt so good. When he told me to imagine my fingers were his, I was lost to the timbre of his voice and the sweet promise in his words.

I wanted him in that moment. I wanted him on top of me, behind me, and inside me. I wanted him to own me. And that was a scary feeling.

No one told me what to do. No one told me what was possible for me. I ran my life. Not some guy. Not that Silas was just *some* guy. He was powerful and commanding and made me wetter than I'd ever been.

Every orgasm I'd ever had paled in comparison to the ones he gave me. Even the one I gave myself on the phone had been earth-shattering.

I drove to his resort, arguing with myself the entire way. The rational part of me wanted to be a professional, and the passionate side of me wanted to fuck him and give in to this insatiable chemistry between us. Normally, I'd be all for it. But Silas wasn't like other guys. He demanded more of me.

It was scary and thrilling all at the same time.

I parked in a visitor spot, wondering what would happen if he truly wanted me as his girlfriend, not someone he had to keep a secret. Everything inside me went soft.

What if we worked together and were able to get along? I had a feeling that wouldn't ever be the case, but *what if* I gave in to this desire?

A knock on my window startled me. Silas stood there in his ever-present suit with a cocky grin on his face. Irritation flowed through me as I grabbed my purse.

Silas opened the door for me, and I told my traitorous heart not to get excited because he'd made one chivalrous gesture. "I thought you might change your mind."

"Why would I do that? I've always wanted to work with you," I asked as he closed the car door.

He stepped closer and lowered his voice. "I thought it might have something to do with what happened the other night."

My skin heated at the memory. "I thought you wanted to keep things professional."

Silas chuckled as he led the way through the front doors. "I do."

His stride was long, and employees greeted him as he walked. He merely nodded and kept going. I kept pace with him, which wasn't easy in heels.

"Today, we can discuss the couple before they're scheduled to meet with us. Then I thought we could have lunch." His tone was professional, and even that was sexy.

I was in so much trouble.

When we entered his office, he moved behind the large dark wood desk and handed me a key card used for hotel rooms. "This is a key for your room while you work here."

"I won't need a room."

"It's a long drive from Annapolis. There may be times when

you won't want to drive home. I'd rather you have a place here. I can make it part of the contract."

Our attorneys had ironed out a deal where I'd earn sixty percent of the fee and would have access to the resort and his staff for the duration. It was limited to the one couple. We'd reevaluate things once the wedding was over.

Silas's expression sobered. "It would make me feel better."

"Okay," I finally acquiesced, because Silas was genuinely concerned for my safety. It might have been out of misplaced loyalty to my brothers, but I didn't think so. And it would be nice to have a room if I needed it.

"You can leave whatever you need to here. The room is yours for the duration."

"Thank you, Silas," I said softly.

His lips twitched. "You can be sweet when you want to be."

"I know how to appreciate a good thing." I meant the room, but I was thinking about how he made me feel when we were together.

Silas's nostrils flared.

"You wanted to discuss the couple before they arrived?"

He picked up the folder on his desk and handed it to me. "I know you prefer working on a tablet, but I'm a paper kind of guy."

"Why doesn't that surprise me?" I asked, smiling. Silas was old-fashioned in a lot of ways. "I'll transfer it to our system. That's how I work."

"That's not a problem. I want you to be comfortable here. Do whatever it is you do that has the wedding couples flocking to you. Work your magic."

I'd always suspected there was something about me that made the business flourish, but it was nice hearing someone else acknowledge it too.

"The purpose of this partnership is to bring the best of both worlds together. And to determine if it makes sense to work together going forward."

My business was based in Annapolis, so servicing couples at Silas's resort would create conflicts and challenges for me. I wanted this opportunity so I wouldn't automatically lose business if a couple chose the resort as their venue. But now that I was here, I wasn't sure it was the best idea for me, and that was the point of this trial period.

The romantic part of my heart that had long ago been cordoned off wondered if Silas and I became a thing, whether I'd handle the weddings at the resort going forward. The idea was ridiculous because Silas never once said he was looking for a girlfriend, and I never wanted a boyfriend distracting me from my business.

It was rare for me to find a man who respected that part of me. Men were usually intimidated by my drive and success. Most didn't want to date someone who could pay their own way. They might say they did, but I suspected it made them feel less than.

"Emma and John have a large budget. The bride's father told Hannah there was no limit. That's why I thought it would be a fun one for you to work on."

"My favorite kind of wedding." I smiled as I scanned the information provided in the folder.

"They are excited that you will be working with them."

"I'm happy to hear that." Although I wasn't surprised. Those with money always wanted the best, and in this area, that was me.

"They haven't made any decisions yet, so you'll need to start from the beginning."

"What are the options you provide for the ceremony?" I asked, and he went through the various locations. There was a large indoor ballroom, a room overlooking the water, a few spots by the water—some more private than others—and the gardens. All were amazing locations, and it was a dream come true to offer all of them on the same property. Most venues had one option, not all of them.

We spent the morning going over the offerings, any limitations, and his personal policy—no request was denied. I limited that with my brides because I didn't want the wedding planners overworked unnecessarily, but Silas's policy was to meet every expectation of the bride and groom, no matter how big. "Are there any boundaries with your couples? Times when Hannah isn't available?"

"That's up to Hannah to set."

"That's good." I'd be setting very clear boundaries at the first meeting. I worked hard for my clients, but not every hour of every day. I wasn't Silas's employee. I was more of a consultant he'd brought in. I'd set my own boundaries and hours.

"If you feel comfortable, we can go to lunch. Then John and Emma are scheduled to meet with us this afternoon."

"Will you be involved in the planning?" I asked him.

"I'll let you do your thing. I trust that you're good at your job."

"I'm more than good." There was a reason I was the number-one wedding planner in Annapolis. But I'd been struggling with the number of high-budget clients choosing Silas's venue. Harper recently came up with the idea of advertising to out-of-state couples with the pitch that Annapolis was a destination wedding. It had added new clients to the mix, but I wasn't satisfied we'd solved our cash flow problem.

This arrangement with Silas could be the answer, and I didn't want to do anything to mess it up.

"That's why we're working together. I only work with the best," he said smoothly.

I smiled, pleased he was complimenting me, and we weren't fighting like we usually did.

Silas stood and rounded his desk, offering his hand to me. "If you're going to be working here, you need to sample the food. I have a table reserved for us overlooking the water."

I put my hand in his, wondering why I was letting him cross this boundary when we were merely working together. The warmth of his palm seeped up my arm and straight to my heart.

He held my hand as he led me through the resort and into his five-star restaurant. Silas nodded at the hostess as he headed straight for a table overlooking the water, where it was relatively private. Silas pulled out my chair. "We're working, so I didn't order any wine."

"That's fine," I said as he sat in the chair across from me. There was a vase of fresh flowers in the middle of the table. It was a nice touch. I had a feeling Silas added details like that to separate his resort from others.

I perused the menu as Silas mentioned the most popular dishes and the ones that were his favorite. I settled on the salmon, and he ordered the chicken.

When the waitress took our order and left, Silas said, "Everything is good. You won't be disappointed."

"I assumed it would be top-notch, and the view is incredible. I can't believe you get to look at this every day."

"My favorite view is the one at my house. It's tucked behind the woods, but the rear of the house is open to the water. I spend most of my time on the deck when I'm there."

"I would too."

He raised a brow. "Maybe you can see it sometime."

"Silas, we're working together now," I chided softly as my heart thumped harder.

"Are you saying that we can't be intimate because of our arrangement? I can be professional and keep things separate."

What he wasn't saying was that he could keep his emotions out of it, but I'd already proven that I couldn't. "I don't think it's a good idea."

Silas nodded but didn't push. "You'll like it here, and you're welcome to stay at any time. Even if you're not working."

"That's very generous of you," I said, and meant it.

"I'm a generous guy."

Normally, I'd have a sarcastic comment to make about that, but as I'd gotten to know Silas, I'd suspected he was a good guy. Generous with both his time and money. I was starting to see that I'd judged him on a surface level, which wasn't fair. But then again, I was protecting myself. I knew if I drifted too close, I'd be sucked into his vortex. I still wasn't sure I'd come out of this unscathed.

There was a business reason we were having lunch together. It would be good for me to know the food and the resort if I was going to advise the couple. I couldn't help but wonder if this was one more way that Silas was getting closer to me.

"I can see why couples choose your resort. The location is magnificent."

Silas paused, his gaze steady on mine. "I think you've given me more compliments in one day than you ever have before."

"I'm sorry if I wasn't always courteous to you, Silas. In fact, I know I wasn't."

"There's nothing to apologize for."

"I don't feel right about it." Especially when my brothers were friends with him. I hadn't been raised to be impolite, and as I scanned over our past interactions, I realized I had been incredibly rude to him.

"I'm just pleased you're here now."

We were getting to know each other on a different level, and some of the animosity I'd always carried with me fell away. We needed to work together, and to do that, we needed to be cordial.

"How are things at Happily Ever Afters?" Silas asked.

"Good," I said, not wanting to get into the business issues with him. He was still my competitor, and if he sensed that there was something wrong, he'd dig until he found something he could capitalize on.

"When you first came to me, wanting to work with my couples, you were a new business and needed the extra income. But now, your business is flourishing. Do you need this?"

I wasn't sure how much I should divulge to him. "I like to explore every possibility. If it doesn't work out, then I'll know it's not the right business move for me."

"Hmm."

The waitress brought us our salads, a spinach salad with

strawberries, feta cheese, walnuts, and a balsamic vinaigrette on the side. We dug into them, and I hoped he'd forgotten what we were talking about.

"I'm not sure I buy it," Silas finally said, startling me.

"Buy what?"

"Your reason for working with me."

I flushed. Could he tell I wasn't telling the truth?

Silas winked. "I think you just want to be closer to me."

I relaxed since he was just teasing me. "Of course, you would think that. Your ego doesn't let you go anywhere else."

"I do have a healthy ego. I have a feeling this is going to be a good partnership."

Was he talking about us working together professionally? I shouldn't have been disappointed. It was what I wanted, yet I couldn't get that phone call out of my head. I wanted Silas in a way I'd never desired anyone else. I was reluctant to let it go, even if it had no future. Yet he'd said the next move was mine. Was I going to take advantage of his offer of a room and stay here, maybe even meet with him one night at the bar, and take it to his penthouse? How many other women had he done that with?

I set down my fork with shaking hands. "How many other women have you taken to your penthouse?" Did he have the penthouse for that purpose? Coldness slithered down my spine. He kept a separate house for his privacy. I suddenly felt cheap.

"What are you talking about?"

"I assume the penthouse is for women you're sleeping with, and the house is yours when you need privacy."

A muscle ticked in his jaw. "I keep the penthouse so I don't have to travel home on late nights, and it's a nice spot to escape to in the middle of the day. It's my hotel. It only makes sense. But I don't keep it to fuck women there."

His harsh words penetrated my shock. "So, I'm not one of many you've taken there?"

He'd bent me over that balcony like he'd done it before. How many women had ridden him in the hot tub? God. How could I have been so stupid? Why did I think I was special? He attracted women who wanted to be close to his wealth, hoping he'd choose them. I wasn't anything like that. I worked hard for what I had and didn't need a man to provide means.

Silas shook his head. "Where is this coming from? Why would you think that about me? I never treated you like you were one of many."

"The women you're photographed with at events at the hotel... It only makes sense."

He leaned back in his chair, considering me, and I resisted the urge to shift in my seat. "You're jealous."

"I'm just feeling cheap."

"Jesus, Gia. You're anything but cheap. You're one of a kind. Gorgeous. I never did anything to make you think that or feel like that. If I did—"

I rushed to reassure him, placing my hand over his. "I'm sorry. I just jumped to conclusions. You always have a beautiful woman on your arms, and then the penthouse and the home on the water... I thought—"

"What we shared was special. I don't take women to the penthouse or to my house. I have to have dates for events, but I wasn't dating those women. I haven't had a relationship in a long time. Maybe since college. Women tend to only want one thing from me."

The immediate thing that popped into my head was sex, but he said, "Money."

"Oh. I can see that."

"They want what I can give them materially, not anything else."

"That's—I'm sorry, Silas." That wasn't okay, and I couldn't imagine it. "If it makes you feel better, men are usually intimidated by me."

His eyes darkened. "I can see that. You're strong. Successful. I find it hot as hell."

I flushed all over, and I was seconds away from begging him to take me upstairs to his penthouse.

The waitress arrived to remove our salad plates. When she left, Silas leaned his elbows on the table. "I want you, Gia. I'm attracted to your brains, your body, and your tenacity. Never think that you're one of many. You're one of a kind."

Nine

SILAS

"Thank you," Gia murmured.

I nodded and leaned back in my chair. "I'm curious why you color your hair blonde." I only asked because she had dark hair as a little girl. Otherwise, I wouldn't have even noticed.

Gia laughed. "At first, it was to upset Papà, and then I liked it. It was a way to stand out in the family. To be different."

I was a little lost in her smile and the pure joy on her face. "You don't need to color your hair for that. You always stand out to me."

Her cheeks flushed pink. "It was just something I did, and it stuck."

She'd be gorgeous no matter her hair color. "I like you as a blonde."

She looked away from me. "I like it too, and it's been so long, I can't remember how I look with dark hair."

"What else did you do to rebel?" I asked, needing to know more. I'd heard things from her brothers, how she drove them crazy when she started dating, but otherwise, they didn't talk about her. They knew how she felt about me and were loyal to her.

"You've probably heard the stories. Leo was supposed to watch out for me, and I'd take off with some guy."

"On the back of a motorcycle," I said lightly, even as it irritated me.

"I did it to drive my brothers crazy. They always kept it from Papà, though."

"That was nice of them."

"They wanted to make sure I was safe, but they didn't have to worry. I could take care of myself. I was always in control of any situation I was in." Her eyes flashed to mine, as if she hadn't meant to reveal that last part.

"I don't doubt that." She could take care of herself, but she shouldn't have put herself in those situations. I had a feeling she didn't do anything like that now. "Do you date a lot?"

"Occasionally, but no one holds my interest for long."

I smirked at that because I was positive I more than held her interest. She was resisting me, but she wouldn't be able to do that forever. I was confident in my ability to wear her down, to drive her crazy until she gave in. And when she did—it would be worth the wait.

She needed a man who was confident and sure of himself. She didn't have to be with someone who was wealthy, but she deserved to date an equal. Someone who'd admire her and not be jealous of her success. I had a feeling we'd push each other to be better in our respective businesses.

I wondered if she got bored with the guys she dated, or if things got too intense, she'd break things off. Maybe she only felt vulnerable with me, and I liked that a lot.

"What about you? You said you don't bring women to your penthouse. Who are the women in the pictures in the newspaper? Are they girlfriends?"

"They're friends. I needed a date for those functions, and they like to be seen on my arm."

Her nose wrinkled. "Why would you need a date?"

I hesitated for a few seconds, unsure if she'd like my answer.

Then I decided to go with the truth. "It keeps women from hitting on me."

She laughed then, her eyes dancing. "You need a date to protect you from women coming on to you?"

"Something like that," I said, enjoying her reaction.

She grinned. "I like that. Maybe I can be your protector next time."

Joy surged through me. I was fairly positive it was a spur-of-the-moment offer, one she'd issued to be funny, but I wasn't going to let it go. "It's a date."

Her eyes widened. "I didn't mean—"

"I'm sure you're a woman of your word, and you offered," I reminded her.

Her eyes narrowed on me. "Fine. I'll be your date."

"There's a charity event here next weekend. You're welcome to use your room to get ready and stay overnight. Unless you choose to sleep in my room."

Gia shook her head. "That's not going to happen. We work together."

"Mmm," I said to get under her skin.

"You don't believe me," she said incredulously.

"I think you believe it. And that's all that matters." I kept my tone light and teasing, with none of the sexual innuendo I usually would have resorted to.

I could tell she couldn't see how to take that.

The server brought our food and asked us if we needed anything, and when Gia said no, he told us to enjoy our meal.

"Everything looks amazing."

"You'll love the way it tastes too," I promised, winking at her when she looked up at me.

Gia shook her head. "Is everything sexual with you?"

"Only when I'm with you. But I can try to keep things PG when we're working."

"I'd appreciate it," she said wryly, but I knew she was enjoying our interaction.

I cut my chicken and popped a bite into my mouth. I chewed and swallowed before adding, "Is it because you don't believe you can resist me?"

Gia groaned. "You're impossible. I'm going to ignore you now."

I chuckled, and we ate in silence for a minute before I asked, "Tell me something about you. Something I don't know."

"Hmm. There's not much to tell. I grew up in my brothers' shadows at school and at the pizzeria. When I went away to college, I enjoyed my freedom. Probably too much. I took some business classes, got the bug, and came home on break with all these ideas to improve the pizzeria, but Papà wouldn't hear me out."

"I'm sorry."

Gia shook her head. "It's okay. My brothers have had the same trouble with him. It's not just me. Although at the time, I thought it was. I knew I wanted to open a business. I just wasn't sure what it would be. I helped some friends in college who'd started an event planning business. I worked as a server, absorbed everything I could, and decided to start my own. I planned parties at first, and then I refocused on weddings."

"I've heard you throw a good party."

"I enjoy creating a fun time for people to enjoy. But I didn't want to spread the business too thin. I wanted to concentrate on one specialty."

"Why did you settle on weddings?" I asked, curious about how her mind worked.

"Money was a big part of it. It's a higher-cost item," she said shrewdly.

"I love it when you talk business to me." She was different than any other woman I'd ever dated because she was a business owner. I hadn't realized before how awesome it was to share business ideas with someone who got it. The other women I'd dated weren't interested in the operations of the resort.

Gia shook her head. "I love planning them too. The couples

have these hopes and dreams for the future, and everything hinges on that one day. If one thing goes wrong, brides think it's bad luck. I love the challenge of creating that perfect day, giving couples their best start."

"I hadn't thought of it like that. You're passionate about your business." I was too, but not in the same way. I didn't give in to the emotions surrounding a wedding. I treated it as a business deal, and maybe that's where I'd gone wrong with some of my decisions.

"You are too."

"I'm not passionate about weddings. It's something we offer because guests want it, and I like money."

She tipped her head to the side, considering me. "What are you passionate about?"

You. But I choked that down. I was supposed to be laying off the innuendos. "I'm determined to create a luxurious experience, from the room to the service to the food and accommodations. Everything should exceed the guests' expectations. I handle all customer service in-house. I've had experiences with other hotels where customer service isn't on-site, and they know nothing about the resort. It happens more with large chains. The advantage of only owning one resort is I can be hyper-focused on the guests' experience here. I'm constantly walking the grounds, introducing myself to guests, and maintaining contact with the managers."

"You sound like a great owner. I bet most don't spend much time on-site. They hire managers for that."

"That's the advantage of living here part time. I know what's happening at all times."

"I think you're doing an amazing job."

I had a feeling Gia didn't give compliments if she didn't strongly believe in them. And I felt her words in my chest. "Thank you."

"You're welcome," she said as she finished her meal.

"Are you ready to meet our couple?"

Gia nodded. Her face filled with excitement. "I can't wait to talk to them. I've always wanted to plan a wedding here. Between the location and the food, it's perfect."

I loved that she was passionate about planning a wedding at my resort. I never cared what other women I'd dated thought about my business. I knew it was successful, and that was all that mattered. But knowing Gia was impressed with my work meant a lot.

She reached across the table and covered my hand with hers. "Thank you for the opportunity."

My heart was racing, and I couldn't seem to form any words. My interactions with Gia had almost always been contentious. I wasn't sure how to handle this softer, appreciative version. I finally cleared my throat and said, "You're welcome. You're doing me a favor."

"Do your clients often ask for me?"

I nodded, not afraid to admit it. "But I thought it was better to keep everything in-house."

"I can understand wanting all the profits. Even if this doesn't work out, we should operate on a referral system. If I send brides your way, you give me a finder's fee."

I was impressed with her tenacity. "Are you saying that you aren't sending them my way now?"

Her lips twitched. "I lose business when I do."

"We might need to change some things." I wondered if I'd let our feud cloud my business judgment. That was something that had never happened before. I prided myself on good business sense, always making the right decisions when other business owners were mired in indecision.

Gia winked at me. "When you know better, you do better."

I nodded. "I think I might have been blinded where you were concerned."

"I think we both were too wrapped up in personal issues to see the way it was affecting our respective businesses."

I wasn't sure I wanted to be business partners with her either.

She'd mentioned not getting involved if we were working together. That it might complicate our business dealings, and I had to agree with her.

I'd never done anything like this before. But then again, I hadn't dated anyone like Gia. Someone who challenged me and encouraged me to be better. I wasn't keen on the idea of a relationship being off-limits.

I was hopeful she'd come around, but first, we had a couple to meet. I stood and held out my hand to her. "Are you ready for this?"

She met my gaze. "I'm always ready."

I chuckled as she stood and curled her hand around my elbow rather than my hand. "I've met my match with you." That was the case in the bedroom, even if we hadn't spent much time there yet. I refrained from saying what was on my mind. We needed to keep things professional, at least for the next few hours. "You should get the full experience next weekend. I'll book you a day at the spa."

Her posture softened. "You don't have to do that."

"You deserve the royal treatment." She bought designer clothes and drove a luxury car, but how often did she take care of herself, her body, and her mind? Maybe she needed a man like me by her side who'd notice those things.

"You want me to like the resort."

I swallowed over the lump in my throat and deflected the only way I knew how—through my business. "If you've experienced the resort firsthand, you'll be better able to make recommendations to the bridal couples and their wedding party."

She sobered. "Of course."

It was only partially true. I wanted to treat her, but I didn't think she'd appreciate that.

Gia squeezed my elbow. "Thank you for thinking of that."

My heart squeezed at her show of appreciation. I wanted more of these kinds of interactions.

The couple was waiting outside my office, and they rose when we approached. "John, Emma. This is Gia Giovanni."

"I thought you didn't allow outside planners?" Emma asked.

"I wanted to make an exception if you're interested. You can talk and see if Gia would be a good fit." I hadn't explained to them the purpose of the meeting before I called them in. I'd wanted to see their reaction.

"That would be amazing. Gia's the wedding planner my friend, Lorraine, used for her wedding last year," Emma said to John.

"Whatever you want is fine with me," John said.

"Then come into my office. Let's talk about the details."

We settled in my office. I leaned on my desk while Gia sat across from John and Emma. Even though she wasn't as familiar with my resort, she seemed to have a good understanding of the amenities. I wondered if she'd studied them. It's what I would have done. Examined my competitor's business for weaknesses and flaws. It made me respect her even more.

I didn't have to add much to the conversation. It was clear by Emma's demeanor that she was delighted to be working with Gia. I couldn't believe I hadn't explored this angle before. I'd been shortsighted by excluding Gia from the resort.

If we only allowed a few brides to work with her, the highest-budget weddings, it would have an exclusive feel to it. I loved it. Her other wedding planners could handle the smaller weddings, and if Gia only offered herself up to the highest bidder, it would make her more valuable. I was positive she'd feel the same way.

They focused on the location of the ceremony and the reception. Those two things needed to be set for them to pick her dress, colors, and linens. Or at least that's what Gia suggested. I rarely sat in on meetings with couples and Hannah.

I could have excused myself, but I felt invested in this arrangement, and I wanted to spend more time in Gia's presence. I told myself it was purely business. I wanted to study how she operated. But it was more than that.

Gia was professional as she guided the couple to the most practical options for the ceremony, given the size of John and Emma's guest list. Ceremonies on the water accommodated the smaller weddings. "There's a gorgeous ballroom overlooking the water. I think it would be perfect for your guests. They want a view of the water without worrying about the weather or bugs. They want to be part of the experience without being in the thick of it. Does that make sense?"

"I think she's right, Emma. Your mother won't want to be so close to the water. She'll complain about the sun on her skin and the bugs. We'll be protected from the elements while still enjoying that million-dollar view," John said.

"It's less stressful for you since the ceremony can be held despite any weather developments. Although I've ordered blue skies and sun for your wedding," Gia said with a smile.

I was impressed with Gia's ability to direct and guide them in a certain direction. She knew the pitfalls and advantages of every possible scenario and seemingly knew what John, Emma, and their guests would want.

Gia was so skilled at it that I wasn't sure they realized she was guiding them in various directions. I was positive it was her years of experience. She knew what to anticipate and how to avoid any problems.

"Before we make a final decision, I'd like to tour the possible locations again."

"Absolutely. Do you have time to do that now?"

John looked at his phone. "I have a work meeting, but we drove separately. Can you take Emma?"

"You should see it at some point, but I can take Emma today," Gia said.

I found it interesting that she wanted the groom present. She wouldn't let him check out of the process.

"Emma can take pictures for me."

Gia frowned, and I knew she didn't like that John was blowing off the decision-making process. Most grooms said the bride could have whatever she wanted, but Gia seemed to prefer when both the bride and groom were involved.

"I can go with you," I said as Emma walked with John to his car.

"You don't have to. I'm used to handling this on my own," Gia said as she gathered her things.

"I'd like to be involved with this wedding. It's an experiment to see if this could work, and I'd like to be involved."

Her cheeks flushed as Emma returned. "Are we ready?"

"Absolutely," Gia said as she led the way out of the room and in the direction of the ballroom with the water view. It was the most expensive space to book. It was also the largest.

Emma stood in the middle of the room, taking it in before moving toward the window. It was where I was always drawn whenever I was here. It was the space I'd fallen in love with when I toured the building.

I knew this resort was money, and I made an offer on the spot. But there was something about watching Gia talk about the space that was enlightening.

"We can hold the ceremony by the windows, hanging flowers from the ceiling to give it a more intimate feel, and during cocktail hour, we'll transform it for the reception. We'll have live musicians, a band or a string quartet, whatever you and John would prefer."

"I love this. I thought I'd want to be outside, but you're right, the guests will be more comfortable here."

Gia smiled. "It has an extravagant feel to it."

"I have to agree," Emma said as she executed a small circle in the center of the room.

When Gia walked Emma to her car, I went to my office, giving them time to themselves. I wasn't sure Emma would want me hovering over every meeting. I just thought it was important to show that the owner was present. Plus, I'd wanted to see Gia in action.

I sat at my desk, intending to answer messages and return

phone calls, but my mind was on Gia. On whether I'd made a mistake the last few years in excluding her from the weddings here. I'd thought for sure I was creating an exclusive experience, but Gia was a dream at her job. If the brides wanted her, I should probably stop fighting them and her.

Gia breezed in. "I thought that went well."

I stood. "You're impressive. It was interesting how you guided her in the direction you wanted."

"The bride and groom usually have only been through this once. I've done it a hundred times. I know what to avoid. What the couple's guests will want and what will work best for them. Some couples prefer the outdoor wedding, but I suspected John and Emma's guests wouldn't. Now she can choose the wedding gown she wants, not one that will work for the outdoors."

"How often will you need to meet with them?" I wanted to know how often to expect her on-site.

"We'll talk over the phone and have Zoom calls, but I prefer to meet in person. It allows me to get to know the bride and groom better and anticipate their needs."

"I'll want to know your schedule."

Gia nodded. "I'll have Harper enter the information and share it with you. I'd better get back. I have a drive to get home."

"You should stay. Enjoy the suite I reserved for you." I'd given her one of the one-bedroom suites with a view of the water. I didn't mind reserving it for her for the next few months. I knew she'd enjoy it, and I wanted to entice her to stay.

"I can't tonight. I have plans."

I wanted to ask what they were, but it wasn't my place. We weren't dating, but my mind ran wild with possibilities. Was she seeing someone else?

I walked her to her car and held her door open, saying good night as I closed it. I watched her drive away, my jaw tight and my back knotted with tension. Working with Gia was both the best and the worst idea I'd ever had.

Ten

GIA

I doubted my ability to resist Silas. I'd assumed Silas would give me space to work and not hover in the background, paying attention to everything that happened.

There was no way I could stay in that suite he'd arranged for me. It was sweet and thoughtful and completely unnecessary. But staying at the resort meant being close to him.

I needed space after spending the day with him. First our meeting, then sharing an incredible lunch at his five-star restaurant, and then planning time with John and Emma. I was exhausted, both mentally and physically. I was hyperaware of Silas's every move as the day went on. And every time I checked, his eyes were on me.

I wasn't sure what he was thinking. Did his offer to continue our physical relationship still stand if I made the first move? But I knew if I'd stayed overnight, I wouldn't have been able to stop myself from knocking on his door. It was safer to keep distance between us, and I needed the space to regroup.

I needed more of these contracts, and if I had to work with Silas to get them, then I'd need to do it. I just couldn't be involved with him while working together. It would complicate everything. No matter how much I wanted him, we had to keep things professional. And since he seemed incapable of that, I needed to be the one to set those boundaries.

When I got home, I headed inside and drew a bath. I filled it with lavender and bubbles and got undressed as the water level rose. I kept my phone nearby in case Harper needed me for something. She sometimes worked after her daughter, Evie, was asleep at night.

I'd just eased my tired body into the warm water and rested my head on the back of the tub when my phone buzzed.

> Are you home, beautiful?

I smiled, enjoying the way it felt to be called beautiful, even if Silas had no business doing it himself. He wasn't my boyfriend, even if he'd been my lover for a short time, and I wanted him to be my full-time one.

> I'm at home, taking a bath.

There was a delay in his response. I wondered if he'd left his phone to do something else or if he was thinking of what to say.

> I'm going to need proof.

I barked out a laugh. Silas was fun.

> You wish.

> Come on, beautiful. I've seen it before, and I'd love to see it again. If you won't let us be together, you can at least tease me.

I was positive he wanted more than that. I wanted to drive him crazy. He asked for it, after all.

I held up my phone, testing angles so that my nipples weren't showing. I gave the camera my most seductive look, and the result was glowing skin and the globes of my breasts visible above the bubbles.

I double-checked the image, satisfied it was sexy, and sent it to him. I don't know what it was about Silas that brought this side out of me.

Why did the first man I wanted have to be Silas Sharpe? It was like the universe was laughing at me.

> Gorgeous. I want to be in that bathtub with you. I'd sit behind you and cup your breasts, making your nipples hard, aching points.

I wanted that too.

> Then I'd slip my hand lower to your pussy.

My breath came in short pants as I mimicked his words.

> Are you there?

I fumbled with the phone and almost dropped it in the water.

> I'm a little busy making that a reality.

The phone rang. Silas's voice filled the small room. "Are you touching yourself?"

"What do you think?"

He broke off a curse. "If you were in the suite, I'd be knocking on your door."

"That's why I came home. It's not a good idea." But my words were slow to come to me because I'd slid one finger inside and circled my clit with the other.

"Are you making yourself feel good?"

"I miss you." The words wouldn't have left my mouth, but I was lost in the sound of his voice.

He groaned. "Are your nipples hard peaks?"

I glanced down. "Want to see?"

I was a little surprised he hadn't called on video to begin with.

"Hold on. I'm switching to a video call."

I took the time to set up the phone so it was propped against my cup of tea and showed my breasts. I lifted myself out so he could see, and the cold air made me harder.

"I'm so hot for you, Silas."

"It's like music to my ears."

"Where are you?"

"I'm on the balcony of my penthouse, imagining you bent over my railing. Your legs wide as you wait for me to fuck you."

I let my head fall back. "Yes."

"Are you fucking yourself, beautiful?"

I lifted my head to meet his eyes on the screen and raised a brow. "Are you?"

He smirked and lowered the camera so I could see him fisting his cock. He was sitting on a chair with his legs spread wide.

"That's hot." I wasn't sure what was hotter: him fisting his cock or his smirk.

He gripped his cock tighter, giving it one stroke. "I wish I could see you. The water covers everything."

"I don't want to let out the water. I'll be cold."

"We'll make the best of it."

I spread my legs and used two fingers to fuck myself like he suggested and used the other hand to tweak my nipple.

"If I was there, I'd suck on your nipples and rub my cock on your pussy."

I licked my lips as he drove me higher with his dirty words. "If I was with you, I'd get down on my knees and suck your cock."

"Fuck, baby. I love it when you talk dirty."

"I don't usually." I wasn't one for words. I usually took control and didn't allow my partner a chance to make any moves.

"I can't wait for you to be on your knees for me."

Normally, I'd see that position as subservient, but it wasn't when I knew I'd drive him crazy with my mouth. "I want that too."

His face drew tight, his eyes wild with desire. "Are you going to come for me?"

There was something about his words and his voice, hard with want, that sent me over the edge. I bit my lip as my body spasmed with waves of mind-numbing pleasure.

"Fuck, yes," he barked out as he went over too.

He relaxed into his chair, his eyes meeting mine. "I still want you."

"I do too."

This was hot, but it was a poor substitute for the real thing.

"I want to be in the same room with you. When are you going to give in and give me what I want?" His voice was low, seductive.

"And what is it that you want?" I asked carefully.

He raised a brow. "I'd settle for a kiss but wouldn't turn down your mouth on my dick."

"I love it when you talk dirty."

"I love it when you send naughty pictures."

I considered him for a few seconds. "This thing we're doing is dangerous."

He grinned. "It couldn't be more innocent."

There was no chance of pregnancy, but there was still a very real chance of me losing my heart. "You know what I mean."

"You feel like you can't trust me, but you can."

"I can trust you with my body. But what about the rest of me?"

His forehead wrinkled. "What do you mean?"

"How can I trust you with my heart?" I swallowed down my misgivings. I shouldn't have admitted it was a possibility, but it was the reason I was holding back.

"I don't know what this thing is between us. I can't guarantee you anything except I'll always protect you and put you first. I'll take care of you and make sure you feel good."

It was something but not enough. "What about our businesses, my brothers?"

"I don't have all the answers. But why do they have to be involved in our relationship?"

I liked that he'd referred to us as being in a relationship. "I need to think about it."

"Let me know at the fundraiser. I can't wait any longer."

I nodded. That was the night when everything would change. When I'd make the first move, or I'd erect a wall between us. "Aren't you worried about what it could mean for our business arrangement?"

"I'm always considering the angles, weighing the risks and benefits. But what I know is, whatever happens is worth it. I just want a chance with you."

I just want a chance with you.

"Everything about you drives me crazy. You make me see things differently. You make me want things I've never considered before. And the one thing I've learned is that when something special comes along, you have to go for it. Take what you want, no matter the consequences."

A tingle ran down my spine at his words. "You're very convincing."

"I've never wanted anyone or anything the way I want you. You're worth pursuing. You're worth blowing up everything."

"Wow." Silas didn't mince words. He said exactly what he was thinking, and it was enlightening.

"I go after what I want, Gia, and I want you. I won't back off. Not unless you tell me you don't want this."

"You know I do. I'm trying to be good."

"What's the sense in being good when we can be very, very naughty?"

My face flamed at the intensity in his voice. He made me want to be reckless for him. To forget everything that was on the line and let go with him. But I knew it would be a mistake to make any decision tonight when we'd spent the day together.

Silas leaned back in his chair and sighed. "I'm a patient man."

After his speech, I wasn't so sure about that. But after our initial hookup, he had given me space.

"Let me think," I finally said, because everything felt disjointed. If I chased a thought, it disappeared. I felt like I was coming apart at the seams, and I wasn't sure how I'd ever get myself together. Panic bubbled up in my chest, making it difficult to breathe.

"Take a breath, Gia. It'll be okay."

Tears pricked my eyes because it wasn't. Silas had changed everything, and I had a feeling he'd change me if I let him. I couldn't let that happen.

I'd worked too hard to build a life I was proud of. I wouldn't let a man come along and make me think I didn't need it anymore. He wanted to distract me and dull my focus, and I wouldn't let that happen. "Give me some time."

Silas's expression was disappointed, and it hit me in the sternum, stealing my breath. "You can have all the time you need. I'll see you on Saturday."

He hung up, and I instantly felt searing regret. Silas wanted me. He wasn't intimidated by my success or my confidence. He was one of a kind, and I liked him.

But I couldn't help but think it wasn't enough. That I couldn't have it all. The guy and the business. I couldn't be independent with a man by my side, especially not one like Silas. They shined like the sun, and everyone around them paled in comparison.

I didn't want to be some trophy wife or a woman supporting her man. I wanted to keep my focus where it belonged—on my business.

I'd been working hard to impress my father, and it hadn't happened yet. But if I could take Happily Ever Afters to the next level, maybe then Papà would respect me. Maybe then he'd tell me I'd done a great job.

My chest ached as I emptied the water. I should have been

basking in the aftermath of another amazing orgasm, but I wasn't. Instead, I ached for a different reason.

I wanted to connect with Silas. I wanted to be all in with him. I wanted to see where it could go. For the first time in forever, I felt like I'd met my match. I just wasn't sure he was good for me.

* * *

I needed to talk to Harper about the new contract with Silas. I put it off because I wasn't sure she would think it was the best business decision. I worried she'd see right through me and know exactly what I wanted, and it wasn't to increase revenue.

"You seem jumpy today," Harper remarked during our morning meeting.

We usually spent the time going over the schedule for the week, finances, and business expenses. We brainstormed ideas and talked about our lives. It was the benefit of working with your best friend.

"I have something on my mind." Or more like *someone.*

She raised a brow. "Are you worried about cash flow?"

I smiled ruefully. "I'm always worried about that."

"Did something happen?"

I took a shuddering breath. "Yes, but I think it's a good thing. Silas came to me with a proposition."

Harper rolled her eyes. "He's famous for those. You turned him down, right?"

When I didn't answer, Harper's startled gaze flew to mine.

"He wanted to partner with me to plan the wedding of one of his high-profile wedding couples."

"You said you'd never work with him."

I sighed, hating that I'd lied to my best friend. But I didn't want to admit to anyone that I'd been rejected. "Early in the business, I suggested it to him, and he turned me down."

Harper's mouth opened, then closed. "I had no idea."

"I didn't want to admit that I'd failed."

"I wouldn't see that as a failure." Harper considered me for a few seconds. "But why wouldn't you tell me?"

"You didn't work here then, and Silas never mentioned it. I didn't want anyone to know I'd gone to him."

"Whatever issue you have with Silas is personal, and I know you keep business separate."

"Not this time."

Her eyes widened comically. "You agreed to his proposal?"

"It's what I've always wanted. We need high-paying clients to float the rest of the business. It's everything we've been talking about."

"But we're starting to see traction with our marketing around Annapolis as a destination wedding. I thought that was the answer."

"I don't believe in relying on any one thing. The money could come from anywhere, and everything in me was saying I should do this."

"Your intuition."

"Exactly." It's never steered me wrong.

"Are you sure your intuition had your business needs in mind, and not something or someone else?"

"What are you saying?" I asked, not surprised she could see right through me.

"It's clear to anyone who's been in the same room with you and Silas that you're attracted to each other."

"So?" I asked, my cheeks hot. Did everyone know I couldn't resist Silas?

"Do you like him?"

I closed my eyes, remembering how sweet he always was with me. He made sure I got home safely. "He's a good businessman."

Harper huffed out a laugh. "You know that's not what I was talking about."

I sighed. "I'm attracted to him."

"Was that so hard to admit?" Harper teased, her expression pleased.

"Yes, because it's Silas. If it was anyone else—"

Harper rolled her eyes. "Please. You wouldn't have patience for anyone else. You need someone like Silas. He's smart, strong, and successful, and the best part is that he's not intimidated by you."

"He's not." I knew that about him, but it was still refreshing to think about. That Silas was my equal in every way. He was a businessman who had good instincts. The difference was, he had the capital to buy the resort outright and renovate it.

I built my business from nothing. There was an art form to figuring out where to spend your money and what would have the best return. There were times when I didn't have enough, when I thought I'd failed, and it was coming out of those scary times that made me the businesswoman I was today. I was fearless and strong in my focus. I wouldn't let anyone, or anything, derail me from my goals.

"You're worried he's a distraction."

"You know he is," I insisted as I moved around the desk and sat next to her. We weren't talking business anymore. This was purely personal, and there was no one I trusted more than Harper. We'd been friends since we were kids. She was practically my sister, especially now that she was engaged to my brother.

"Love isn't a distraction. It's this amazing thing that lifts everything around you. It motivates you to be and do better. It makes you see everything in a different light."

I laughed without any humor. "I didn't say anything about love."

Harper grinned. "Lust, then."

"That sounds right," I said, not willing to disclose my feelings.

"So, you don't have any feelings for him?"

"We aren't close," I said, carefully skirting around the truth.

Harper stood and moved her tablet to the desk so she could pace. I was surprised there wasn't a path worn on the wood floors from her doing that during our brainstorming sessions. "Of course, you're not close. You won't let him be."

I frowned. "You have it all wrong. It's purely a physical attraction, and maybe there's some mutual respect there. But that's it."

She stopped moving. "Tell me what happened. I need to know everything."

I let out a breath. "It was at Chris and Naomi's wedding. The night you went home with Leo."

Eleven

GIA

Harper's face flushed. "Nothing happened between me and Leo that night."

"I didn't say it did. I'm not upset that you're engaged to my brother. You're going to be my sister. What better outcome could there be? Just don't tell me any intimate details about you and my brother. Because that's—" I shuddered.

"Got it. Now, tell me about Silas. I had a feeling something was going on, but I wanted to give you space."

From her expression, I could tell she was preoccupied with Leo at the time, and I couldn't blame her. "We hooked up."

Harper sucked in a sharp breath. "I shouldn't be surprised, but I am. I always had a feeling about you two. You burn hot when you're together."

"I can attest to that. But I left in the middle of the night. I didn't want to face what we did."

"Gia." Harper sighed, her expression falling.

"I needed space."

"Did he give it to you?"

"I didn't see him again until the night that Leo proposed to you." I didn't mention that seeing my brother so in love with my best friend, him getting down on one knee in front of our family,

99

pierced my heart. It made me want something that I had no business even considering. A future with someone by my side. Someone strong and fierce and steady. Someone like Silas.

In my fantasies, Silas wasn't my enemy. He was the man who challenged me and supported me. He cared for and protected me.

"That night, he kissed me in the kitchen, but then he said I'd have to make the next move."

Harper's expression was hopeful, but then it fell. "You haven't. You're too scared."

I bristled. "I'm not scared."

"You're afraid of being close to someone, of letting someone in. You think he's going to hurt you."

I couldn't argue with her assessment because it was true.

Her shoulders lowered. "So that's it? Nothing's going to happen?"

"We're working together now. We have to be professional."

"I have a feeling he's not concerned about any of that."

"He's confident he can keep business separate."

"You think he wants something physical."

"He hasn't said, but I assume."

"You're afraid you'll feel too much, and your emotions would get involved."

I hated to admit it, but I nodded miserably.

"Love isn't a bad thing."

"It is when the other person doesn't feel the same way." We both remembered my first boyfriend in college. I'd fallen hard and fast, giddy to be out of my father's house and free for the first time in my life. I'd fallen into the arms of the first boy who'd showed me attention. We were inseparable that first year, until the new flock of freshmen arrived. Then he'd moved on to another girl, and I'd been devastated.

"You always fall hard for your first love."

"I didn't love Jeff."

"You thought you did."

The pain of that breakup was still fresh, even though I'd long ago realized I was better off single. I vowed not to let go with another man again. I was always in control of any relationship, and Silas made me feel very much the opposite. "I was young and naïve. Desperate for a guy's attention."

"You're not that now. You're strong and independent and fully capable of having an adult relationship with Silas."

"I won't survive it."

"How do you know if you don't try it?"

"You're high on love because of my brother. Just because it worked out for you doesn't mean it will for me." It was clear how much Leo loved Harper, but Silas wasn't looking for love.

"Is that what you want? Love?" Harper asked gently.

I snorted. "Of course not."

Harper sat, her gaze on me. "Then what are you afraid of?"

I twisted my hands in my lap. "I'm afraid I'll blur the lines."

Harper's gaze was understanding. "You're afraid you'll fall for him."

"Something like that." I hated to admit any weakness, but I needed to talk it out with someone.

"It's okay to like him. Maybe even love him."

I shook my head. "I'm not looking for love."

"Then I don't see the problem. Enjoy him. Have a good time. Don't let it interfere with your business relationship. How are you working with him now?"

"He's allowing me to have a room there to work with one couple. If it works out, we'll reevaluate things. But for now, it's just the one."

"That's good. You can figure out if it's feasible to hold weddings both in Annapolis and at his resort."

I nodded. "We have Ireland and Aria covering here."

"I don't want you working too much again."

"I can handle it. It will be fine." Except I wasn't sure anything would be fine.

"I'll run the numbers and see if it makes sense to have you

focused solely on Silas's resort, while Aria and Ireland handle Annapolis. Are you planning to move there?"

"What? No." My family was here.

"Mmm. It's just a lot of back-and-forth for you. It's an hour away."

"I can stay in that room he's reserved for me."

Her lips twitched. "That's generous of him."

"I think he wants me to give in. There's a fundraiser this weekend. I'm going as his date."

Her eyes widened. "How did that happen?"

"He said he needed dates for these events. I offered to be his next one. I don't know what I was thinking, but he promised to schedule time for me at the spa on Saturday."

"Go. Have a good time. Explore whatever's going on between you. It might surprise you."

I shook my head. I couldn't stay in control with Silas. He wanted me to come undone.

"I think this is a good move. You've always wanted to work with Silas, and now you have your chance."

Was it that simple? Was I overthinking everything? Could I have a casual relationship and keep my emotions out of it?

"How amazing would it be to work with him and not against him? You won't have to turn away any clients."

"It would be nice." It was a source of consternation for me. If a client wanted to hold their wedding at Silas's resort, I couldn't be their wedding planner. But this arrangement had the potential to change everything.

The more I thought about Saturday night, the more I was leaning toward going to him. To making that next move. I convinced myself I could stay in control. I always had in the past, and if he was going to let me make that move, then maybe I could this time too. I said it to myself so many times I started to believe it was possible for me to take that next step without losing myself.

"Can we handle it? Or will it be spreading us too thin? This is all hypothetical because he hasn't agreed to anything more than one wedding."

"Would you limit the number of weddings you'd handle? Maybe make it an exclusive thing? When you started out, everyone was able to work with you. But now it's a special thing. You can only handle so many weddings, and to do the best job possible, you need to limit it to just a few a year. If you charge more for that exclusive option, then you'd be okay. Plus, you'd be protecting your time too."

"I make money by either handling the clients myself or hiring wedding planners who can do the work for me."

Harper's brow furrowed. "Right."

I moved behind the desk. "What if there was a way for me to help more people, but it didn't take much more of my time?"

"What are you thinking?" Harper asked eagerly.

"What if we offered a wedding planner course? We give our best practices, our tips for starting a business, maintaining it, and how to build it?"

"How would that work?"

"I wouldn't want to be doing a live course every time. We could pre-record the videos and have a portal for the written material. The planners could go through the content at their own pace."

"We can do lives in the beginning to entice people to sign up, and we could always add to the course later."

I snapped my fingers. "Yes."

"Oh my God, Gia. This is genius."

"You don't think it's crazy? I don't know if others are doing it already."

"Even if they are, you do things differently than someone else. They're paying for your unique knowledge. No one else can do it like you can. Your business acumen is what makes you stand out. You're willing to take risks and pivot when necessary. So many businesses fail because what was working stops, and they can't try it a different way. But you've expanded, and now you want to add more income streams. It's amazing. I think you should do it."

"It'll take time to develop."

"Gia, I've got this. This is what you hired me for. I can research the options for course platforms. You provide the content, and I'll build it and create the images and marketing materials."

"How soon do you think we can get it up and running?" I asked, excited now that Harper was on board.

She thought for a few seconds. "A few months?"

"I want this to be your top priority. We already have the marketing set up for the destination wedding advertisements. I can handle the interviews with the new couples."

"I'll get started right away," Harper said, standing up and gathering her things.

"I want to offer you a bonus once the course is completed."

Harper paused. "Let's see how it goes. We don't even know if we can do it."

"I'm confident you'll make this happen, and it will be better than I'm imagining."

Harper raised her brow. "You have a lot of faith in me."

"I have faith in us."

"That's why you should trust yourself when it comes to Silas. How does he make you feel?"

I chewed my lip. "I feel amazing when I'm with him. Like I can do or be anything."

"Then go with your gut. Just like you do your business. You can trust your instincts. Looking back, I bet there were a few red flags with Jeff you ignored."

I sighed. "You're probably right. I was just so eager to have his attention that I overlooked the signs that I was just another girl to him. I wasn't special."

"Does Silas make you feel that way?"

"No. In fact, he's said I'm different from other women he's dated."

"Then I think you have your answer. Now, let me get started on your course."

"Thanks, Harper. For listening to me and being a great friend."

Harper's face softened. "Always, Gia. You'll be my sister soon."

I hugged her. "You always have been."

Was I strong enough to make a move on Silas and not lose myself in the process?

* * *

I was busy the rest of the week between issues with various weddings, new client meetings, and planning the course with Harper. There were so many decisions to be made. Did we need a separate website, or should we create a separate page on the current one? Which course platform would work for the long term? I had a few moments when I thought I was losing my mind, but for the most part, I was excited for the future. I wanted stability. I needed consistent income. I didn't want to be affected by the slow seasons.

I didn't want the roller coaster anymore. I hoped this would be the thing to take me to the next level, and maybe, just maybe, I wouldn't need Silas's partnership. There was power in that. And I went to his resort on Saturday with more confidence than the last time.

I didn't need Silas. I had everything I needed inside myself to take my business to the next level. I'd packed a few dresses I thought could work for the event. And I'd even packed my sexiest lingerie, confident Silas wouldn't be able to resist me.

I thought about teasing him with another picture of me in them, but I wanted to keep him guessing as to what my answer would be this weekend. It was more fun this way.

When I checked in, a bellhop took my things to my room, and I was immediately taken to the spa for the treatments Silas had booked for me. I was delighted to discover he'd booked time but not actual treatments. I was able to enjoy a massage, pedicure, and manicure. Usually, I had a hard time relaxing at spas, but Silas's was next level. I felt pampered the entire day. When I was escorted to my room, there were a few dresses hanging, shoes, and another box wrapped in a ribbon.

There was a note on the box. I opened it, my heart beating rapidly in my chest. It was from Silas.

I picked a couple of dresses for you to wear tonight.

My immediate thought was to wear one of the options I'd brought. But I was curious to see what Silas picked out. I would have thought a stylist had chosen them, but the note made it seem like he made the choice.

The first dress was black and draped over my body like a second skin. When I moved from side to side, it shimmered in the light. It was gorgeous and fit like a dream, but I wanted to see the second.

This one was red and bold, and I wondered if that was how Silas saw me.

It was strapless with a sweetheart neckline, an embroidered bodice, and a trumpet silhouette. As soon as I put it on, I fell in love with it. It was bold and sassy and hot. It was a designer dress that must have cost a fortune. I wasn't one to be impressed by a man buying me something this extravagant, but then again, it had never happened before. I couldn't help but be impressed by both the cost and the intent behind it.

When I turned in the mirror, I noticed the large bow in the back. It wasn't something I would have picked for myself, but it was on trend, and I felt gorgeous. I tried on the different shoe options, settling on a strappy silver pair that wouldn't be visible under the full-length dress.

There was even a small Chanel clutch. It was vintage, and my heart was tripping at the implications of this entire night. It wasn't just the *Pretty Woman* feeling I got from the clothes and spa day. It was the implication that I was taking a risk with Silas.

But I refused to worry about tomorrow. The only thing that mattered was tonight.

I removed the shoes and dress so I could quickly shower and do my hair and makeup. When I was dressed, I smoothed a hand down my stomach, trying to quell the butterflies. It didn't work.

When the knock sounded on the door, I wasn't prepared either mentally or physically. My hand trembled as I unlocked it and opened it to find Silas looking handsome in a black tux.

I'd seen him dressed in a suit in the pictures in the paper, but in person, he was devastatingly handsome. He always had a dusting of scruff lining his jaw, but tonight he smelled faintly of soap and cologne. It was intoxicating.

"You wore my dress."

A tingle ran down my spine. "I love it. Thank you."

"I knew it would look gorgeous on you," he said as he cupped my jaw with his palm.

"You always pick out dresses for your dates?"

His expression was serious as he gazed into my eyes, as if he couldn't believe I was here. "No. Never."

"I should feel special then."

"I wanted to create the perfect day for you, where you didn't have to worry about anything."

"You did," I managed, even as my throat was dry, and my eyes stung with an emotion I couldn't quite name.

Instead of kissing me, Silas let go of my jaw, closing the door behind him. He moved to the bar, pouring ice and water into a glass and handing it to me.

"Thank you," I said gratefully as I soothed my dry throat.

I'd eaten at the spa in between treatments, but it had been a while.

"Are you ready?"

I took a deep breath and smiled. "As ready as I'll ever be."

"We only have to stay as long as you want."

"I want to do whatever you need. I assume you need to stay

for the duration." I wanted to be supportive. I wanted to be like those other women in the pictures.

"We'll see how the evening goes," he murmured, and I wondered if he was thinking about the challenge he issued.

It was all I could think about this week. I turned the idea over in my mind, trying to figure out some way to put a stop to it, but I was determined to see this through. I wanted to enjoy this time with Silas. If I was only going to meet one man who made me feel this way, I should take advantage of it for as long as I could.

I just hadn't anticipated how he'd make me feel over something as simple as a date to a charity function. "I feel a little like Cinderella with the spa day and the dresses."

"I wanted to pamper you."

My face flushed. "Thank you. It was unexpected."

"I loved both dresses, but I hoped you'd pick this one. I knew it was you the first time I looked at it."

"What about the shoes and purse?" I asked.

"I let my stylist pick those. I gave her some pictures of you, and she guessed what you'd like. She's fairly good at that."

"She has good taste."

"She knew you liked designer bags, and she thought you might enjoy the vintage Chanel."

"Are these borrowed? I'll have to be careful with them."

"They're yours."

"I couldn't accept it. It's too much." Everything had a designer label, but there were no price tags. I couldn't even imagine what it cost.

He pulled a velvet box out of his pocket. "These are on loan. But don't worry; they're insured."

He popped open the top before I could respond, and I was dazzled by the dangly diamond earrings.

I drew in a breath and looked up at him. "These are gorgeous."

"Put them on. I want to see how they look with the dress."

I carefully took the earrings and moved to the mirror by the front door to put the first one, then the second one, into my ears. It was just enough bling to complete the ensemble. "I love it."

Silas stepped behind me, his hands on my bare shoulders, and my gaze was drawn to his in the mirror. "You don't need anything else."

I knew he was talking about my bare neck and wrists, but I couldn't help but feel it in my chest. I was enough just as I was. Maybe with the addition of designer clothes and diamonds. "It's too much."

"It's not enough." He brushed my hair off my right shoulder and dusted his lips over the skin, sending tingles through my whole body. I turned, and his hands drifted down to my hips. I felt feminine and desirable in the dress and the bling.

"You make me want to stay in tonight."

His eyes darkened with desire. "I want that too. But I also want to show you off."

My face flushed with pleasure that he thought I was just as beautiful as the other women he'd had on his arm. He'd done an admirable job of making me feel different, special even, and I intended to enjoy the night. To not worry about what came after. I wanted to soak up everything that happened today and tuck it into a memory box for later.

Cinderella only had one night. I would take advantage of the evening and enjoy it to its fullest.

Twelve

SILAS

When she stood in the doorway, she stole my breath. It had nothing to do with the makeup or fancy updo or even the designer dress. It was her.

I'd hoped she'd wear the red one. It was her. I wanted to make the entire day special so that she felt like a princess. I'd never done anything like this before.

She deserved all of it and more. I didn't care about designer names, but I knew Gia preferred them. I suspected they were a symbol of her success.

We needed to leave this room before I lost control entirely. I held out my elbow. "Are you ready?"

She took a breath and smiled. "As ready as I'll ever be."

"Don't forget, the room will be full of businesspeople. It might be good networking for you."

"I hadn't even thought of that."

"Someone's daughter might be getting married and looking for the right planner."

"You know this is too much."

"I don't know what you mean," I said as I led the way to the elevator.

"The dress. The bag. The spa day."

"It wasn't enough," I said as the door opened, and we made our way downstairs, through the lobby, and into the ballroom.

Lights flashed as we stopped to take pictures for local media outlets. I was used to the attention, but Gia wasn't. I was proud to have her on my arm, but I was hyperaware of the tension in her body. If it was too much, I was prepared to whisk her out of the spotlight. Instead, she practically glowed as she glided down the hallway on my arm.

I'd never felt prouder to be with someone. I didn't like to go to these things alone. The press speculated, mentioning that I was the most eligible bachelor in the area, and I didn't like the attention.

But now, I was getting attention for a different reason. For the gorgeous woman on my arm. "Everyone is going to know your name by the end of the night."

Her eyes widened. "Are you serious?"

"They're going to want to know who you are."

"I'm nobody," she whispered.

"I think we both know that's not true."

We paused at the entrance to the ballroom so they could introduce us. I'd provided the announcer with Gia's name earlier in the day. Once our names were read, I led the way to the first group of donors, introducing Gia.

"Gia runs a wedding planning service, Happily Ever Afters in Annapolis. This is Stu Schrader. He owns various marine businesses in the area."

They shook hands.

"My daughter just got engaged, and she's looking for a wedding planner. I've heard you're the one to talk to."

"I'm happy to speak to your daughter and her fiancé about the possibility."

Stu nodded. "Perfect. I'll have her do that."

As we made our way around the room, I introduced Gia as a successful business owner and a sought-after wedding planner. I listened with pride as they inquired about her services and availability. I pressed a glass of champagne into her hand. I wanted her to enjoy this evening, and she might need something to take the edge off.

When it seemed like Gia was tired of socializing, I asked her to dance. She let me lead her to the dance floor.

I drew her into my arms and ducked my head so I could whisper in her ear. "This might be the only time we'll be alone tonight."

She smiled at me. "I understand why you wanted to dance, then."

"Who wouldn't want to dance with the most beautiful woman in the room?" I said honestly, feeling the truth in my chest.

She tipped her head slightly. "You know that sounds cliché."

I replayed the words in my head and then said, "It might sound that way, but it's the truth."

Gia straightened in my arms. "You've been amazing and attentive. This almost feels like a real date and not a favor for an almost-friend."

"This is a date," I insisted, a little surprised that she didn't think that.

She shook her head, a rueful grin on her face. "I don't know what I expected, but it wasn't this. I feel pampered and beautiful, and at the same time, I'm generating business contacts. It's surreal. I don't know how I can ever thank you."

"That wasn't why I did it. I just wanted to return the favor and make the evening worthwhile for you." Her words did something funny to my heart. I felt her appreciation, but I wanted more. I wanted her to like me. But I wasn't sure if she'd ever let go enough to realize what was right in front of her.

She fell silent, and we resumed our dance.

I pulled her tight against me, ducking my head slightly so that our faces were close to each other.

She looked up at me and licked her lips. "*Cosa mi fai?*"

Everything inside me stilled at the Italian phrase. I'd heard her brothers and parents speak Italian from time to time, but never Gia. It made me feel like the words were just for me. "What did you say?"

She blinked but finally repeated in English, "What are you doing to me?"

I wondered if she'd said the words in Italian as a form of self-protection. If it was a shield for her feelings. "Can you say that in Italian again?"

She met my gaze and held it with a lift of her chin. *"Cosa mi fai?"*

"I wish I could say it as eloquently as you, but you're doing the same to me. You drive me crazy."

Gia stopped dancing, and everything inside me pulled taut. "Will you take me to your penthouse?"

"Are you sure?"

She smiled softly. "I've never been surer of anything."

I curled my hand around hers and led the way through the partygoers into the hallway.

Gia placed her hand on my bicep. "Do we need to stay?"

"The evening is winding down," I said, not really caring about the party anymore.

In the elevator, I swiped my keycard to gain access to the penthouse.

"I don't want to interrupt anything for you."

My jaw tightened. "We mingled. We talked. We're done."

On my floor, it opened directly to my suite, and my heart was beating hard in my chest. I paused in the foyer. "I said when you were here next, you'd make the first move."

Gia moved closer and curled a hand around the back of my neck, tangling her fingers in the hair there. *"Ti voglio."*

I needed more than just the words. I'd asked her to make the next move, to take control and kiss me.

Gia lifted on her toes as I lowered my head. Her lips were tentative at first, as if she was testing me out or tasting the champagne that lingered on my lips.

Remembering the Italian words she'd said, I asked, "What did you say just now?"

"I want you," Gia repeated in English.

My jaw tight, I said, "I want more than one night."

Gia blinked as if she hadn't anticipated me making demands. "What do you want from me?"

"I want everything." Then I kissed her, stealing the breath from her lungs as my tongue plunged inside her mouth, taking and claiming her as mine.

I should have been worried about her intentions, but I was lost in her. Her scent, her passion, and her obvious desire for me.

I'd tried to show her she wasn't just another woman on my arm who I used for photographs or a public image. I'd attempted to make her feel special, creating a relaxing day and an extravagant evening. Gia wasn't attracted to my money, but she appreciated expensive things.

I wanted her to feel just as much as I was. I wanted her to lose herself in me. "I want to take this dress off." Yet at the same time, I never wanted to see her out of it.

"Please don't rip it." Her voice trembled.

I ran my hands over her shoulders and spun her around so I could ease her zipper down. Inch after inch of skin was bared to me. I ran a hand over her spine—no bra—and down to the lace of her thong, the same color as the dress.

"You are gorgeous."

She drew in a shaky breath as I pushed the dress down. When she stepped out of it, I draped it over a nearby chair. I didn't care if it was ruined, but I hoped she saw it as a gift from me and wanted to wear it again.

She stood in silver heels and that red lace thong that barely covered her pussy. "I know I keep saying it, but I've never seen anyone more beautiful than you. I want to take a mental snapshot of this moment and keep it forever."

"You certainly know all the right words today."

I gave her a sharp look. "Make no mistake, when I say something, I mean it. I'm not saying some line to get you to sleep with me."

"I'm sorry, Silas. I'm not used to this."

I was still fully dressed, and she only wore a scrap of lace, but I didn't think that was what she was talking about. "You can let go with me. I'll catch you."

That seemed to assuage a place deep inside her, and she stepped closer, her body pressed against mine. I could imagine how the stiff material of my jacket felt against her hard nipples. I cupped her jaw and tipped her chin up so I could kiss her, softly at first and then exploring. I'd never get enough of this. Of her.

She encircled my wrists. "*Ho bisogno di te*. I need you."

"I want to do crazy things to you. I want to throw you down on my bed, spread your legs, and feast on you for hours. I want to bend you over my bed and pound into you. I can't go slow."

"*Voglio farti le pazzie*. That means I want to do crazy things to you."

I repeated the phrase as best I could, *voglio farti le pazzie*, and a shiver ran through her body. "Take me to your bedroom."

I lifted her, her legs wrapping naturally around my waist. I knew how big that was for her to say. Last time, we'd fucked everywhere but my bedroom. I'd only cuddled with her there, admiring her in the moonlight before she ran. But tonight, I'd savor her.

She kissed me as I moved, and when we got to my room, I carefully lowered her to the bed, hovering over her.

"What I want to do to you sounds so much better in Italian. I want to wreck you."

She widened her legs underneath me. "That sounded pretty good in English."

I knew how hard it was for her to be here, to trust me to take care of her, and I didn't take that lightly. I'd said I wouldn't be able to control myself, but I would. I wanted to make this perfect for her. But first, I needed her bare. I moved, kissing her chest, then sucking on her nipples, before I moved lower, hooking my fingers in the band of her panties and pulling them over her hips and down. I flung them somewhere over my shoulder, hoping she couldn't find them in the morning.

I wasn't one to hold on to a woman's panties as a keepsake, but I liked having her colorful thongs in my drawer when I opened it in the mornings. It was too much to hope she'd ever leave anything here on purpose.

I wouldn't get ahead of myself. I'd enjoy where we were, and right now, I had a naked woman under me, waiting for my mouth. I didn't want to disappoint her. I wanted to blow her mind.

I shucked off my suit jacket and unbuttoned the sleeves of my shirt, rolling them up before palming her ass and lifting her to my mouth.

"Silas," she breathed.

I blew over her pussy. "What? No pretty Italian words?"

She moved onto her elbows, looking down her body at me. *"Ti voglio."*

"I'm starting to recognize that one. Keep saying that, baby."

Then I licked her, and her head fell back. I wanted to see every reaction to my touch. I circled her clit, not touching the bundle of nerves, and she fell back onto the bed. "I'm going to make you feel so good."

She fisted the comforter as I used a finger to ease inside her. "You already are."

That statement went to my head, and I used a second finger, mimicking my cock fucking her. "I want to see you come on my mouth and then my cock."

"Yes," she breathed.

"You're so fucking sexy laid out on my bed for me. You're so wet for me."

Her thighs trembled as I kissed them. Her skin was impossibly soft. I reached up and palmed her breasts as I sucked on her clit, moving my fingers inside her, curling when I found that spot. The one that would send her over the edge.

Her breathing grew ragged, and her muscles tightened.

"Let go for me, baby." I sucked hard on her clit and used a third finger before she finally jerked, her hips arching off the bed, her pussy tight against my mouth. I eased her through the aftershocks before wiping my mouth and quickly removing my clothes. I caught her gazing appreciatively at my body, and I kissed my way up her body, loving how soft she was now.

She bit her lip. "I need you inside me."

I loved the raw honesty in her words. I'd been with women I suspected were putting on an act, pretending they wanted me, when what they really wanted was my lifestyle. But this thing with Gia was real. She did her best to resist me, and the fact she couldn't only made me want her more.

"I'll take care of you," I said, sensing she needed to hear that from me. It was past time for her to allow someone to care for her, and I'd be honored to be the man she chose.

I lined up at her entrance and then paused. "Do you want me bare?"

She hesitated and then nodded.

"I don't mind wearing a condom if it makes you feel more comfortable."

"No. I like feeling you inside me. It feels so much better, more intense somehow."

I suspected a big part of that was that we were connected on a level we hadn't been with anyone else. But I wasn't going to mention that to her. She wasn't ready for the emotional side of things. Or at least, she wasn't ready to acknowledge what we meant to each other. I could only hope she would, eventually.

She gripped my forearms as I slid the tip inside her. It felt so good I groaned. "Nothing feels as good as you." I'd give up everything to be with her like this forever.

I needed to be closer to her, though. I slid an arm under her and lifted her so that she straddled my thighs, and I rested on my heels. "Lower yourself onto me."

I held the base of my cock and helped her sink down over me.

Her walls closed around me, hot and wet and amazing. "I need you to move."

Every muscle in my body was pulled taut as I waited for her to adjust and start a rocking motion. I let her set the pace, and I sucked on her nipples. It was the perfect position for me to touch her and see all of her. She couldn't hide from me, and I loved that.

This was so much more than what we'd shared last time. If she tried to run this time, I'd chase her. I'd follow her anywhere. She was it for me. And the realization didn't scare me; it only made me want to hold on to her tighter.

She bit her lip as she gazed down at me, her hips rolling, whimpering as her clit brushed against the base of my cock on her descent.

"You're so sexy. I can't get enough of you." I hope she realized my words were genuine and my feelings were real.

"Yes, yes, yes," she said as an orgasm seemingly took her by surprise, and she shook around my cock. I took over, tightening my grip on her neck and back as I drove into her from below. I couldn't hold back any longer, and I didn't need to. I groaned, sinking my teeth into her skin.

She shivered from the bite.

I soothed the sting with a kiss and held her tight to me. I wouldn't let her go, no matter how far she ran or how deep she hid her emotions from me.

I eased her off my cock and laid her down on the bed. I went to the bathroom to clean up and threw cold water on my face.

When I returned, I asked, "Do you want to take a shower?"

But her eyes had already drifted shut, and she rolled onto her side. *"Voglio il tuo profumo."*

I drew her into my side and held her, not needing to ask what she'd meant because I could loosely translate *profumo* to scent. I figured she wanted to keep my essence on her skin for a little while longer, and I was all for that.

Her fingers curled over my forearm that was wrapped around her middle, and I realized I'd never felt more content or happier.

Thirteen

GIA

I woke slowly, a heavy weight on my side and warmth on my back. I slept better than I had in a long time, and it probably had something to do with the very hard body pressed against mine.

I should have slipped out from under his arm, put on my clothes, and left, but I didn't want to. I didn't want to run like I had last time. I believed him when he said he'd follow me.

As much as I liked the idea of that, it was childish to sneak out again. This was an adult relationship, and I was aware of the implications when I agreed to come to his room last night.

He kissed my shoulder, his voice gravelly with sleep. "Are you awake?"

"Mmm," I murmured, not ready to get up yet.

"Good. I've been waiting all night to do this." He moved me so that I was flat on my back.

"Waiting for what?" I asked, still feeling somewhat drowsy as he moved between my legs. My nerves tingled at the first contact of his wet mouth on me. I gripped the sheets, quickly becoming lost in the sensations. He used his tongue and teeth to quickly drive me up and over. I was surprised at how quickly I came for him.

I was still shaking and panting when he moved up the bed and slid inside me. He felt just as good as last night, if not better. I kind of loved the freedom of forgoing condoms.

"It's. So. Good," he punctuated between thrusts.

"Yesss," I hissed as his cock hit a few places that were still sore from the night before.

He lowered himself until his chest was pressed against mine, making shallow thrusts and grinding against my clit when he bottomed out. We couldn't get any closer, and instead of feeling panicked, I felt good. Content even.

I couldn't remember feeling like this with another man. With Silas, I was in over my head, and falling deeper with every minute I spent with him.

I should have gone back to my room. I should have run as far and as fast as I could, but I stayed, enjoying a few more minutes with him. Last night, I wasn't sure what the morning would bring, but it wasn't this.

I thought one of us would leave, and that would be that. I hadn't expected him to continue the intimacy. Didn't he see how dangerous this was? How out of control we were? One of us was bound to catch some feelings, and then it would hurt.

I couldn't let that happen to me. I needed to shore up my emotions and strengthen my walls. Somehow, Silas managed to infiltrate everything.

"You feel so good," he murmured, placing kisses on my collarbone before sucking one nipple into his mouth. I arched into his mouth, holding him to me. The scrape of his teeth over my hard peak sent me careening toward ecstasy.

His name tumbled out of my mouth despite my best efforts to stifle it.

"I love my name on your lips," he said as he kissed me, thrusting harder now. It still felt good, satisfying a deep ache inside, one that longed to be filled by him.

I wanted to say *Don't get used to it,* but I couldn't seem to form words.

"I love you like this, all soft and sweet."

I wanted to protest, to say I'd never been soft or sweet, but I loved that someone saw me that way. I'd hardened myself over the years, first as the youngest of four siblings and then later after my first boyfriend broke up with me so callously. I vowed never to let anyone else in. I focused on my school and then later on my business.

If I could keep my focus on work, everything I'd ever wanted would be mine. Success. Wealth. Happiness.

When he thrust deep one more time, I bit my lip against the words that wanted to spill out. *I like you. Being with you is the best thing I've ever felt.* Nothing good would come from being brutally honest. It would only put me in a position I didn't want to be in. I hated being vulnerable, and I'd already let Silas see more of me than I'd ever shown anyone else.

I'd been open and carefree once, and it had blown up in my face. I'd never let another guy in, especially not Silas Sharpe. I couldn't forget that he wasn't an easygoing, nice guy.

He lifted off me slightly and brushed a strand of hair off my forehead. His touch was tender, his expression a little awestruck. This was too much. My breath got caught in my throat.

"You okay?" he asked, his voice laced with concern.

"Never been better." At least that much was true. My body was in heaven while my mind was a tangle of ever-tightening knots.

He looked like he wanted to say something more, but I breathed a sigh of relief when he shifted off the bed and held his hand out to me. "Shower with me."

I couldn't come up with a valid reason not to, and it wasn't really a question.

I vaguely remember him asking last night and me telling him I wanted to keep his scent on me. My cheeks heated as I recalled that slip. I hoped he hadn't remembered.

Who says something like that to a man? Only someone who

was completely gone over one, and I would never be that girl again.

"I know you want to keep my scent on you—" he began lightly.

"You remember that?" I asked, purposely keeping my voice light as he led me into his large bathroom. I'd never been in this room before, but it was huge, almost as big as my bedroom at home with a huge walk-in closet and leather chair on the right, a tub with columns, and a rain shower along the back wall.

He turned on the various showerheads, and I wondered why he needed so many. It was a waste for one person.

"Come on. It feels good." He pulled me to the one in the middle and angled the other showerheads so that they were aimed at us. The steady pressure felt good on my sore muscles. I'd never experienced anything like it. It felt decadent.

I stayed silent as he lathered his hands and washed me from head to toe. Emotion clogged my throat as he took his time, massaging sore muscles and even gliding gently over my core. I almost expected him to go for another round, but he kept his touches light, as if he didn't want to spark anything.

Instead, his hands were gentle, his kisses featherlight as he covered every inch of me as if I was special, something to be cherished. It wreaked havoc on my brain. This was supposed to be a onetime thing, or a two-time thing, not a relationship.

I couldn't ask what he was doing because I was afraid of his answer. A part of me wanted more, and that was the scariest thing of all.

When he was finished, I returned the favor, my heart beating out of my chest at the unfamiliar gesture—one I'd never performed on a man before. I wondered if this was something Silas did with other women. But I couldn't bring myself to ask.

When we were finished with our bodies, he turned me to lather my hair. His firm touch sent tingles down my spine. I barely contained the moan that rose from my throat. When he was finished rinsing my hair, he said, "Grab one of the heated towels from the rack. I'll be out in a minute."

I wrapped myself in a fluffy towel and lathered lotion on every inch of my body. Even the products the hotel provided were top quality. I left the room as he got out to get dressed. I hadn't moved my overnight bag to the room, so I settled for grabbing a T-shirt and shorts from his drawer.

"I like seeing you in my clothes," he said when he entered the bedroom in a towel knotted low on his hips.

"My things are in my room." I'd never felt more naked than standing in his room in his too-big clothes.

"We'll eat and then get them."

I brushed my hair with the hairbrush he'd left on the dresser. I wondered if the hotel kept spares, or if he did. But again, I didn't want to ask. This was just an awkward morning after. Except if I was being honest with myself, it felt nice.

"What do you normally do on Sundays?" Silas asked as he led the way into the kitchen. It was modern, with gleaming stainless-steel appliances and smooth white cupboards.

"I catch up on work while the office is quiet." I was used to spending weekends alone. Harper spent all her time with Leo now, and I hadn't really fostered other friendships. The women at Happily Ever Afters were more employees than friends.

Silas flashed a smile at me. "I do that on Saturdays, but Sundays are for relaxing and clearing the mind."

I sat on the metal stool as he grabbed a pan and a carton of eggs from the fridge. "You like eggs?"

"Of course." I'd never had a man make them for me before. But I kept that tidbit to myself.

"How do you like 'em?"

"Any way, but I love omelets," I said, a little surprised that I'd revealed that about myself.

Silas flashed me a bright smile. "Omelets it is."

Who was this guy, and why had I been avoiding him for all these years? Maybe I was afraid of the inevitable fall. I didn't want to get hurt again, but I couldn't seem to make myself walk away. I should have made some excuse as to why I needed to go to work, but it was Sunday, and even I knew it was lame to use work as an excuse after the amazing night we'd shared.

"Surely you do more than just work," Silas chided.

"I get up early, work out, and drink my coffee. So, it feels like a lazy morning."

He raised a brow as he cracked the eggs into a bowl and whisked them. "You ever go to brunch with friends?"

My throat tightened, and I attempted to clear it.

"Let me grab you a water. I'll get the coffee going in a minute." Silas filled a glass with ice and water from the fridge and handed it to me.

The cold glass felt good against my forehead. Why did I feel feverish suddenly? Then I drank the cool liquid, almost wishing it were alcohol so I could numb myself for this conversation.

When he raised his gaze to mine, I realized he hadn't forgotten the question. "I work the rest of the day."

He raised a brow. "Even I'm not that hardworking."

"What do you do?" I asked, desperate to get him off the subject of my habits.

"I'll go out on my boat with friends or tinker around my house."

"You're handy?" I asked, impressed. Silas struck me as a suit type who hired out for any needs he might have.

"It doesn't come easily to me, but I know how to watch how-to videos online. I'm a pro at that." He flashed me a devastatingly handsome smile.

"That's impressive." I was hopeless at anything that needed to be fixed if it wasn't related to marketing, business, or weddings.

He transferred the eggs to the pan and said nonchalantly, "You should come with me."

"Go where?" I asked, watching as his muscles flexed as he moved around the kitchen, grabbing a bag of coffee beans and scooping them into the machine.

"On my boat."

My eyes widened as he hit start on the machine, and the sound of beans grinding filled the air. When the noise died down, Silas arched his brow. "Well?"

I was tempted. "I should get home and catch up on things from the week."

"I'm going to guess that you have a housekeeper, someone who does your dry cleaning, and maybe even a physical trainer."

"Yes, to the cleaner and the laundry, but no to the trainer. I prefer to lead my own workouts."

He grinned. "Of course, you do."

"It's just that I know my body best," I insisted, not wanting him to think I was a control freak when I was.

"After last night, I feel like I'm intimately familiar with it," he said, with one eye on me and the other on the pan.

My body flushed with heat and desire, and something else I couldn't define.

He focused on me. "You're really going to pass on a chance to go out on a boat to work?"

"That's what I should do," I said, rethinking my stance.

He turned and braced his hands on the counter. "When was the last time you did something fun?"

I panicked at the word *fun*. I wasn't even sure what that meant. I enjoyed working. I loved working out. It felt good, but was it fun? I didn't have time to read or watch TV. I didn't have any friends except for Harper.

Silas shook his head. "That's just sad."

"I have a great life." I loved building my business. I could relax when it was successful, which I defined as bringing in a significant profit. I took care of myself by working out and eating healthy, at least most of the time.

"Yet you can't recount one time that was fun."

I racked my brain, trying to find one memory that could be characterized as fun. "I enjoyed the pizzeria's opening."

He shot me a disbelieving look. "Unless you're talking about our kiss in the kitchen, I don't believe you."

I shrugged. "I don't have to go on a boat to have fun."

"Probably not, but I want to take you. Will you let me?" Silas asked, and despite all my very valid reasons not to go, I found myself nodding.

He grinned, and the light from that one smile lit me up from the inside.

Extending our time together was not a good idea, but I couldn't come up with a reason to disappoint him. It seemed important that I go with him. He wanted to share this one thing with me, and who was I to deny him?

"You brought a spare set of clothes?" Silas asked.

I nodded. "And a bathing suit because I wanted to try out your pool."

"You can wear it on the boat. I know a cove where we can swim. It's private, and most boaters don't know about it."

"That sounds nice." It actually sounded kind of amazing, but I didn't want to admit that to him.

He slid the omelet from the pan to the plate. "I just added cheese."

"That's perfect."

He pushed it across the counter toward me and then poured the coffee. "Cream or sugar?"

"Cream if you have it," I said, trying not to think about how domestic all this seemed.

He grabbed a few cream pods from the fridge, the kind hotels stocked. "I get them from downstairs for when I have guests."

"You have guests often?" I asked, trying to sound innocent. He'd said he didn't bring women here, but I wasn't sure.

Silas shot me a knowing look. "My parents like to stay here from time to time."

"They stay here and not in one of the other rooms?"

"It's a two-bedroom suite, and it's like a condo. It doesn't feel like a hotel room."

For the first time, I looked around as he started his eggs. There were framed photos on the wall of his brothers and parents on his boat and standing in front of the hotel, probably at the opening, and others of him when he was little. "Your family is close?"

I didn't know much about him. If my brothers had mentioned his family, I didn't listen.

"We are. All of us live in the area, and we see my parents often."

"That's nice," I said, wondering why his words sent a pang through my heart.

"It's very similar to your family."

That felt like a lie because I hadn't gone to family dinner on Sundays in a long time. My mother was disappointed, but she'd given up on pressuring me to go. There was a rift between Papà and me, and no amount of family dinners would fix it.

"Leo mentioned that you don't go to Sunday dinners anymore."

"Remember? I'm usually working." I shifted in my chair, uncomfortable with him asking questions about the situation.

"And your parents are okay with that excuse?" Silas asked.

"They aren't, but they don't have a choice."

"What's the real reason?" he asked, his hip cocked against the counter as he crossed his impressive biceps over his chest.

"My dad doesn't respect my choice to open a business separate from his. He thinks I should be working with him."

Silas frowned. "That's tough."

"I couldn't work for him anymore. I felt stifled. I had all these ideas, and he didn't want to hear them."

Silas raised a brow. "He approved the expansion of the restaurant."

"Only because my brothers would have gone out on their own if he'd said no. I get the irony. He didn't care about me leaving because I'm just one person. But my brothers run the other restaurant. He needs them."

"I'm sure he needed you too."

"As a waitress? I have more to give than being a server." I sighed and put my fork down. "It doesn't matter because I didn't want to work for my parents or the pizzeria."

"He doesn't respect your dreams."

"He doesn't respect my business. He thinks everyone in the family should work for him. But I couldn't. There wasn't a place for me in it, and it wasn't what I wanted. But he wasn't listening to what I wanted."

"And you want to prove yourself to him," Silas observed, his voice gentle.

I laughed without any humor. "That's impossible. Nothing I do ever seems to impress him. He still sees me as a rebellious teenager. No amount of monetary success or good grades seems to alter his opinion of me. It's like he doesn't see me." That admission came from somewhere deep, somewhere I hadn't accessed in a long time.

Silas's expression softened as he came around the counter and pulled me into his arms. I rested my cheek against his hard chest, sinking into him and savoring the feel of his arms around me. "I see you."

I closed my eyes against the feeling behind his words. I thought this conversation was about family and parents, not about him.

"Sometimes you have to do things for yourself. Not to impress others around you. If you're always seeking his approval, you might be disappointed."

He eased back, and I smiled to cover the emotion I was feeling. "Yeah, I get that. I don't need his approval, or at least I shouldn't." It was something I struggled with because a part of me would always want it. Even if I thought it was a pipe dream.

Fourteen

SILAS

"When no one is cheering for you, you have to clap for yourself," I said. A desire to be the one by her side made my chest tighten.

Her lips twisted. "That's kind of sad."

"You're your biggest cheerleader," I said, leaning against the counter and sipping my coffee.

"I suppose that's always been the case. It's not like my family supported my decision to open Happily Ever Afters. Harper's always been by my side, encouraging me, but you're right. I don't need it."

"You're like me. You're driven by an internal force, not an external one. That's the best way to be."

Gia smiled. "We're a lot alike."

I winked at her. "That's why we didn't get along."

She gestured between us. "I think it's because we both knew this would happen."

"You mean on a subconscious level?" I was very much aware of my attraction to her and how bad of an idea acting on it would be.

"Yeah."

I leaned on my elbows, and she raised her brow in surprise.

This thing with her was a game. It was a balancing act of getting close one minute and giving her space the next. I wanted to draw her in, but not so much that she bolted. "You can tell yourself that."

She blinked at me. "Are you saying you know you were attracted to me?"

"That's right. No point in pretending I wasn't." I straightened and checked on my omelet. Seeing it was almost done, I sprinkled shredded cheese on it.

"I had no idea."

"You had this way of pushing me away whenever I was near. But that's in the past. All that matters is what's happening between us now."

Then I tensed, waiting for her response. I busied myself sliding the omelet onto a plate and then turned to face her, eating while standing up.

She arched one delicate brow. "And what is going on?"

I could smirk and say something cocky, but I had a feeling that wouldn't be a good move. She'd made herself vulnerable by asking. "Whatever it is, I like it. I want to keep enjoying it. No pressure. No labels. Can you do that?"

She sighed and finally nodded. "Yeah, okay."

I wanted to pump my fist in the air, but I restrained myself. I was positive she wouldn't appreciate it. "We'll eat, get your stuff, and spend the day on the water."

Gia smiled softly. "I'm actually looking forward to it."

Her shoulders had relaxed a bit. I could tell she was worried about staying overnight and when she should make her escape. But I'd changed everything with my impromptu offer of a boat ride. I usually went with friends or on my own. I'd never taken a woman out on the boat. I'd never wanted to before, but Gia was breaking all my rules.

I wanted to do something for her, pull her out of her usual routine. Make her see there was something more out there for her than proving herself to her family. She was incredibly successful and should be proud of her hard work, but she needed to enjoy life too.

I was positive I was the man to show her.

We finished eating, and I cleaned up, and then we went to her suite, where I waited while she got dressed.

I looked up from my phone when she came out of the bathroom and almost swallowed my tongue. She wore a red string bikini and cutoff jeans, a throwback to the day I saw her when she was sixteen. There was no way she could know how much that outfit affected me. There was a lot of bare skin, and when she turned around, the cheeks of her ass were visible.

I cleared my throat.

"Is there a problem?" Gia asked.

I gestured in her direction. "Those shorts—they seem to be missing something."

This time, she smirked. "They're on trend."

I stood and moved closer to her. "Your ass hanging out is a trend? What do your brothers have to say about it?"

Her face clouded over. "My brothers have no say in what I wear. Nor should they."

"That's not what I meant. I just—it's going to be hard for me to keep my hands off you." And I didn't want anyone in the hotel to get a glimpse of her.

"That was the point," she said, moving past me to grab a bag and stuffing sunscreen and a book inside it.

"You think you'll have time to read?"

She raised her brow. "You said this trip was for me to relax, and I can't remember the last time I was able to. I've been carrying this paperback around with me for a long time. So far, all it's accomplished is building my shoulder muscles."

I moved toward her, kissing her softly. "If you want to read, I'll make sure there's time for it."

I wanted to swim, eat lunch, and just relax with no destination in mind.

"Perfect." She smiled, and she looked so much younger.

I liked this look on her. I loved her in the morning, soft and pliable from her orgasm, and I liked her even more like this. I wouldn't talk about work or what any of this meant. I wanted to enjoy it, and I wanted her to do the same.

She slung her bag over her shoulder. "Are you ready?"

I draped an arm over her shoulder as we headed out. "For someone who didn't want to go, you seem eager."

She hung her head, hiding her face from me. "You convinced me this would be fun."

I squeezed her shoulder. "You're going to love it and want to go every week."

She grinned but tried to cover it. "You wish."

"You know I'm right. You can't resist this or my boat," I said, touching my stomach.

She laughed. "You're ridiculous."

I grinned, enjoying myself. "But just what you need."

She sobered. "I'm starting to think you're right."

"It's just you and me today." I'd called ahead and had the kitchen staff pack snacks and a lunch for us, so we headed straight for the dock. Since I owned the marina, my boat was in the largest slip at the end of the dock.

When we reached the end, Gia paused, taking it in. "This isn't a boat. It's a yacht."

I shrugged, feeling slightly uncomfortable about the one flashy thing I owned. Besides a five-star resort. "Labels are just semantics."

Her lips twitched. "Yeah, okay."

I held out a hand for her to board the boat.

"I was expecting something smaller, like a sailboat."

"What's the fun in that? I like to entertain," I said lightly.

The box of food sat on the bench, so I took it below to refrigerate it.

Gia followed me as I set the box in the kitchen galley and turned on the air. "Does someone drive it for you?"

"Sometimes, but I wanted to be alone today. You can help me

drive to the cove, and then we'll anchor for a bit." It was the only destination I had in mind. I wanted her focus on me.

Gia relaxed even more, and I liked to think that she enjoyed spending time with me. She moved around the room, touching the wood. "I bet you impress women with this baby."

It was large and comfortable, with several levels to enjoy. There was a large master bedroom that I hoped we'd get to experience today, but I didn't want her to think this was a regular occurrence for me. "You're the first."

Her wide gaze met mine. "Are you serious?"

"The yacht is my baby, and it's my time to relax. I don't bring dates here." I moved closer, her chin lifting so her gaze could remain connected with mine. "Until you."

"Does that mean I'm special?"

"It's whatever you want it to mean. I like spending time with you, and I wanted to share my favorite thing with you."

"Wow. You sure know how to smooth-talk a woman."

"Everything with you is natural. I never could control my reaction to you."

She finally nodded as I leaned down to steal a kiss. I loved having her near, kissing and touching her whenever I felt like it. I had a feeling she wouldn't be so free with affection when we were around others, so I wanted to take advantage of her relative comfort when we were alone.

"Let me get things ready so we can get out on the water."

"I can't wait."

Hope bloomed in my chest that I'd finally found someone who was not only a match for me but could be that soft place for me to land too. I never thought I wanted a relationship, but Gia was making me rethink everything.

"Relax while I get everything ready."

She pulled her book out of her bag. "I can read?"

"There's a hammock on the front end of the boat."

Her eyes lit up as she went on deck to search for it, and I enjoyed the view of her ass cheeks peeking out of those cutoffs. I adjusted myself before focusing on the task of preparing the boat for the day. When I was finished, I called one of the staff members from the marina to untie the lines from the dock.

When we were sailing out of the marina, Gia moved out of the hammock and into the cockpit.

I slung an arm over her shoulder. "You enjoy the hammock?"

She cradled her paperback against her chest. "It was amazing. I could lie there all day."

I tucked her into my side and kissed her temple. "Feel free."

She rested her head on my chest and didn't move away from me. I took the opportunity to explain the various things we saw as we traveled toward the cove.

"I love hearing about the history of the area."

"I always wonder what the story is for every family that lives inside." There were large homes lining the shore.

She rested a palm on my chest and looked up at me. "Are they rich? Do they live here all the time, or is it a vacation home?"

I loved being close to her, breathing in her flowery scent and wondering if this could be an everyday thing. "I'd love to know."

She smiled mischievously. "You can make it up. That could be fun too."

I pointed at a particularly sizeable house with a large deck and patio. To get to the dock, you needed to move down a big hill. "What about that one?"

She tapped her chin with her finger. "Mmm. The dad is an attorney at one of the big firms in Baltimore. The family summers here, and he comes for a week when he can."

"Wow. You have an imagination."

She shrugged. "I like to think about what other people's lives are like."

I wondered if she wanted a different one when she was growing up. If she felt stifled at the pizzeria as the youngest of so many siblings. "Did you want to be someone else?"

She laughed. "I love myself, and I'm happy with where I am."

Maybe that's why Gia was so attractive to me when other

women weren't. She was extraordinarily confident in herself and didn't need a man to fulfill anything inside her. "Have you thought about creating your own life story outside your business? Like falling in love and starting a family."

She shook her head. "I'm focused on the business."

"Have you had any long-term relationships?"

She stiffened in my arms. "Just one in college. Looking back, it was only serious for me. He was just having fun."

Was this the man who'd changed Gia's outlook on life?

She elbowed me in the side. "What about you? Any girlfriends?"

"I dated a girl in college for a couple of years. I thought it could lead somewhere, but she wanted to move back home to Oregon. This will always be my home. I love the bay and crabbing. Oregon doesn't have Old Bay."

"You gave up a woman over Old Bay Seasoning?"

"It was more than that. I couldn't imagine living anywhere else, and neither could she. It was a realization over time that we wouldn't work out. But it was fine. We had fun in college."

"I wish I could see things so easily. When our breakup happened, I was surprised. I thought we had something, and he didn't see it that way at all."

"You fell for him."

"Yeah, I guess I did. At home, I felt looked over. As soon as the first boy paid attention to me, I was a goner."

"I bet it was nice not having your brothers there to stop anything from happening."

"That too. Although they protected me from heartbreak. I see that now. I couldn't have gone through that in high school."

"It was a learning experience." Except I worried it might be a wound for her, the thing that was keeping her from opening up to me. I hated that for her and for me. We had so much potential, if she just had the courage to reach out and grab it.

"Thank you for bringing me. This is so much fun."

I loved her like this. Relaxed and happy. Enjoying life. I

intended to do many more outings, just like this. Maybe we could make boating a weekly thing. I wouldn't mind having someone to share this with.

"Let's head to the cove so we can swim and relax."

"That sounds perfect."

I showed her how to steer and let her do a little of the driving until it got trickier near the cove. It was a larger cove that accommodated my boat, but few people spent time here. That's why I loved it so much. I dropped anchor, grabbed the food, and took it on deck.

We ate on the deck, the breeze rustling our hair. There were sandwiches, fruit, cheese, and crackers with water. It was the perfect day.

After we cleaned up lunch, I asked, "Want to rest in the hammock for a bit?"

We managed to both get in the hammock, my arm under her neck, as it swayed in the breeze. I'd put this hammock here for relaxation, but I rarely ever used it. We stared up at the mostly cloudless sky, content to be together.

We must have drifted off, waking up a short time later. "Are you ready to go swimming?"

"Yes," she said as I helped her get out of the hammock without falling. We went to the back of the boat, and she pushed down her shorts, revealing red bottoms that curved high on her waist.

I wanted to strip the suit off her and taste her, but I promised her a day on the boat, and I wanted to give her the full experience.

I took off my shirt and waited while she put on sunscreen and offered to spray my back. I would have preferred she use her hands to smooth lotion over me, but the spray was quicker. When we were ready, I took her hand and led her onto the diving ledge at the back of the boat. "So, we just jump?"

"You can, or dive."

She let go of my hand and executed a perfect dive into the water. Her form was smooth. I dove in after her, eager to see how well she could swim. She emerged on the surface, swimming a perfect freestyle.

When she eased up, I stopped alongside her. "Were you on the swim team?"

Gia smiled. "For a few summers. I liked the competitions."

"You're a good swimmer." I drew her into my body.

She wrapped her legs around my waist and tightened her arms around her neck. "I feel a little rusty, but it's coming back to me."

I loved that she enjoyed swimming. I had a feeling most of the women I'd been with would have stayed on deck, sunbathing while I brought them food. None of them would have dived off the back.

She smiled down at me, so effortlessly filled with joy. It was a moment I wanted to remember forever.

She lowered her mouth to mine and said, "Thank you for inviting me."

Her appreciation washed over me.

"Any time, sweetheart."

We kissed in the water until I couldn't keep us afloat anymore, and then we swam for a bit, racing each other to a buoy and back to the boat. On the last race, she pulled ahead of me, and instead of increasing my speed to beat her, I dove underwater and snagged her ankle, pulling her to me.

She gasped. "What are you doing?"

"Capturing you."

She arched a brow, then wiggled away from me and dove underwater. I easily followed her as she darted here and there, trying to lose me. But I was a strong swimmer too, and whenever she came to the surface, she couldn't stop laughing. It greatly reduced her ability to escape me.

I finally got her, wrapping my arms around you. "I've got you now."

"What are you going to do with me?"

I bit her earlobe and tugged as a shiver ran through her body. "I'm going to keep you captive on my boat."

She laughed. "I might like that."

I ran my nose over her neck. "You're supposed to be scared of me."

She tipped her head, giving me more access to her skin. "But it sounds so enticing."

I bit her neck, and she melted into my arms. I swam with her over to the diving platform, allowing her to pull herself out, and then I followed. Water fell from us as we kissed, stumbling our way down below, where we finally landed on the bed. I didn't care that we were wet or that the bedding would be soaked.

All I could think about was her mouth and her wet skin. Chasing her in the water brought out this primal need in me to claim her for my own. All the talk about capturing her was real when I thought about how elusive it felt to be with her. I wanted to grab on to her with both hands and hold on tight, never letting her go.

I untied her top and then her bottoms, letting her suit fall away. I took a few seconds to take her in, her body beaded with water, her nipples hard points. "So beautiful."

She reared up, kissing my chest. "Silas, I need you." Then she attempted to shove my swim trunks down. They were wet and wouldn't budge, so I stepped off the bed to do it for her.

I loved that we'd forgone condoms a long time ago. I didn't need to stop to find one or worry about having one. Everything with her flowed naturally from one step to the next.

I kneeled on the bed, kissing her and touching every inch of her, kneading her breasts, tweaking her nipples, and finally sinking my fingers inside her.

She widened her legs in an open invitation for me to sink inside her. But I held back.

"Silas, please, let go. I need you."

I knew what she wanted. She felt just as wild and desperate as I did. So I withdrew my fingers and lined up my cock. With one thrust, I was inside her, filling her up.

Her eyes widened, and her skin flushed; her hips lifted,

enticing me to move with her. "I love you like this. Wet and wild. Desperate for me."

Her nails trailed down my back as I leaned over and kissed her roughly, letting go of finesse. This was rough and raw and primal. I was barreling toward my release, and I couldn't stop it if I tried.

I reached down to touch her clit, but she eased off my cock and rolled onto her knees.

"Fuck, yes."

There was nothing more primal than this position. I wasted no time in getting my cock inside her, my fingers gripping her hips as I thrust inside her.

She was gorgeous on her knees for me, her ass tipped up to meet my cock. The orgasm built again, and I knew I was in danger of going over before her, so I reached around to circle her clit with my fingers, pressing hard.

She spasmed around my cock, sending me over too. I groaned into her shoulder, and she slumped onto the bed. I lay there, exhausted from the swimming and the sex, unable to move or think.

I kissed her shoulder as I eased my weight off her and to the side.

"That was nice," she finally murmured, and I couldn't stop the bark of laughter that flew from my lips.

"Nice? I must be doing something wrong."

She touched my chest with her palm. "Your ego doesn't need any boosting."

I leaned in for a quick kiss. "With you it does."

"You wouldn't have it any other way," she said before falling silent, and I knew deep down she was right. I more than liked this girl. I was falling hard. I just hoped she was following me down.

"Mmm. That was amazing," she said as she rolled onto her back and stretched her arms over her head.

"Much better than work."

Gia smiled. "Much."

"I'm going to show you how to have fun if it's the last thing I do."

She moved into my arms and wrapped her arms around my neck, pressing her breasts into my chest. "I just like being here with you like this."

I stroked her back, closing my eyes and knowing that I wanted this—her and me—forever. It wasn't going to be easy, but I was relentless when it came to getting what I wanted.

Fifteen

GIA

We stayed in bed for a while, reminiscing about our childhoods. I relayed what it was like to grow up in the pizzeria, doing homework in the office and learning to cook next to my father. Back then, I absorbed everything he had to say.

"I can't imagine growing up the way you did. For me, it was more about tutors and activities, the ones that would improve our résumés for college. Everything we did was to impress other people. Even when it came to volunteer work."

It didn't sound warm and loving to me, but I had a feeling his parents thought they were preparing him for the real world.

"There weren't a lot of hugs or expressions of love. But we were financially supported. We're successful business owners, so it paid off."

"What do your brothers do? I'm sure you've mentioned it, but I wasn't paying attention."

"Sebastian owns a few farm-to-table restaurants. He never liked having a boss, so he bought a few failing restaurants and made them into what he wanted."

"I can't imagine having that kind of money and freedom," I

said, running my hand over his chest, loving the feel of his hair beneath my fingers.

"You're successful."

"I sink most of my money back into the business. I only pull enough of a salary to cover living expenses."

"Is that necessary?"

"We don't all have money to fall back on. I built the business from scratch. No loans. I need to work hard for a few more years, then it will get easier, and I can relax." Not wanting his focus on me and my business when I wasn't as successful as him or his brothers, I said, "What about your other brothers?"

"Liam's in corporate. Wells is a musician. Our music lessons were meant to be a supplement to our education, not our career. Our parents never approved of Wells majoring in music, but if a Sharpe is going to do something, he must be the best at it."

"That's a lot of pressure."

"We're used to it. We should head back. You're probably getting hungry."

"That's a good idea." I needed to salvage the day and get something done. I'd never taken an entire day off before. Anxiety built in my chest.

"Let me feed you, and if you still want to head home, I won't stop you."

I rolled my eyes. "Like you could."

It was a bluff because he'd already convinced me to spend the day with him, not working.

He pulled up the anchor and started the engine so we could head back. He sat in the captain's chair with his legs spread. "Come here."

I went to him easily, standing between his legs and leaning into his chest. He easily steered around me. We didn't speak, just enjoyed each other's company. We'd shared a bit about our pasts, and neither of us felt the need to fill the air with unnecessary chatter.

I felt like I belonged here in his arms. Like we could do this every Sunday from now on, and I'd be content. It was stupid and ridiculous, but I wasn't ready to let go of this vision.

Silas called ahead, so a couple of workers met us at the dock and quickly had the boat tied to the pilings. We gathered our things, and I waited for Silas to lock up before we headed to the hotel.

In the lobby, he stopped in front of the elevator. "I was thinking we could order room service."

My stomach grumbled.

"But what do you think about going back to my place? I could cook for you. I want to cook for you." His gaze flicked to mine, and I saw a vulnerability there I'd never seen before.

No man besides my father and brothers had ever cooked for me. "That would be nice."

"I'll run up and get our things."

I waited for him in the lobby, wondering how I'd gotten sucked into an evening with Silas. I couldn't resist him. Was he like this with every woman, or just me?

Silas stepped off the elevator, scanning the lobby for me, his shoulders relaxing when he found me.

I approached him, and he wrapped an arm around my shoulder. "Were you worried I left?"

He chuckled. "You have a history of running."

"I'm sorry if you were worried." I wanted to reassure him I wouldn't freak out again or have second thoughts about us, but I couldn't make that promise. Everything was okay when we were together, but I couldn't predict how I'd feel when I left.

He must have called to have his SUV brought around because it was waiting for us at the curb. He opened the door, and I stepped inside, pleased he hadn't allowed the valet to do it. I liked that he treated me as someone to be respected and taken care of.

When he climbed inside, he reached over the console and interlaced his fingers with mine. I couldn't take my gaze off the sight of his long fingers wrapped around mine. My heart squeezed, and I had to look away. I let out a breath, trying to steady my rapidly beating heart.

"We'll take it one step at a time," Silas said, as if he sensed my discomfort. "We're in this together."

I didn't say anything, just felt grateful that he got how hard it was for me to be here.

He drove down a stone lane lined with trees. We came upon a large cluster of trees, and then there was a clearing for his house.

"The best part is that it backs to the water."

"I can't wait to see it," I said as we got out.

He grabbed our bags and held out his hand to me.

The house was a two-story with a large wraparound porch. I'd already fallen in love with it, and I hadn't seen the view from the back or anything inside. I loved that he had a respite from the resort. A place he could go and be quiet.

Inside, he dropped our bags and led the way through the large family room and kitchen, through French doors to the deck. It was more of a covered porch with steps leading to the backyard and the water.

We stopped at the railing, looking over the lake. "This is gorgeous. I'd never leave if this was my place."

There was a moment of silence, and then Silas moved behind me, surrounding me from behind and kissing my neck. "One more reason to keep you here."

I leaned back into his chest as he straightened, wishing we never had to leave.

He sighed. "As much as I love this view, I promised you a home-cooked meal."

"You don't have to. We had a long day. We could just order in."

"I never do that here. The point of being here is that I'm off the grid. Room service isn't a call away, and there's no one rushing to do my bidding."

"Life is so tough for you," I teased, though I respected him even more for it.

He led the way inside, opening a bottle of wine and pouring me a glass. "Have a seat while I whip something up."

I sat at the island with the windows displaying the water behind him. "I have the best view."

He cocked a brow. "Watching me cook?"

I laughed. "The water."

"Hmm. I don't know if I like the competition."

"I love both." Every minute with him made it easier to stay. I forgot the reasons why I should be at home, working on my next big project.

He pulled out some chicken, adding seasoning before putting it in the oven, and then boiled a pot of water for the pasta. While everything was cooking, he cut up tomatoes.

"Are you sure you don't need any help?" I asked, feeling lazy for sipping wine while he did all the work.

Silas glanced up at me and winked. "I love cooking, and I want you to relax and have a good time. You can help next time."

Warmth spread unheeded through my body at his sweet words. "I'd like that."

"I assume you know how to cook?"

"It was a requirement for everyone in the family. It wasn't an *only girls cook* kind of family. Mamma always said she wanted her boys to be able to impress their women."

Silas barked out a laugh. "I like your mom. She's practical."

I smiled, enjoying sharing about my family. "She never let the boys get away with a messy room or not putting away their dishes. And I think they turned out okay. They're respectful of women."

Silas tipped his head. "Matteo?"

I laughed. "He seems like a player, but he has a huge heart. I was always the one he'd talk to after one of his dates." Then I stopped, thinking I shouldn't be spilling Matteo's secrets to his friend.

Silas lifted his head from the chopping. "I won't tell him you said anything. He can keep his street cred."

"Matteo would make a good boyfriend. If only he'd be willing to show who he is underneath all the bluster." He had been hurt by his first girlfriend, and I watched as he pretended everything was okay. He put on this persona, one that said he was a good time. But he was so much more than that.

"I think that's true of all the Giovanni kids."

"Are you talking about me?" I asked, not sure I wanted the answer.

"I think you have a heart of gold, and I'm the lucky guy who gets to see it."

"Who says I've shown it to you?" I teased.

A smile spread over his face. "Oh, I've seen it."

I should have been scrambling to protect myself, to shore up my walls so he couldn't see through, but I was enjoying this time we were spending together, and it was better now that I was more at ease with him.

Then he sobered. "You can trust me with your truth, Gia. I won't hurt you."

I scoffed. "No one can promise that."

He paused, his knife pressed flat against the cutting board. "Let's put it this way. I don't *want* to hurt you."

My heart beat a steady rhythm under my rib cage. "You might not intend to, but it's still possible."

Silas shook his head, lifting his gaze to meet mine. "Anything's possible, but that's not the way to live your life—so afraid of the worst-case scenarios that you can't live your life to the fullest."

"And you think my being here and spending time with you is living my life to the fullest?"

He smirked and said, "Something like that."

"I'll admit I had fun today."

He finished chopping tomatoes and scraped them from the board into a serving bowl. Then he rounded the corner and stood in front of me. "That's a start." Then he placed a featherlight kiss on my lips and dropped his forehead to mine.

Something passed between us then, heavy and meaningful,

and before I could analyze it fully, he'd moved away to check the boiling water and add the pasta to the pan.

"You need more wine?"

I pushed the empty glass toward him, wondering what I'd gotten myself into. I worried about what would happen tomorrow. Would everything go back to normal? Would we be able to work together after everything we'd shared?

"Can you stop worrying about the what-ifs and enjoy our time together?" Silas asked as he poured wine into my glass.

"How do you know I'm doing that?" I asked as I reached for the now-full glass and sipped it.

"You get this pensive look on your face."

"Mmm." He read me like no one else could, or it was more likely that he took the time to get to know me. I was able to push everyone else away. I was usually so strong that no one worried about me. Not even my family.

They assumed I had everything handled, and while that was nice, it was better to have someone who saw underneath. Who read between the lines and knew what I needed before I did.

He poured a second glass for himself. "This will pair well with dinner."

"Do you ever take those boats on the water?" I asked, pointing to a kayak and canoe I noticed lying along the shore.

"I love going early in the morning or at dusk. It's quiet and peaceful."

"I'd love to go with you sometime." I wasn't sure where that came from or if it was a good idea, but how he described it was too enticing to ignore.

Silas flashed me a smile. "I'd love that."

The warmth that had filled my chest all day expanded to the rest of my body. I watched while he finished dinner and then helped him get the food onto plates before we carried them onto the porch to eat at the large table there.

He kept the lights low so we could see the water as we ate. I was starving, and we ate quickly. Afterward, Silas left the plates and asked, "Would you like to see the water up close?"

I nodded eagerly. "Yes."

He stood and held his hand out to me. It was natural to take it and allow him to interlace his fingers with mine, his palm flat against mine as we walked down the wooden steps and across the short expanse of lawn to the water that lapped on the shore.

"The only downside to this property is I can't have a dock here. If you already have one, you can keep it. Apparently, they're not good for wildlife."

"I can imagine."

"It would be nice to sit on it in the evening, though."

I lifted my chin, taking in the sight of the moon in the distance. "I get that, but I can't imagine that being a downside. It's so peaceful here." I could almost forget Silas was the owner of a luxury resort. Here, he didn't have to keep an eye on whatever was going on or nod at every manager he encountered. Here, he was able to relax.

Silas led us to a couple of Adirondack chairs by the shore. He sat in one and tugged me onto his lap. I draped my legs over his and curled into his body, content to be near him and the water.

After a while, I said, "I could sit like this all night."

His voice rumbled through his chest and into my shoulder. "Me too. But eventually, the bugs will find us."

I snuggled deeper into his chest, keeping my gaze on the water. "Let's stay for as long as we can."

He kissed the top of my head. "Whatever you want."

When had a man ever anticipated what I needed and delivered it? I couldn't remember a time anyone took care of me. I did such a good job of it—or maybe I acted like I did—that it didn't leave room for anyone else. But I enjoyed being here with him like this.

Clouds rolled in, and the air started to smell like rain by the time Silas suggested we clean up.

I was drowsy from the day on the water and the big meal. When I offered to help clean the remnants of our dinner, Silas waved me off, telling me to get ready for bed. I didn't argue because I was swaying on my feet.

I followed his directions to the top of the stairs and down the hall to the master. The room had soft-gray walls and natural wood furniture I thought might have been handmade. I brushed my teeth with a spare toothbrush I found in the bathroom and brushed my hair with my fingers before washing my face.

I climbed into the king-size bed, and the bedding was so comfortable, I almost drifted off by the time the bed dipped and Silas joined me. His breath was minty fresh, as if he'd just brushed his teeth. "I like having you in my bed."

I rolled into him, resting my forehead on his chest, loving his warmth and solid presence. He tightened his arms around me like he didn't want to let me go.

Who would have thought a few months ago I'd be in Silas's arms? It was incomprehensible, yet I felt more comfortable with him than anyone else.

He kissed my forehead. "Go back to sleep."

At his insistence, I closed my eyes again and fell asleep, content in his arms.

Sixteen

GIA

The next morning, I woke up feeling slightly panicked to find myself still at Silas's house. I needed to get to work early, but I had to drive home and shower.

Silas's arm tightened around me. "What are you thinking about so hard?"

I shifted in his arms so that I could see his face. "I can't believe I stayed overnight. I need to get to work."

"I'm positive you hire competent employees who can handle things if you're running late one day."

Anxiety curled in my stomach. "That's not the point. I should be there. I'm the face of the company."

"And it's a beautiful face," he said as he rolled me so I was flat on my back, and then he was kissing me.

"You're distracting me."

"That was the point." He shoved my shirt up and palmed my breast. I was putty in his hands when he touched my nipples. There was a zing that traveled straight to my clit, and I lifted my hips, seeking friction.

He obliged by moving between my legs and grinding his cock where I needed him most.

"Too many clothes." I needed to feel him.

He raised a brow as he hovered over me. "You're not worried about work?"

"Hurry," I demanded as I pushed up his shirt.

He reared up to remove it himself. "I can be quick and thorough," he said as he shoved his sweatpants down and off, and I hurried to remove my T-shirt and shorts sleep set. When we were naked, he settled between my legs, the scruff of his chin scraping my skin as he placed wet, open-mouth kisses on my chest and stomach. But I needed him lower.

I placed my hand at the nape of his neck and widened my legs. "I need you, Silas."

I knew when I said his name he couldn't resist.

He devoured me as if I was his breakfast and he was starving. It wasn't a slow buildup, but an onslaught of his tongue, teeth, and fingers.

Then he stopped, and my skin heated as he moved up my body, wiping his mouth on his hand before settling his cock between my legs. I wrapped my legs around his waist as he slowly sank into me. As always, it felt amazing. As if no one else could fill me as well as he could.

He surrounded me with his presence and scent.

He wrapped an arm around my back and pressed me to him as he moved inside me. I felt so close to him, so open and vulnerable, I couldn't seem to catch my breath.

Nothing about this morning was slow. There was no sense of savoring the way it felt. Instead, it was fast and quick, as if it was a rush to the finish line. It also had the added effect of not letting me think about what was happening. All I could do was feel his skin pressed hot against mine, his cock impossibly hard inside me, and his mouth covering mine.

We went over together, his tongue tangling with mine as my muscles squeezed him tight. He groaned when he finally lifted himself off me and held his hand out to me. "Shower."

I went with him because I was hot and sweaty and needed to get ready for work. In the warm shower, we washed quickly and efficiently. There were no lingering touches or teasing words. Then we got dressed.

"I'll take you back to your car. Do you have time for breakfast?" Silas offered as he got dressed in slacks and a button-down shirt.

I glanced at the clock and winced at the time. I was usually at my desk working by now, waiting for Harper to join me for our morning meeting. I sent her a text to let her know I'd be late.

"I'll call ahead and have something made up for you."

Without looking up, I said, "You don't have to do that."

"I want to."

I gathered my things and went outside with him to his SUV. He drove me to the hotel, not saying anything.

"Are you going to work?" I asked him.

"I'll see you off and then check in."

I wanted to ask him more questions like what his workday was usually like, or how he spent it, but it wasn't my place. Besides, we were in an awkward spot this morning. I was distracted by work, and he had to be too.

This was another good reason to keep my wits about me. Sunday was an anomaly, a break from the norm, but it couldn't happen again.

When we arrived, a hotel worker met him at the curb with a bag of fragrant food.

Silas took the bag and carried it to my car. "I ordered a bit of everything. I hope you like it."

"I'm sure I will."

At my car, he placed the bag on the roof and spun me so that my back pressed against the metal. "I'll miss you."

I smiled despite my misgivings.

Then he kissed me, one of those toe-curling ones that you wanted to place in a box and remember forever. I forgot that we were kissing in the parking lot of his resort.

When he finally eased back with small kisses, I wanted to take him upstairs to his penthouse and try out a few more positions.

"We both need to get to work," Silas murmured, his voice low and tempting.

"Work. Right." How had he made me forget the most important thing in my life? I felt a little shaky as he put my bag in the backseat, and I slid into the front.

"Don't be a stranger this week," he said, his hand on the doorframe.

"I'm working with John and Emma."

He smiled, but it didn't quite reach his eyes. "Right."

"I'd better go. I have a long drive." It was more of a reason why we weren't a good idea. We lived too far away from each other. This would never work long-term.

"Have a good day."

"You too," I said evenly as my heart thumped its own rhythm inside my chest.

He shut the door and stepped back, his hands in his pockets as I backed up and drove away. I felt like I was leaving more than memories in that lot. I felt a little torn. As if it was possible to stay with Silas when I had a business to run. As if he could take a break when he had the same responsibilities.

Silas was fun while it lasted. We had a good time, and he showed me how a man could be in the bedroom. He'd raised my expectations for what a relationship could be.

But he and I weren't in the right time or location in our lives to pursue anything other than what we'd already shared. One great day, a few amazing nights, and that was our story.

I told myself the same thing as I drove home, and when I arrived, I almost believed it. I quickly changed, throwing my clothes into the hamper and grabbing a coffee before heading to the office with my now-cold breakfast.

I heated it up in the office kitchen and took the plate to my office. Silas had ordered eggs, waffles, fruit, and potatoes, and it smelled heavenly.

When I walked by, Harper came out of her office and followed me into mine. "Where have you been?"

"I worked with that couple yesterday at Chesapeake Resort." I refrained from saying Silas's resort, but just barely. "We worked late, and I used the suite Silas reserved for me."

Harper's eyes narrowed on me as I sat at the desk and picked up my fork. "You met with the couple on Saturday."

How had I made that slip? "We had more to work on, so I stayed Sunday."

Harper raised her brow. "Gia Giovanni, are you lying to me? How stupid do you think I am?"

I threw my hands up in the air. "I don't want to talk about it. Can you just let it go?"

She shook her head as she plopped into the chair across from my desk. "Nope."

"You kept your relationship with my brother a secret for weeks," I exclaimed.

She shook her head again. "You are not using that against me. Silas isn't my brother."

"How do you know I spent the day with Silas?" I asked, trying to bide myself time to think.

"Where else would you be? Am I right? You spent the weekend with Silas Sharpe—your archenemy, the bane of your existence."

I gave her a look. "That's a little over the top."

She dropped her chin. "Yet completely in character for you."

I thought about what I should say for a few seconds. "I'll admit I've been a little harsh over the years when it came to him."

"A little?" Harper's voice was raised.

"Okay. A lot. I may have misjudged him. Slightly. I slightly misjudged him."

Harper snorted. "You hated him, and you told us we had to hate him too."

I waved a hand in her direction. "You're being overly dramatic."

"I don't think I am, but I was right about you two. I knew there was something there—something explosive."

"I'll admit there's chemistry. Whether it's smart to act on it, that's another story." I sipped my coffee.

"I don't know. I think that's the best way to start a relationship."

"There's no relationship. We aren't together. So get that out of your head." I dug into the eggs, enjoying the breakfast.

"Is the food from his resort?"

"Yeah, we didn't have time for breakfast," I said before I realized my mistake.

"You spent the night with Silas?"

"At his house," I decided to admit. Harper was my best friend, and I couldn't keep this from her. Not after she'd already guessed it.

"I thought he stayed in the penthouse?"

"He has a house. It's really nice." I was surprised that it wasn't modern. Instead, it was traditional and cozy, and I suspected a lot of his furniture was handcrafted, which made it even more appealing. Silas wasn't as flashy as I thought he would be.

She ticked off the events on her fingers. "He took you to his house. You spent Saturday night, Sunday, and Sunday night together. Then he ordered you breakfast because you quote 'didn't have time.'"

"That's right," I said nonchalantly, even as my cheeks heated.

She dropped her hands to her sides. "Okay. I can read between the lines. So, you're just sleeping together?"

"I guess. I don't know. We didn't discuss labels or what any of it meant." I was pretty sure I was the one who had set the tone for that kind of talk. I wasn't open to discussing it.

"What did you do?" Then she held up her hand. "Nope. Don't answer that."

I wanted to share something with her. I needed to get someone else's take on the situation. "He took me out on his boat. We went to this secluded cove, swam, and ate a picnic lunch. He has this hammock on the boat deck, and I was able to read my book finally. It was the perfect day. When we came home, we were hungry, and it was late, so he took me to his house and cooked for me."

"Am I right that he doesn't bring everyone to his house?"

"That's what he said, but he doesn't date around a lot either."

"You're defending him."

"He's not who I thought he was, but it doesn't mean there's a future for us. I don't want to get your hopes up."

"Are you sure it's not more like you don't want to get *your* hopes up?"

I sighed. My stomach was full from the food. "I'm just realistic. He works an hour away, and I'm here. It's far."

"You don't have to get to work so early. Surely, there's a way you can make it work."

There was no way to get around the geographical distance between us. I needed to be near my office, and he needed to be near the resort. "There are a lot more reasons than geographical for why it won't work."

Harper shook her head. "Because you're not willing to try."

"We don't make sense. We're both strong-willed people who are wrapped up in their businesses."

Her brow furrowed. "Doesn't that make you a good fit?"

"We're both busy. Neither one of us will compromise." Although I wasn't so sure about that.

"Do you know that to be true, or are you assuming?" Harper leaned forward in her chair.

"We haven't discussed it, so there's no point in wondering what if. If Silas wanted more, he would ask for it."

She raised a brow. "Maybe he's taking his cue from you."

I gestured between us. "We need to focus on work."

"Gia, be honest with me. How do you feel about Silas?" Her voice was gentle, and I couldn't deny her.

I sighed. "Truthfully, I like him more than I've ever liked anyone else, but I can't forget—"

"No one said to forget your past, but you can move on from it and have a fresh outlook on life. Forgive Jeff for not being the boyfriend he should have been and let him go. Stop letting him control your life."

"Is it that easy?"

"You've been closed off to every guy since, and I haven't said anything because you've never met anyone who was worth letting go for."

My shoulders lowered. "How do you know that Silas is worth it?"

"You're acting differently than you ever have before. You didn't work on Sunday, and you were late today."

"That just means he's good at distracting me."

"It's more than that, and you know it."

"Fine. I like him. I enjoy spending time with him. But the more I'm with him..." I couldn't form the words.

"The more you fall for him. Sweetie, that's not a bad thing. That's called falling in love." Harper's expression was sympathetic.

"I don't want to be in love. We're starting this new course. I have no idea what's going on with the Monroes and their Christmas tree farm. I can't afford a distraction right now." I felt a little whiny listing all of that out, and I didn't like it.

Harper bit her lip. "Maybe you can work less and make more money."

"What?" That went against every one of my values and beliefs. I worked hard, always had. I was willing to do what others weren't. I never gave excuses, and I never missed work. Not until Silas. I couldn't get around that uncomfortable truth.

"Think about it. You've hired me to handle the course. You have wedding planners to handle the local weddings. It leaves you free to work solely with the couple at Silas's resort. You can outsource. You can trust us to do our best job, and you can focus on what's important."

"The Chesapeake Resort couple?" I asked, knowing she really meant exploring something with Silas.

She shot me an exasperated look. "Let yourself have this. Take your time and enjoy it. Don't worry about how it's going to work."

"I don't know if I can do that."

"Think about it."

"Fine." I would, because I couldn't stop my mind from wandering to that scenario.

"Good. Now, back to the Monroes."

"What's going on with that?" I asked, cleaning up my trash and sending a thank-you via text to Silas for the tasty meal.

He immediately sent back a flower emoji.

Silas: Nothing but the best for you.

I smiled, the feeling of being cared for and maybe even loved sweeping like wildfire through my body. I lifted my gaze to Harper's exasperated one. "Can we work now?"

I set my phone aside. "Of course."

"I have a feeling the Monroes are putting us off. Lori wanted to work with us, but her son, Emmett, is—"

"A pain."

I should handle this myself, but I wanted to train the newer wedding planners too. "I need to pay them another visit. I'll take Ireland. You stay here and work on the course." I found that in-person visits were better when you were closing a deal. It made it more personal. It was much easier to dodge someone via email and phone calls. But when you found me standing on your porch, I was harder to disregard.

"It would be amazing if we had another holiday venue to offer couples."

"I agree. We need to secure that location. At the same time, let's reach out to other farms in the area to see if those could be an option." I'd offered Lori an exclusive, but if she wasn't willing to agree on a contract, I'd need to explore other options.

"I already did. I'll forward you the information."

That's what I loved about Harper. She was quick and efficient and anticipated my needs.

"Where are we with the new course?" I asked, eager to get it started.

"I researched the options for a host. I sent you a spreadsheet on the various options and prices."

"Which one is the best?" I asked as I pulled up the email on my laptop.

"The one I put at the top. It's mid-priced, but it has the features we'll need, and it's user-friendly."

"Let's go with that one," I said, looking away from the screen.

"You don't want to review everything?"

"I trust you, Harper." I hired her, and she'd only impressed me more with every task I gave her. I intended to pay her a bonus for taking on the course because I had a feeling it was going to be huge for me.

I hadn't felt this excited about anything in a long time. It reminded me of how I felt when I first decided to open an event planning business. Back then, I was scared to do the thing I wanted, which was to focus on weddings. Instead, I advertised as a party planner, thinking I didn't have what it took to handle just one type of event. After I gained a reputation as a great party planner, I expanded into weddings, and once that took off, I limited my services to weddings.

But this seemed even bigger than that. I'd be marketing to other wedding planners, telling them everything that worked in my business and giving them advice. I felt like I was on a roller coaster. One minute, I felt like I was qualified to teach, and the next, I felt like an imposter. Who was I to teach about wedding planning? What certification did I have?

I had to remember that couples came to me because they heard I was the best. I'd built this business in only a few years because what I created was magical. I had what it took. Brides wanted to work with me. I just needed to remind myself a few times a day that I was on the right path.

It was either the biggest risk I'd ever take, or it would be wildly successful. I was hoping for the latter and planning for the former.

"This is going to be amazing. You have so many tips you could impart. I'm excited about getting started on the content. Do you have any ideas for how to organize it?"

"I have an outline in our shared folder. It's something I've been thinking about for a long time, and I started taking notes when I first started out. I was worried I wouldn't remember what it was like to start out if I didn't write down the details at the time."

"Wow. That was smart. And you knew back then that you wanted to teach?"

"I was thinking about writing a book. Online courses weren't a thing then. Or at least not a respected thing."

"You should write a book," Harper said.

"Really?"

"It would bring attention to your course. While we plan it, you should be writing your book at the same time. Then we can release the book before the course."

"Wouldn't I need a publisher for that?"

Harper shook her head. "I don't know if you know her, but Hailey writes fantasy books and publishes them herself. She works at Brooke's store, Market Tavern."

"Could you find out more about self-publishing? I would think we'd need a publisher to get the word out."

"Hailey always says the publishing industry moves very slow, and even if you get a deal, it takes a year or more to publish your book. If you did it yourself, you could put it out quickly."

I bit my lip. "I wasn't planning on writing a book right now."

"You're writing down what you already know. Just make sure you don't give out all your secrets in the book. You want them to get a feel for you and make them want to buy the course. Then you'd have to narrate an audiobook. Everyone loves audiobooks. Especially nonfiction."

I held up my hand. "Hold up. I'm willing to think about the book. I've always wanted to write one, and you're right. It would just be writing down what I know. But let's focus on the course, and if the book makes sense, I'll do it."

"I'll call Hailey and do more research for you. I want to see how feasible it is. I know she mentioned she was selling her books on book distributor sites but that she preferred selling in her own store. Something about one-on-one contact with her readers."

Harper gathered her things and rushed out of the office, excited about a new thing to research. I suspected it was her favorite part of her job.

I hadn't expected to write a book. I'd always been a service provider, but a course and a book would allow passive income.

I couldn't help but think this would be my big break. I wouldn't be reliant on couples choosing me. I'd have another stream of income that might be more reliable. I felt a pang when I realized I hadn't shared any of this with Silas.

I justified it because he was my competitor. But it felt like something you'd share with a lover or someone you were getting to know better. I had a feeling he'd support it. But I couldn't bring myself to share it. Not yet. Not when it was so new.

Seventeen

SILAS

On Sunday, something changed between me and Gia. It felt like she was it for me. The only problem was that Gia probably didn't feel the same way. Every time we were together, we grew closer, and when she left, she created distance between us.

I kept putting off her brothers coming on the boat because I didn't feel right about lying to them.

During the week, Gia traveled back and forth between her business and my resort. When she wasn't with Emma and John, she was in constant contact with Harper, as if they were working on something big. But she hadn't told me what it was, and I wasn't sure she was planning to.

I had an uneasy feeling she was working on something that could negatively affect me. I didn't want to believe she'd do that after how close we'd gotten, but she was a savvy businesswoman. She'd mentioned a few times that things were different for me. She didn't have family money to fall back on, and she had something to prove to her father. I just hoped she wasn't using me or plotting against me for her next big win.

I hadn't managed to get her alone all week. On Friday, I joined her in her meeting with Emma at the restaurant. They were discussing the dinner menu with my chef, Brad.

"Surely, you don't need to be here for this," Gia said pleasantly, but I heard the underlying question: *Don't you have something better to do?*

There were various options for salad on the table in front of them.

"I always eat lunch in the restaurant. It only makes sense to join you."

"I don't mind," Emma said, smiling at me.

I was positive she thought it was her money and her family's standing in the community that had me paying extra attention to her. In reality, I was here to see Gia.

Usually, I had no interest in weddings outside of the revenue they generated. People were more than willing to part with their money for a wedding. The fathers were all too eager to indulge their daughters in the one-day party.

Brad discussed the various options for salads and dressings before disappearing into the kitchen while we sampled them.

When we'd finished sampling the salads, Emma excused herself to go to the bathroom.

Gia hissed, "What are you doing here?"

I set my fork down, pleased that I'd finally gotten her alone. "You've been avoiding me all week."

She narrowed her eyes on me. "I've been busy working."

"What have you been working on?" I asked nonchalantly, as if my heart was beating out of my chest.

Gia rolled her eyes. "John and Emma's wedding."

I carefully watched her reaction. "You seem to be preoccupied with something else. You're always on the phone with your office."

"This may come as a surprise to you, but when I'm here, I can't be working at my office. I need to be in contact to ensure things are running smoothly."

"I can understand that, but it seems like something more than your usual workload." Gia had been buzzing all week with this energy. It was how I felt when I got the bug to try something new.

Her shoulders lowered slightly. "I promise it has nothing to do with you."

"So, you're not plotting against me?" I asked her casually.

Her brows raised. "No. Of course not."

I tipped my head to the side. "Then why can't you tell me?"

Gia's voice softened. "We're in the process of researching to see if my new idea is feasible. I promise it has nothing to do with you or the resort. It's something else entirely."

"Is it something I'd want to do too, if I had the idea?" I couldn't help but ask.

Gia barked out a laugh just as Emma returned.

"What did I miss?" Emma asked.

"Gia is working on something big but won't tell me what it is," I said.

"It's not something you'd want to do or would even be able to do. Maybe Hannah, but not you."

"Ah, it's something about being a wedding planner." Relief flooded my system. Her explanation made me feel better, but I was still dying to know what it was, and a part of me wondered if she was telling me the truth. How could I trust her when she was my biggest competitor? I thought we had a connection, but she was slower to have those same realizations. What if she didn't see me as anything more than a physical release?

Any time I remembered what we'd shared on Sunday, I couldn't believe it was true. I had to keep the faith that she'd eventually realize what we had.

The waitstaff cleared our salad dishes, and Brad appeared with several options for soup. When he left, Gia said, "I don't recommend soups for summer weddings. It can feel very heavy, and you want your guests to feel light."

"I agree," Emma said as she sipped her Maryland crab soup.

It was delicious, but I had to agree, if the weather was warm, soups wouldn't be ideal.

Next, Brad brought out a serving tray of the entrée options, ranging from filet mignon to lobster to crab cakes and the more expected chicken.

"You'll want two options in case someone is allergic or doesn't like seafood, but in my opinion, every Maryland wedding should offer seafood. Especially when your wedding will be held on the water."

Emma nodded. "I agree. Let's go with the filet mignon and the crab cakes."

Once that was settled, Brad brought out the options for the sides. There were several different types of potatoes and veggies, and I lost interest.

"Ladies, it's been nice, but I need to get back to the office for a meeting." I stopped in the kitchen to praise Brad and thank him for a job well done. I was almost to the elevator before Gia joined me. "Did I forget something?"

"You just happened to jump into my meeting with a bride, and then you leave early?" Her tone was exasperated.

"I'm a busy man."

"You did that just to get to me." Gia's body was tense, and her eyes were filled with irritation.

With a hand on her elbow, I pulled her to the side so no one saw us arguing. I was always professional in front of my employees and guests. "I wanted to see you. I missed you."

Gia's entire demeanor relaxed, her shoulders lowered, and her face smoothed out. "Are you serious?"

"Is it so hard to believe that I could miss you? What we shared this weekend was next-level, and I haven't seen you since. I'm starting to question my sanity." I figured the best plan of action with Gia was honesty.

"Silas," she said, shaking her head, and I braced for her denial of what I already knew to be true. "I'm sorry, but I'm preoccupied with this new project at work. You know how it is when you get an idea, and it's all you can think about."

I knew exactly what she was talking about. I became

consumed with seeing it to completion. "You're so preoccupied with this new project that you've forgotten about us?"

I dropped my head slightly so my breath ghosted over her ear.

Breathlessly, she said, "I promise, I haven't."

I leaned back slightly to see her face. "Did you forget that I'm good for bouncing ideas off of?"

She stiffened. "I'm confident in my business ideas and actions. I didn't need to."

I straightened, realizing my mistake. I assumed she needed my help when what I admired about her was her independence. "I'm sorry. I didn't mean to insinuate that. I just meant I'm here if you need to talk to anyone about it."

Her expression softened. "Thank you."

"You'd better get back to Emma. She's going to wonder where you went." I stepped back, regretting I hadn't kissed her when I had a chance. My anxiety about her new business idea had bothered me more than I thought.

"I'll see you later," Gia said as she walked away, and I wondered if that was true. Lately, she disappeared from the resort without stopping in to see me. It was more than her being busy; she was still fighting whatever this was.

I'd like to think I had a plan where she was concerned, but I kept changing course. I never encountered a woman who wasn't completely enamored with me and what I could do for them. Gia was strong and independent, but I wanted her to need me in her life.

I couldn't seem to get her out of my mind, and I wanted to spend time with her. I just hoped she felt the same.

I immersed myself in meetings that afternoon, and at some point, Gia texted to say she'd checked in with my secretary, who said I'd be tied up in meetings for a few more hours, so she left. I appreciated that she made the effort, but next time, I'd let my assistant know she could interrupt me.

Later that night, Gia texted to ask if we could spend our

Sunday together, and I immediately said yes. I wanted more time with her outside our respective businesses and responsibilities. It was the only way I saw the real Gia, the woman beneath her armor.

I had a feeling Gia wanted to spend time on my boat, but I wanted to spend time with her on her turf. I wanted to see her house and get to know her town better. If we were going to have a future, we needed to figure out the distance between us and make it no big deal.

It had to be possible these days with virtual meetings. I refused to believe that there were no options for us, not with our money and resources. We could get work done and spend time together. I was sure of it.

I researched things to do in Annapolis and suggested brunch and then a boat tour. After that, we could play it by ear. But for dinner, I had a surprise I wasn't sure she was going to be happy about. I hoped she'd understand that I just wanted the best for her.

When I picked her up at nine in the morning on Sunday, I was surprised to see she lived in a historic home downtown. Gia wore a sundress with strappy sandals. She looked cute and fresh. If I didn't already know she was a business owner, I'd never suspect it. After she locked up, I pulled her into my arms and kissed her. "You look beautiful today."

"Thank you," she said as I took her hand and led her down the sidewalk.

"We can walk from here, can't we?" I'd looked at the map, and it looked possible, but I'd never done it myself.

"That's what I like about this location. I can walk anywhere, including work."

I remembered that her business was on Main Street, with the restaurants and tourist shops. "Your house is a bit off the main path."

"That's why it's perfect."

"Have you thought about living outside of town?" I asked her as we set a leisurely pace. I had made reservations at a place called Iron Rooster, but we had plenty of time to make it there.

Gia frowned. "This is so convenient, and when I bought it, I wasn't worried about school districts."

"Were you supposed to be?"

Gia rolled her eyes. "My realtor mentioned it for resale value, but this property will always be attractive because of the location."

"I agree."

"Why drive to work when I can walk? Not only that, but I can pick up coffee on the way."

"It's convenient." It had the added benefit of being close to the water.

She chewed her lip. "I love your place too. The one on the water. It's so secluded and private. I can see myself wanting something like that someday."

Would someday ever be today?

Gia snuck a glance at me. "Why did you want to spend the day here instead of on your boat?"

"The boat is usually what I do on Sundays, but I wanted to see your place and get to know Annapolis."

"You have plans to move here?" Her tone was light.

"I'm not sure yet."

Gia paused on the sidewalk and faced me. "What are we doing?"

I stepped closer, cupping her jaw. "I enjoy spending time with you, and I wanted to see you on your turf. Can you enjoy the day with me?"

Her face smoothed out, and she nodded. "As long as you feed me soon. I'm starving."

"You didn't eat anything this morning? I wouldn't have lasted."

She laughed and shook her head. "Nope. I was saving it for brunch."

We resumed walking, and as we got closer to the restaurant,

the sidewalks were more crowded with people, and we could smell the water from the harbor. There was a light breeze from the water as we turned the corner onto Dock Street, where several restaurants were lined up in a row. I opened the heavy wooden door of Iron Rooster and went inside.

The buildings were older and narrow. This one had seating on two floors and an option for outdoor dining too. It was already crowded, so it was loud as the hostess led us to a table on the second floor by the windows.

"This is a nice view," Gia said as I held her chair out for her.

"I asked for a table with a view."

Gia smiled. "That was nice of you."

"I try to be a thoughtful date."

Gia glanced up from her menu, her cheeks slightly pink.

I snapped my fingers. "Although I forgot to bring you flowers. That's something girls like, isn't it?"

"How can you describe yourself as a thoughtful date when you overlooked that important detail?" she asked.

"I can bring you flowers next time."

"There's no need. I love fresh-cut flowers and have a subscription to a company that sends them monthly. I usually get more around holidays, and I love sending them to my employees on their birthdays."

"I already learned something new about you. You love flowers."

"But I can buy them myself."

"Is this going to be an argument we have continually in this relationship? You want to provide for yourself when I want to treat you? I think you have to wrap your mind around the idea that you get both."

She considered me for a few seconds and then finally nodded. "This is new to me."

"Dating a man or being with someone like me?" I was positive she hadn't dated anyone like me before.

"Someone like you. I've never been with anyone who was my

equal, both intellectually and in the business world. Plus, you are independently wealthy." She said the last sentence with a flick of her hand that made me feel like my accomplishments weren't my own.

"My family has money, but everything I've built with the resort is mine."

Gia let her menu fall to the table as she leaned across it to cover my hand with hers. "I'm sorry. I didn't mean to insinuate you haven't worked hard for what you have. It's just different when you start from nothing. We're successful no matter how we started out."

"I knew what you meant. It's an old wound of mine. People assume my life was easy, and that I haven't had to work hard for anything I have. As if my last name gets me everything."

"I don't believe that."

"I know you don't." It's what made her so special. There was a lot more to business than having the capital to start it. It's why so many failed.

The waitress stopped by for our orders. I ordered the crab hash, which was a bowl of crabmeat, eggs, veggies, and spices, and Gia ordered the poached eggs over crab cakes.

"You can't get brunch without seafood here. It's what I love about Annapolis."

"It is unique." This wasn't the first time I wondered how this would work between us. If she ever accepted that we were a thing, would we alternate weekends? Or would one of us move? My resort was an hour away, and I needed to be on-site. I wasn't positive she needed to work in her office all the time. Not that she would see it that way.

"What's that building there?" I asked as we gazed out the window. There was a road that went around it, but it was the only building between this one and the harbor area.

"It's a market. It's been renovated a few times. They open it to grand fanfare, and then they close it down, renovate it again, and reopen it. I haven't been inside in a long time, but each time, they try to make it work as a traditional market, like you'd see in Boston."

"I've been to that one. It's a neat idea."

She sipped her mimosa. "If it worked."

"I'm sure you have ideas on how to make it work."

Gia shook her head thoughtfully. "I don't pretend to know anything about a food court. That's not my area of expertise."

"Be honest. When you go into a business, you evaluate how they operate, how good the customer service is, how clean everything is, and how fast your order is brought out, and then you think of all the ways they could improve."

She laughed. "I get frustrated with small businesses. I've heard people say that if someone is a musician, it's okay that their instrument and lesson shop is disorganized. Because they're a creator, not a businessperson."

"You need to be both. If you have no background in business, you can still learn."

"Exactly. I listened to my father growing up, but I learned so much more by just doing my own thing. It was a lot of trial and error."

"I agree."

"I bet you're continually coming up with new ideas for your business."

"Some work and some don't. But I usually act on them immediately. I don't wait and think about it. Maybe that's a mistake, but I've always gotten that spark and immediately figured out what I needed to do to make it happen."

"I know what you mean. I've had to slow myself down a few times to make sure I'm making the right decision."

"Is that what you did with your newest idea?" I asked, wanting to know more.

She laughed. "We immediately started researching it and getting everything in order. I'm excited about it. I think it could be the thing that keeps my business afloat."

My forehead wrinkled. "You were worried you wouldn't make it?"

"I don't like being dependent on seasons or trends. I want a consistent and steady income."

"I hadn't thought about how, as a service business, you have dips and valleys."

"My employees expect to be paid monthly regardless of how many weddings we booked that month."

"I have a fairly steady income between the rooms, the restaurants, and the weddings."

"You diversified just by the nature of owning a resort. You have locals coming for the spa and restaurant and for weekend getaways, and then you have tourists looking for a getaway. I'd thought about writing a book in the beginning, and I'd put it to the side. I didn't think I'd ever do it. I kind of let it go, but Harper said it would be a good idea."

"What would you write about?" I asked, genuinely impressed she wanted to write a book.

"What it's like to be a business owner, but specifically a wedding planner. It would be a mindset business advice book for wedding planners. Or do you think that's too limiting? Should I open it up to all business owners?"

I was pleased she'd confided in me and wanted my input. "I think you should write what you know first. If there's interest in something more, then do another one that's open to all businesswomen. I've heard women lament the lack of business conferences and books on money and business too."

"There's an opening in the market. I've seen a few women be successful with books about money, but I don't see any for event planners."

"I think it's an amazing idea." She was so smart and innovative. I was continually in awe of her. It made me want to tie her down even more. This woman was perfect for me. If only I could convince her of that.

Eighteen

SILAS

"I'm not sure if I can write a book, but Harper said just to write down what I know. I kept a journal of my journey so I could remember what it was like when I was first starting out."

"I love that you're doing this. I think it will be good for you."

"I'm still struggling with whether it will be advice for wedding planners or more business focused."

"I think once you start writing, it will become clear."

"I hope so. It's been keeping me awake at night."

I hated that she was stressed about this. "Why don't you just have fun with it? Write what you wish you'd known starting out."

"That's an interesting idea," she said thoughtfully.

"If you come from that perspective, maybe the writing will be easier."

She smiled. "I'll give it a try."

Our food came, and we dug in. It was good, not as tasty as my resort, but I was biased.

We talked about how the food compared to my restaurant, and other business things surrounding the resort. It was nice to talk to someone who understood.

When we finished eating, we headed toward the harbor area,

where the tour boat was docked. While we waited to board, I asked, "Have you taken the tour before?"

Gia shook her head. "I never did the touristy things in town. We were always too busy with the pizzeria and now, my business."

"That's good to know." Since I hadn't done it either, it would be something fun for us to do together.

We boarded, and I led her to the top deck to look over the railing at the others boarding.

"I wonder if this is what it feels like to be on a cruise ship."

I gripped the railing, my eyes riveted on her, not the view. "It's much bigger though."

She glanced at me. "I've never gone on a cruise. Have you?"

I shook my head. "I've only seen them when I was in Key West. They're huge. I like smaller boats."

Her brow furrowed. "It's not like your boat is small."

"But it's easier for me to handle. The cruise ships are massive. I can't imagine being in a hotel that moves. I prefer to see places from the ground."

"That makes sense."

We fell silent as the captain went over the safety features. The boat honked, and then it pulled away from the dock. We stood by the railing as someone talked on the loudspeaker about what we were seeing on the shore, including a nice view of the Naval Academy.

Gia was engrossed in what the captain was saying over the speaker, the history of the area, and the things we were seeing.

When we turned around and made our way back, Gia said, "This was neat. I really enjoyed it."

"I did a good job with planning our date?" I asked her.

Gia smiled. "You did. I'm glad we did this."

I almost hesitated to ask. "You're not missing work?"

Her smile fell. "I probably need to be writing. The book is on top of my regular work, and I hadn't anticipated doing it right now."

"Sometimes the best plans are the ones that pop up out of nowhere."

She wrapped her arms around her middle. "I hope so. I could really use something right now."

She mentioned needing a steady income, and I wondered if her business wasn't doing well. "What's going on that's making you worry?"

"Spring and summer are our busy months. We can barely keep up with the weddings scheduled, but then it slows down, moving from fall into winter. We're trying to partner with a Christmas tree farm to offer holiday weddings, but the owners are dragging their feet."

"What do you mean?" I asked, in full business mode now.

"Well, at first the owner, Lori, was interested. She wants to expand the business, including the gift shop, but her sons—well, one of them—seem to have put a stop to the idea. I can understand their concerns. We'd be holding an event on the property that requires parking and guests to be present during their busy season. But it's an additional income stream for them too."

"You'd increase your weddings during your slow season."

"Exactly, and we lose a fair number of couples to your resort. They want to work with me, but they want the one-stop resort more."

I knew we were in competition, but I hadn't thought about the direct effect on her business. I'd only been worried about my bottom line. "That wasn't my intention. I never wanted to make things harder for you."

Gia shrugged and looked out over the water. "It's business. If you treated me differently, I wouldn't respect you."

I didn't like that my choices affected her business. I guess on some level, I knew I was taking business from her, but I thought she was doing fine. Her brothers never mentioned that she was struggling. "Do your brothers know?"

"Know what?" Gia asked, focusing on me.

"That you struggle sometimes." I was pleased she'd confided

in me when I suspected she viewed being vulnerable as a weakness.

She shook her head. "I'd never mention my business to my family. They'd tell me to quit and work for them."

"Would they?" I couldn't see her brothers doing that. They seemed to respect her tenacity.

"My father takes every opportunity to tell me to work for him. He thinks it's just a phase. That people don't want to pay for someone to plan parties."

"He hasn't changed his position over the years?"

"To be honest, I avoid him and talking about the business. I can't remember the last time I went to a Sunday dinner."

"You think he doesn't respect you and what you're doing?"

She laughed without any humor. "You could say that."

I wondered if that was true. Was Mr. G. so shortsighted that he couldn't see how he was hurting his daughter? I'd been invited to Sunday dinner tonight, and I was hoping to convince Gia to go with me, but now I was doubting my intentions.

Would she be mad at me for asking her or that I went without her? I wasn't sure what to do. I'd been so confident that she'd go, even if we couldn't talk about our relationship. I hadn't realized the extent of her fallout with her father. I didn't want to push her, especially if her father was only going to hurt her. Maybe Mr. G. didn't see how his words had already hurt his daughter.

When we disembarked the boat, we walked through town, stopping to get ice cream and buy fudge to eat later. When we walked past the shop Petals, Gia dragged me inside.

"Is Lily here?" Gia asked the clerk.

"She's in the back," the girl at the counter said. "Let me get her."

A few seconds later, a blonde woman came out with a huge smile and a hug for Gia. "What are you doing here on a Sunday?"

Gia flicked a hand in my direction. "We went to brunch and took the boat tour."

Lily's eyes widened when she saw me. "You went to brunch with Silas Sharpe?"

I leaned over to shake her hand. "The one and only. Why do I get the impression that people are surprised to see me with Gia?"

Lily's lips twitched. "I mean, you're kind of enemy number one around here."

"Lily," Gia chided, as if she was embarrassed.

I kind of knew that by the way she treated me, but it was interesting to hear others talk about it.

Lily raised a brow. "What? It's surprising, and I can't believe you're doing touristy things and not working."

Gia threw a thumb in Silas's direction. "That's his fault. He insisted on hanging out today."

I stuffed my hands into my pockets and rocked back on my heels. "Sunday's my day to relax."

"Well, if you can get this one to do the same, I'll love you forever," Lily teased.

"You're already in love with Jake. Stop teasing Silas."

Lily smiled easily at me. "Jake's the mechanic over at Harbor Garage if you ever need work done."

"I've heard of it. They've built quite a name for themselves, especially with classic vehicles."

"That's right," Lily said with a bright smile. "Were you coming in for a bouquet? I have one you'll adore."

Lily pulled a vase out of one of the fridges that was filled with sunflowers and other ones I couldn't name.

"This is perfect," Gia said as she reached for her purse to pay for it.

"I'll get it." There was no way I'd let her pay for flowers when I was here.

Gia frowned at me. "You don't have to do that. This is my addiction."

"I'm buying you flowers," I said to Gia, placing my card in Lily's outstretched hand. She seemed all too willing to help me out, and I appreciated it.

Gia was a tough woman to treat. I was surprised when she allowed me to schedule her that spa day and that she'd worn the designer dress and shoes I'd picked for her.

I waited while Gia and Lily talked about some developments in an upcoming wedding. I gathered that Lily was her flower supplier. When they said their good-byes, Lily said to me, "I hope to see you around more."

I wasn't sure how to respond to that. I wanted the same thing, but did Gia? I carried the vase outside. "Is that where you satisfy your flower addiction?"

"The monthly subscription service is hers, but I like flowers more often."

I draped an arm over her shoulder. "You should always have fresh flowers."

"That's a dream of mine. I'd love to have them on my desk and in every room of my house. But that's ridiculous. This is already too much."

"Why would you say that?" I asked as we headed down a side street with uneven sidewalks.

"Cut flowers only last so long. Some say it's a waste of money."

"It's not if it brings you joy, and I, for one, love seeing you happy."

Gia smiled, and her cheeks turned pink. "You're sweet when you want to be."

"I'm sweet, period. This isn't an act, baby." I pulled her into my side and kissed her upturned lips. This had been the perfect day.

We walked around town like we were a couple. I guess I should have been more worried about running into her brothers, but I knew they were busy with the new restaurant, which was out of town.

When we reached her house, she unlocked the door and led me inside. "This is my place."

It was small but updated. There were wood floors throughout. A small living room was on the right, with a fireplace and sofa, and the dining room was on the left. She led me to the kitchen in the back that overlooked a small backyard. She arranged the vase on the counter, looking a little uncomfortable to have me in her space.

"It's perfect for you." It was just the right amount of space for one person.

Gia smiled. "It's hardly a house on the water or a penthouse, but it's mine."

"That's what I meant," I said as I moved closer and turned her so she faced me.

"What now?" Gia asked, and I loved that she hadn't immediately kicked me out.

I glanced at the clock on the microwave. I had a little bit of time before I needed to leave for the Giovannis', but I didn't feel right not telling her where I was going.

"I have dinner plans, but we have a bit of time before I need to leave." I leaned down to kiss her, but she stepped back.

Gia frowned and pulled away from me. "Oh, I wouldn't want to keep you."

Did she think I was seeing someone else? I guess we hadn't had a discussion about expectations. "When I'm dating you, I'm not seeing anyone else, and I expect the same from you. I know we didn't talk about that—"

She swallowed hard. "That sounds good."

I kept my gaze trained on hers. "Your brothers invited me to dinner."

She frowned. "You're going to my family dinner night?"

"Is that a problem?"

"Of course not." She hadn't physically moved any farther away from me, but I felt the distance between us.

"I've gone to dinner there in the past."

Gia smiled, but it didn't quite reach her eyes. "You should go."

My heart thudded in my chest. "I'd like it if you'd go too."

"But my family doesn't know about us, and I doubt they'd understand it after I've hated you all these years."

Hate felt like a strong word. But I suspected she was creating more space between us. "We wouldn't have to come out to them, but I'd like to spend more time with you."

"I don't do family dinners. I told you why. I have to protect my energy. My father doesn't believe in me, and I can't be around that."

I hated that for her. My parents had always supported me and my brothers in our business endeavors. They never once doubted that we'd be successful. "I understand that, but I was hoping it would be better if we went together."

She cocked one brow. "Are you planning on telling them about us?"

"No."

She crossed her arms over her chest. "How will it look when you all of a sudden take my side?"

I hadn't thought about that. We were usually arguing, not supporting each other. "I guess I didn't think it through."

She waved me off. "You go. Nothing should change because we spent some time together."

We'd just had the exclusivity talk, and she was already pushing me away. "I don't want to leave you like this."

She led the way through her house and opened the front door. "I'm a big girl. I can handle it."

I had other ideas for how to spend the time before dinner, and they had everything to do with seeing her bedroom, but I wasn't sure how to breach this void between us. "I don't want to go."

She crossed her arms over her chest. "I think you should."

"This doesn't feel right." I shut the door gently.

"I need some space." Her lips pressed into a tight line.

I placed my hands on her shoulders. "I want you to feel comfortable going to your parents' house."

Her gaze lifted to meet mine. "Your going doesn't change anything. Don't worry about it."

That was probably true, but it still didn't sit right with me. "You won't try to ease this rift between you and your parents?"

"Is it a deal-breaker for you? If so, we don't need to see each other anymore." Her voice raised with every word.

My heart stutter-stepped. "You don't mean that."

"I don't like the way you're pushing me into something with my family."

I held up my hands and stepped back. "I didn't mean to make you feel like that."

"I'd like you to go now." Her eyes were glimmering with unshed tears, and I hated leaving her like this.

"Okay, but this isn't over. I like you, Gia."

She nodded but didn't respond. I opened the door and walked out, even as everything in my body was urging me to go to her. To make her feel better. But I didn't know how to do that. I'd overstepped with her family, but I had a relationship with her parents and her brothers separate from her. That wouldn't change. It would be easier if she got along with them.

But she was right. What did it matter when we couldn't come clean about our relationship? Was I ready to tell her brothers?

I headed toward my car, wondering if I'd made a big mistake with Gia. Should I have approached it another way? Would we recover from this? I wasn't sure about anything.

I drove to Mr. and Mrs. G.'s house, pleased to see that Leo, Harper, and her daughter, Evie, were already there. I headed to the backyard, where Evie was swinging on the swing set.

"Higher. Higher," she cried as Leo pushed her.

I never thought Leo would date a woman with a child, but they were perfect together, and, according to Harper, she'd crushed on him as a teenager. So, it felt like it was fated. Was that what Gia and I were to each other? Were we circling each other for years, and our relationship was inevitable? Or was it all a mistake? Were our issues too insurmountable for us to overcome?

"You came for dinner?" Leo asked, clasping my hand.

LEA COLL

Evie shot a look over her shoulder. "Daddy Leo, what are you doing?"

"I'm pushing. I'm pushing. Hold your horses."

Evie frowned. "I don't have any horses."

"Daddy Leo, huh?" I asked him.

"Yeah, it's a new thing," he said proudly.

"You like it."

"I love everything about Harper and Evie. They're it for me."

"Yeah, I got that when you proposed." That was the evening that Gia and I got back together, and I'd never forget it. I think a part of me was a little jealous that my friend had found happiness.

"What about you? You seeing anyone?"

I cleared my throat, uncomfortable with the conversation. "Kind of."

"Who is it?" But before I could answer, he continued. "There were pictures of you and Gia at the fundraiser, but Gia said she did it as a favor. Some tit for tat because you're letting her work with one of your wedding couples?"

"That's right." It was close enough to the truth that I didn't feel like I was lying. But I still didn't feel great about it.

Evie jumped off the swing, stumbled, and before I could reach out to steady her, she ran for the house.

Leo turned to face me. "I hope you're not dicking her around."

I flushed hot because I most certainly was, just not in the way he was insinuating. "I realized I was doing my brides a disservice by not allowing them to work with the planner they wanted."

Leo frowned. "What about all your talk about exclusivity and business, and how you were making all this money?"

"It wasn't what the brides wanted. They want to work with Gia. Besides, this is just a trial thing. It might not work out."

Leo stepped closer. His face was stony. "Gia wants this so bad. If you fuck her over—"

"I don't plan to fuck her over." I wasn't so sure what Gia wanted from this. I had a feeling she was going to break things off.

She was so closed off to the idea of love that she'd never even consider it, especially not with me. That thought sank like a rock in my stomach.

It felt worse that Leo was threatening me about treating her right when he didn't even know the whole story. I hated having to keep my true feelings from him. But what could I say? *I love your sister, but she doesn't love me.*

He wouldn't understand. He'd blame me. They all would.

I knew better than to mess with my best friends' younger sister. But then I hadn't been thinking with my brain. My heart had led me here, and I'd hoped I hadn't made a huge mistake in falling for Gia when she wasn't capable of anything more.

Nineteen

GIA

My chest ached when Silas left. I couldn't believe he thought I'd go to my family's dinner. It was like he hadn't been listening at all.

I couldn't be upset that he was going. He'd always been close with my family, separate from me. I wasn't sure why I was so twisted up inside. When I thought he was seeing someone else, I felt something I hadn't in a long time—jealousy—and I wasn't sure what it meant.

We couldn't tell my family we were together. They'd think I was crazy after how angry I'd been at Silas all these years. My brothers would be mad at Silas for hooking up with me. The whole situation was a disaster. We didn't have a future, so why did it hurt when I sent him away?

I wanted to see him. I wanted to smooth things over, but I couldn't go to my parents'. Every time I did, I got into an argument with my father.

I didn't like how I'd left things with Silas. I'd needed space, room to breathe, but his leaving hadn't helped. It only made everything worse.

We were in this weird limbo, where I wasn't even sure we were seeing each other anymore.

I couldn't pinpoint the moment that things went wrong. It could have been when I thought he was seeing someone else or when he said he wanted to be exclusive or that he was going to dinner with my family. It was probably all of it together. I'd felt this pressure build up, and it was like everything imploded. I couldn't be around him anymore. I needed space and time to think.

But now that I had it, things weren't any better. I wanted to go to him, to make sure he was okay, even if it meant going to my parents' house when they weren't expecting me.

I brushed my hair, washed my face, and reapplied my makeup. I wasn't prepared to out Silas and me to my parents, so I'd have to pretend nothing had changed, and there was nothing between us. That might be harder than being with my family.

I took several deep breaths before I got into my car and drove the short distance to their house. They'd moved out of town when we were older to get some space from the restaurant.

But they still spent most of their time in the pizzeria, even though they claimed they wanted to retire.

I pulled into the driveway, where there was already a cluster of cars. Leo was with Harper and Evie now, but Matteo and Carlo were still single, or so they said. Mamma pressured them to get married and have kids, but she seemed slightly appeased with the addition of Evie.

When I walked into the house, the lively conversation in the kitchen stopped. Harper was the first one to recover. "Gia, I'm so happy to see you."

She hugged me and whispered, "What are you doing here?"

I squeezed her in response, not sure what to say.

"We weren't expecting you," Mamma said. "We have plenty of food."

"Are you sure it's okay that I'm here?" I asked Mamma when she hugged me.

"Of course. You're family."

Tears sparked in my eyes as I moved to kiss Papà's cheek.

There had been this wall between us since I said I was going to start my own business. He'd never approved, and the worst part was how he'd kept bringing up how I could come back at any time.

I moved around the room, hugging Matteo first, who gave me a playful wink, and then Carlo. When I came to Leo, he asked, "What are you doing here?"

"I heard there was a family dinner tonight," I teased.

"The more the merrier," Mamma said, making me feel welcome again. It hurt her the most when I stopped attending family dinners, but she'd understood. She'd said Papà was stubborn, and he'd eventually come around, but he hadn't.

Not that it mattered. I didn't let anyone's opinion of my business affect me anymore. All that mattered was how I felt about it.

Silas stood next to Leo, with Evie in his arms. I squeezed her knee. "Good to see you, squirt."

She leaned down to hug me, and Silas's body came with her to prevent her from falling out of his arms. His chest pressed into my shoulder.

I saw the question in Silas's eyes, but I couldn't let on that we were intimate. To maintain everyone's expectations, I should have said something snarky to him, but I couldn't manage it. I was too torn up about what happened earlier.

Slowly, the room filled with talking and laughter again, and I didn't feel like I was being scrutinized as much. Mamma kept shooting me concerned looks, and Harper gave me a reassuring smile. Harper wanted me to come home more often too. We were like her second family since her mother hadn't been around much growing up.

"Why did you come?" Silas asked once he'd set Evie down.

My heart pounded in my ears. "I didn't feel right about what happened earlier."

His expression was stoic. "We can't discuss it here."

"I know."

He squeezed my shoulder but didn't say anything else. We

helped Mamma put the food on the large dining room table, and we all sat down to eat.

Silas sat next to Carlo and Matteo because Mamma knew enough to keep us separated. It was a good thing, but I hated being so far away from him after our fight.

We ate, and the discussion focused on the new pizzeria and its success.

"I'd like to offer the family-style items on the menu, not just for parties and catering orders." Matteo spent most of his time in the kitchen.

The table fell silent. No matter how much Papà said he wanted to take a step back from the restaurants and retire, he was still the one in charge, and everyone knew it.

"I don't think that's necessary."

"Let's say you have a large gathering or party scheduled, and you don't have time to cook or clean your house. You can order the meals, and it's taken care of."

"When someone has a party, they order ahead of time."

"But that requires forethought and planning. What if it's an impromptu party or someone waited too long to order the food in time? This will allow for more orders." He continued without waiting for Papà to respond. "I'd like to see if it would work. We can start with chicken parmesan. I'm thinking it will be eight chicken breasts with pasta. The salad and breadsticks can be add-ons. If it works, we can offer other options, but I would keep it to three or so entrées. We can package the salad dressings and sell them on the side too."

"I love that idea," I said to the quiet room. "It doesn't hurt to try it. You're already providing these types of meals for parties and catering. What's the harm in allowing other customers to order the meals? I can see the appeal of a busy mom not wanting to cook for a large gathering."

"You can't just come home and offer us advice. You wanted out of the pizzeria. You made your choice," Papà said.

My face flushed as a shocked silence fell over the table.

"This is a family matter," Papà said stiffly.

I hadn't planned to come tonight and cause a fight. "Am I not family?"

"You didn't want to be part of the family business. I don't understand why you do now."

It wasn't a question. Instead, his statements were intended to stop any further comments. I threw my napkin onto the table. "I don't know why I came."

It was only to see Silas, but it was shortsighted because my father wouldn't change. Different ideas wouldn't be welcomed. My brothers were better at convincing him to see their side.

"Papà didn't mean that," Mamma began as I stood.

"You don't have to stand up for him. He said what he did. Nothing has changed. My opinion isn't welcome here."

"If you want to come back to the pizzeria, then we can talk."

I stood by the table, my hands braced on the flat surface. "We've been over this a million times. I love running my own business. If I think something's a good idea, I don't have to run it by three brothers and my parents before I implement a new idea. Matteo's idea is genius. With the increase in curbside pickup and online ordering, it's the logical next step. It will add another income stream for the pizzeria. It's forward-thinking, and I'm confident it will work. Not that you'll listen to me."

Then I walked out, despite my mother's protests. I would never be welcomed in this family for who I was. I was almost to my car, my heart thundering in my chest, my frustration with my actions at an all-time high when someone grabbed my wrist.

I pulled it away from Silas. "What do you want?"

"I wanted to make sure you were okay."

"You wanted me to come tonight. Was it everything you hoped it would be?" I couldn't stop myself from asking.

He let out a breath and looked away from me. "I'm sorry."

"You don't understand how it is with me and my family. Papà respects my brothers' opinions but not mine. If I ever came back to work at the pizzerias, I could only do it if I was okay with no one listening to me."

"I'm sorry, Gia."

"Now you know." I pulled open my door.

"What are you doing out here, Silas?" Leo asked, with Harper at his side. Evie must have been inside with my parents.

I looked from him to Silas. What could he say? He certainly couldn't admit the truth.

"I was—"

Leo's eyes widened as he looked from Silas to me. "Is something going on between you two?"

Harper's expression filled with guilt.

"Silas was just leaving," I said, trying to salvage the situation.

"In the middle of dinner?" Leo asked and then looked at Silas. "Did you come out here to see if *my sister* was okay?"

The way he emphasized *my sister* meant he was not okay with what he suspected was going on between us.

"Someone had to," Silas said stubbornly, and I wished he'd lied. I wasn't prepared to deal with my brother's wrath.

"First, you can't seem to get along with our parents, and now this?" Leo asked.

I sucked in a breath. "What are you talking about?"

"You just can't stop causing trouble, can you?" Leo's voice raised.

"Leo," Harper said with rebuke in her voice.

I blinked back tears as I sat in my car and turned on the engine. I had to get away from here. I couldn't deal with my father's disdain, and now my brother felt the same way.

There was a roaring in my ears, and my fingers trembled as I closed the door, blocking out Leo, Harper, and Silas. They all thought I was the problem, and maybe I was. I didn't act how they wanted me to or talk how they wanted me to. I wasn't enough for them.

I pulled away. My vision blurred with tears. I tried to calm down enough to drive home. I couldn't believe I'd come tonight. I knew better than to place myself in the line of fire. And now Leo knew about me and Silas and thought I'd done it on purpose to cause trouble between him and his friend and my family.

Is that what everyone thought about me? That I caused trouble wherever I went? I said things no one wanted to hear. When I was separate from them, I could rationalize it and block it out. I could protect myself. But right now, it felt too raw, too close to the truth for me to keep it at bay.

I would never fit in with my family. I wouldn't say the right thing or be quiet when they wanted me to, and apparently, I wouldn't date the right guy either. Everything I did was calculated to cause other people in my life pain.

Was that why I had so few friends, and I kept my employees at a professional distance? Was I afraid of them rejecting me too?

I didn't go home because I didn't want Silas showing up, even though I had a feeling he wanted nothing to do with me. We had that argument earlier, and why would he want to date someone who couldn't have a simple dinner with their family without causing an argument?

I'd always been too much for people. Why was this any different? Silas was probably happy he'd dodged a relationship with me. It would never work. Not when he was closer to my family than I was.

Instead, I drove to my office—my sanctuary—and sat at my desk in front of my computer and let the tears roll down my cheeks. I hadn't even bothered to turn on the lights. My chest felt like there was something on top of it, pressing down, crushing me. I could only manage short breaths.

I looked at the screen for a long time, not seeing anything. Finally, I blinked away the tears, got up to wash my face, and ate one of the meals I kept in the fridge for when I worked late. Afterward, I felt a little better.

I was used to being alone. Things would go back to normal. I'd be able to work without any distractions. No mind-blowing sex or relaxing Sundays with Silas. I could focus on my business, the only thing that mattered. The one thing I could help flourish and grow. The one thing I didn't destroy with my actions and words.

It would have to be enough because my family and Silas wanted nothing to do with me. I saw the email message from Harper, asking about my input on the content of the course, and I settled down to work.

I could write the book as I created the content for the course. The book would have smaller tips and less explanation than the course. If readers wanted more, they could buy the course when they finished reading the book. They were a perfect complement to each other.

It was the perfect project to focus on. Everything fell away but the knot in my stomach as I wrote what I wished someone had told me when I was starting out. I even outlined a quick chapter on small business and tax advice and when to form an LLC or an S-corporation.

The main message was to trust yourself and your intuition and then price your services equivalent to what you're worth. I went with my gut on a lot of business decisions, and I didn't believe in failure. When I tried something new, it either worked or it didn't. Then I tried something else. There was no failure. No disappointment. I recommended that they keep track of their numbers, what was working and what wasn't, and pivot accordingly.

Now that I knew what my book and course were about, the words flew easily. I stayed up all night getting everything down. By morning, I still had gaps to fill and other chapters to add, but I'd gotten a decent amount done. I felt good.

Then I rested my head on the cool surface of my desk to rest my eyes.

"What are you doing? Did you sleep here all night?"

I lifted my head, blinking away the sleep. My neck was tight, and my back ached. "Harper, what are you doing here?"

"It's Monday. A workday." Then she continued without

letting me respond. "But I've been worried about you. We were looking for you all night."

I stretched my neck and then my arms over my head. "I parked in the garage."

"The lights weren't on."

I shrugged. "I wanted to be left alone."

"And I guess you weren't checking your phone."

"I don't even know where it is. It might be in the car." I wasn't awake yet, and Harper was firing questions and observations at me at a pace I couldn't keep up with.

"I can't believe you just left like that and didn't answer your phone. We were worried about you. Silas was worried about you."

I snorted, the night coming back to me. "I cause trouble wherever I go. Does that ring a bell? I figured no one wanted to see me. So I came here." Where there was no judgment, and every decision I made seemed to have some magic powers. Why had I ever ventured out of this sacred space and tried to have a relationship with Silas? It was a ridiculous waste of time.

Except thinking that about Silas hurt, so I dismissed him from my mind.

Harper shook her head. "Leo overreacted last night. He was shocked when he found out about you and Silas."

I shrugged as if I didn't have a care in the world. "It's none of his business, and it's over now anyway."

"You broke up with Silas?" Harper lowered her voice and moved closer.

"We were never really together. We had one conversation about being exclusive, but that was right before we had a fight. I don't think it applies anymore."

"Of course, you'd get into a fight after a guy wants to put a definition to what you were doing."

I frowned as I got up to brew some coffee in our work kitchen. "What are you talking about?"

"As soon as Silas dared to define what you were doing, you bolted."

"He walked out." After I told him to, but she didn't need to know that pesky detail. She seemed like she was on a roll, and I wasn't going to be able to stop her.

I scooped the fresh beans into the grinder, added water, and pushed the button to brew. I needed coffee five minutes ago.

Harper was either wired from last night or had been drinking coffee all night.

"You heard my father and Leo. I'm not wanted there."

"Your father is as stubborn as you are."

I blinked at that comment.

"Leo made a mistake he is currently paying for, but what about Silas?"

"What about him?"

"Why are you avoiding him?" Her tone was full of exasperation.

"He feels the same way. He's friends with my brothers and doesn't want to do anything to ruin that relationship." I said the words, even as it shredded my heart as I did.

"You really think he believes that your business advice isn't spot-on?"

A tingle ran down my spine as I remembered how we'd always discussed business. It was always as equals. He never put me down or belittled my opinions. Instead, he valued them. He believed in me. "It doesn't matter what I think. He's friends with my—"

"Brothers. Got it. And you think that your love isn't enough to overcome some stress?"

"Love? Who said anything about love?"

"You are literally impossible. You can't see what's right in front of your face. I'd say you were like Leo, but you're worse. At least he acted as soon as he realized he liked me. He didn't pretend it didn't mean anything."

I frowned, wondering if she was right. "That's not what I'm doing."

"That's exactly what you're doing."

"I came here to work. Not rehash one of the worst nights of

my life," I said as the machine whirred and sputtered. It was the longest brewing machine ever. It couldn't finish fast enough for the rate this conversation was flying off the rails.

Harper's expression softened. "How do you feel?"

There was a headache threatening at the base of my head. "Like I was run over by a truck. But I got a lot of work done on the course and on my book."

"That's what you want to talk about?" she asked as the machine finally beeped its completion.

I didn't waste any time grabbing my *Lady Boss* mug and pouring the coffee. I grabbed the creamer from the fridge and poured a generous amount to cool the coffee enough to drink. "It's a workday."

She threw a hand in my direction. "You haven't slept or showered."

"I'll take a shower. I always keep clothes here in case I work through the night."

Harper sighed. "Is this a common occurrence for you?"

"More so before I was seeing Silas." I hadn't even realized it, but I'd kept more reasonable hours when we were together so I could get home and sext him from the bathtub or send him other naughty images from the privacy of my home. And I hadn't worked the last two Sundays. "He was a distraction. Now that he's gone, we can focus on work."

I picked up my mug and tried to move past Harper, but she blocked the exit. "Do you hear yourself?"

"What?" I asked.

"You're ignoring what happened."

"I have to, Harper. If not, I'll start crying and never stop." I allowed myself to feel the loss of Silas. It filled every crevice in my chest with a throbbing pain before I shook it off.

Harper's shoulders lowered as she moved out of my way.

"I'll take a quick shower before our meeting."

I sucked down my coffee while the water in the shower heated up. I scrubbed myself, not remembering any of the times I shared a shower with Silas. I was proud of myself by the time I dried off and got dressed in a power outfit—a tailored white blouse, pencil skirt, and black stilettos. Feeling better than I had when Harper walked in, I stepped out of the bathroom and called Harper in for our morning meeting.

Harper didn't bring up Silas or Leo the rest of the morning, and I was pleased with the progress I'd made with the content for the course and the book. I didn't want to lose any momentum, so I immediately got back to writing as soon as Harper left. I drank coffee and ate when Harper brought in some food, but I still hadn't looked for my phone. I had no desire to.

I didn't want to know if Silas tried to reach out to me or if he was done with me. Every time thoughts of him crept in, it hurt too much to continue. I had to focus on the book and write.

If only my life came together as easily as this book was. But then, work had always been easier for me. Relationships were complicated and messy and made me lose focus on what was important.

I'd always believed that I didn't have anything if my business wasn't successful. I tried to prove to my family that I'd made it. But I didn't think that was the case anymore. My sense of success came from inside, not from my family anymore. And maybe from Silas. It felt good when he supported my ideas and encouraged me.

He was a successful business owner, and he wasn't clouded in his opinions like my father was. It was like Papà wanted me to be his little girl forever. I wasn't allowed to grow up and have opinions different from him.

By dinner time, I'd written so much that my fingers and wrists ached. But I was satisfied with the progress I'd made, even if it felt empty.

Twenty

SILAS

Last night, I told Leo I owed him a conversation but needed to talk to Gia first. I couldn't reach her, so I figured she was at work and sat outside her office to make sure she was safe.

I was surprised when she showed up at Sunday dinner. I wanted her to have a good relationship with her family, but I saw firsthand how awkward it was between her and her father.

Once Harper arrived at work this morning, she texted me to say Gia was inside, sleeping on her desk, and was as fine as she could be for now. I checked into a hotel and used the change of clothes I kept in my car for nights when I wasn't sure where I was sleeping. Then I picked up breakfast and took it to the new pizzeria.

"How'd you know I'd be here?" Leo asked when he opened the door.

"You're the same place I would be, or where Gia is now —work."

Leo chuckled as he locked the door behind me. "That's the Giovannis. We bury ourselves in work."

I followed him through the dining room, down the hall, and

into his office. He sat across from me and held his hand out for the egg bagel sandwiches and coffee. "I'm still pissed at you."

"For dating your sister?" I asked, already knowing the answer.

Leo shook his head. "I can't believe you just came out and said it."

"I should apologize, but I've kept my distance from her over the years."

Leo ran his hand through his hair. "You've liked her for years?"

"On some level, I must have known. I think she did too. It's why we fought each other so hard."

"Harper said something similar, but I didn't want to believe it."

I leaned forward. "Harper knew?"

"She thought it was just a physical attraction. Is that what this is? Are you just fucking my sister?" His voice rose in volume with every word.

"Fuck no."

Our food sat on the desk between us, neither one of us ready to eat.

Leo threw up his hands. "Then what is it? Because I'm trying to be understanding here, and trust me, Matteo and Carlo won't be as levelheaded."

It was why I'd come to Leo first. He'd recently fallen in love with Gia's best friend, Harper, and was worried his family wouldn't accept their relationship, but he'd done it anyway. Of anyone, he'd be the most understanding.

Carlo and Matteo were still single, and it was more black and white to them. I was dating their little sister. It was unforgivable. There was no excuse for crossing that line, but Leo had already crossed several with Harper, who'd been a de facto member of their family since she was a kid.

"I'm in love with your sister. We might disagree on some things, but we have a lot in common, and I care about her. I knew she'd be hard to convince, but I thought if I was patient, she'd feel what I did."

Leo's brow furrowed. "You don't think she feels the same way?"

I ran a hand through my hair. "She's a tough one to read."

"She's had to be, growing up the youngest of four siblings. We teased her mercilessly, and Papà's the hardest on her."

"Why?"

"He expected her to work at the restaurant, and when she didn't, he was hurt. When she was little, she was his little shadow, but as she grew older, they grew apart. I think he's always wondered why."

"He didn't want her to make her own way?"

"To him, it's more about why she would have to. He'd created this business that she could just step into."

"Gia wouldn't appreciate someone handing her something."

Leo chuckled. "Definitely not. Papà has always been mystified by her. She never does or says what he expects."

"He wants her to return to the restaurant."

Leo's expression was sober. "On some level, yes, but I think he's starting to realize that's not going to happen."

"He had this vision for how things would be, and she's not playing into that. I can understand his disappointment, but it's hurting her." I shook my head. "That interaction with your father was rough. I don't like the way he talks to her."

"I don't like it either. But what can we do? There's always been animosity between them. She isn't what he expected, and he doesn't know what to do about it. Mamma says he'll get over it, but I'm not so sure."

"No one stands up for her with your father?" I asked, the realization pissing me off.

Leo shook his head. "He's the one in charge of the pizzerias. No one wants to upset the balance."

I stood. "I'm going there next."

"You're going to talk to Papà?" Leo asked, standing with me.

I nodded.

"Are you sure that's a good idea?"

"Whether Gia and I end up together or not, it has to be done. Someone has to say something. This can't go on. It's not fair to Gia or the rest of the family."

"I can respect that." Leo shook my hand. "For what it's worth, I hope you work things out with Gia."

"I still need to talk to Matteo and Carlo." I wasn't looking forward to any of these conversations, but they had to be done. Gia was worth it.

"Let me handle them."

"Are you sure?" Leo was easy compared to those two.

Leo gave me a rueful smile. "I was in your position not too long ago."

"And look how it worked out for you." Gia might not realize it yet, but she wanted a man who'd fight for her, who'd protect her. She didn't need it. She could handle herself. But I hoped she'd come to appreciate it. Because this was who I was. And if she cared for me like I did her, then she'd have to accept me stepping in from time to time. Her brothers weren't willing to do it, but it was my place if she'd let me.

Leo walked me out. "I respect what you're doing."

"You don't mind that I'm dating your sister?" I asked, a little surprised.

"I need to talk to her. Make sure she's okay with it. But you're my best friend. I can't think of a better man for her."

"I think we resisted each other before out of self-preservation. We felt the connection and resisted it. Neither one of us wanted a distraction from work. Maybe it wasn't the right time before. But when you came to Naomi and Chris's wedding, I saw her differently."

It was more about touch and taste, but I wasn't going to mention that to her brother. "I want you to know that if she'll have me, I'll take care of her—as much as she'll let me."

Leo laughed and clasped my shoulders. "You'll have your

hands full with Gia. I admire you for doing what you're doing. I hope she appreciates it."

We reached my car, and I turned to face him. "So, you're really okay with this?"

"I'm in love with Harper, so who am I to judge who you love? If she feels the same way, then I'm all for it. I'll check on Gia too."

"I appreciate that."

"I hope you'll be part of the Giovanni family one day." Leo shook my hand.

Contentment flowed through me. "Isn't it the other way around? Gia will be part of the Sharpe family."

"I don't know. You can't resist the pull of our family. It's too strong."

"I couldn't resist Gia, that's for sure."

Leo held up his palm. "Too much information."

"Got it. Sorry." I could talk about caring for his sister, but anything more personal was off-limits.

"I like you two together. It makes sense, and Harper saw it first. I just hope it's the real deal."

"That's all up to your sister. She's focused on her business and resists making time for anything or anyone else. Although she did let me take her out the last two Sundays."

"Life isn't all about work. I could easily have worked more when we opened the second restaurant, but I wanted to spend time with Harper and Evie. I didn't want to be working all the time. And my brothers figured out a way so that I could be home in the evenings with them. Relationships are about compromise, but I didn't see it that way. I wanted to spend a lot of time with them, and I made it happen. If you two want the same, you'll make it work."

"You realize it's your sister that puts up the biggest fight."

Leo laughed. "I don't envy you. I just hope she sees that love is a once-in-a-lifetime thing and grabs hold with both hands."

I tipped my head back. "*If* she loves me."

Leo hummed. "I hope for your sake she does."

"I appreciate it. I've got more work to do."

"Let me know if you need anything. I'll talk to my brothers and check in with Gia."

"I don't think she'll appreciate it."

"Tough."

I laughed. "She's lucky to have you."

"She's luckier to have you. We let her down over the years with Papà, but I have a feeling you're going to do right by her."

"You think this is the right thing to do?"

"How do you feel in your heart?"

"Like I need to have a conversation with her father."

"Then that's what you need to do. I'm a big believer in following your heart. It brought me to Harper and Evie, and I've never been happier. It feels like it was meant to be."

We said our good-byes, and I wondered what he'd meant the whole way to the Giovanni house. Were we meant to be? It certainly seemed like it when I thought back to the years we resisted each other and then to the interactions at my resort. I never acted like that with anyone else. I wouldn't take a woman into a broom closet. I was usually so focused on work, but Gia made me forget everything.

She made me see that there were other things in life, like love and happiness. I just hoped she felt the same.

By the time I pulled up to their house, I was questioning if this was the right decision. What if her father wasn't open to hearing what I had to say? What if he didn't like me for his daughter? Just because Leo was understanding about our situation didn't mean her parents would be.

I knocked on the door, my heart beating harder than the first time I met a girl's parents on a date. Mrs. G. opened the door, wearing an apron, and I breathed in the smell of apples and cinnamon. "Silas. The boys aren't home."

I loved that she called her sons, who were grown men, boys. My parents had a different parenting style. It was less affectionate and more filled with expectations of perfection and success. "I wanted to talk to you and Mr. G. about Gia."

"Is she okay?" Mrs. G. asked as she ushered me in.

There were cooling pies on the countertops.

"Harper's keeping an eye on her." I hated that I couldn't see Gia yet. I had a few things to take care of first, and I had a feeling Gia was going to be stubborn about hashing this out. She probably thought we'd broken up, but I wouldn't back down without a fight. I didn't give up that easily. She wouldn't be able to pretend nothing had happened between us.

"I think Papà is too hard on her, but he won't listen." Mrs. G. opened the stove and pulled out another pie.

I stood awkwardly in the doorway. "I hope he'll listen to me."

Mrs. G. turned and narrowed her eyes on me. "Is there something going on between you and my daughter?"

I gave her the smile women said was charming. "I can't stand up for your daughter without being in a relationship with her?"

She moved closer to me. "Of course you can, but I have a feeling you are."

"We've been seeing each other."

"And you're here to talk some sense into my stubborn husband."

I chuckled, some of the tension easing. "Then I need to talk to your daughter. I have a feeling she's just as stubborn."

"Those two. They were always butting heads. They're nothing like the boys. Their relationship was always harder. I tried everything I could to help them over the years, but they were both too stubborn. They refuse to talk to each other or listen, for that matter."

"Do you mind if I talk to him?" I asked her.

"Are you in love with my daughter?"

I opened my mouth to answer her when Mr. G. walked into the kitchen. "Who's in love with my daughter?"

His voice filled the room, and tension pricked my shoulders.

"I am, sir."

He raised his brow. "Does she love you?"

I chuckled without any humor. "That remains to be seen, but I hope so."

"That's what you came to talk to me about today?"

"That, and your relationship with her. I know it's none of my business, but I want Gia to be mine, and I don't want her to be hurt."

"She's upset?" Mr. G. asked, looking uncomfortable for the first time.

"Your opinion matters to her, probably too much. It's what drives her to work so hard. I think she's searching for your approval. And sure, she needs to learn that the only person she needs to impress is herself, but she also needs to know that her family loves her unconditionally. I wanted you to know how much it hurts her when you don't support her."

"I didn't think she cared what I thought. She's always so strong."

That made sense to me. That he thought she didn't care, so he was harsher with her. "It hurts her a lot. She cares what you think of her more than anyone else."

"I'm proud of her. She built that business from the ground up."

"All she hears is that the wedding planning business is frivolous, and she should come back and work for you."

Mr. G. shook his head. "I think I've handled it all wrong. But it's so easy to fall back into old patterns when she's here."

"She stayed away all these years, and when she comes back, you chase her off again," Mrs. G. said angrily.

This sounded like an argument they'd had before. "I wanted you to know how what you say affects her greatly. She wants your respect above anyone else's."

Mrs. G. sniffled.

"I've made mistakes, and I regret them. Even as I vow to do better by her, I fall back on our old way of interacting."

"She's strong-willed, but I love her for it." I wouldn't be challenged by a woman who didn't act like Gia did. If I wasn't sure about my feelings before today, I was solid in them now.

"I will do better by her. I will talk to her."

"I hope you do. Your opinion matters."

Mr. G. nodded. "Are you here to ask about something else?"

"Gia is my present and, hopefully, my future. But I have a few walls to climb before I can make her mine."

"What do you plan to do with you living where you do? Her business is important to her."

"We'll work it out. One or both of us can work remotely from time to time."

"What about marriage? Kids?"

"Gio, it's too soon for all of that," Mrs. G. Chided him.

"I want all of that with her. If she'll have me." Was she just denying her feelings to protect herself, or was she not as into me as I was into her?

My life was filled with business opportunities and profit margins before Gia came into my life. Now I was worried about work-life balance and how we could see each other despite the geographical distance.

She loved my house. Was it too much to think we'd settle down there eventually? Fill it with our kids, who would inevitably fight and one-up each other? I could see it so clearly now, and it made me smile.

"You're good for her."

"I think so." But it was all up to Gia at this point.

He patted my cheek. "I like you for my daughter."

Did that mean I had his blessing? "Thank you, sir."

I hugged Mrs. G. and shook Mr. G.'s hand. I needed to talk to Gia, but I had to figure out the best way to do it. She'd already had too much time to put emotional distance between us. I had to go about it the right way.

Twenty-One

GIA

I packed up my things, feeling drained. I should have gone home and gotten a good night's sleep, but I knew I'd continue writing on my laptop as long as I could. I had this desire to get everything out on paper. It was motivating to think that I could help someone else by telling my story.

Maybe someone else didn't have a supportive family or didn't come from a family with money and was starting from nothing like I did. It was exhilarating to think I could make a difference in someone else's life.

I opened the door to leave, only to find the girls standing outside with bags of stuff.

"Surprise!" Harper said as she came inside, the rest of the girls —Lily, Abby, Aria, Ireland, and Everly—following her.

"What is this?" I asked as I moved out of their way.

"We're having a *burn the rules* party!" Harper exclaimed as she lifted the bags of supplies in her hands.

"A what?" I asked, confused as the girls quickly put down their bags and pulled out lights. They didn't waste any time moving chairs to stand on so they could hang the strings of lights.

Harper popped the cork on a bottle, lined up glasses, and

poured champagne for everyone. "We're going out back to burn the rules. Now, where are they?"

"What rules?" I asked her.

"You know what I'm talking about. *The* Rules." She pulled open my drawers until she finally found them taped to the top tray. It had been highlighted but never removed. I hadn't referred to it in a long time. But I had a general idea of what it said:

Don't sleep with the wedding party.

Don't sleep with Gia's brothers.

Don't sleep with the vendors or contractors.

Harper ripped the loose-leaf paper off the tray and waved it in the air. "Does this sound familiar to anyone? *Don't sleep with the wedding party. Don't sleep with the vendors or contractors. Don't sleep with Gia's brothers.*"

Groans and eye rolls erupted around the room.

I gestured to each person as I listed the infractions. "Obviously, no one paid any attention to the rules. Abby had a one-night stand with the best man, Lily slept with the mechanic who was charged with keeping her delivery van running, Aria slept with my guitarist at the wedding venues, and finally, you slept with my brother Leo."

Harper smiled sweetly, with a knowing glint in her eyes. "But all of us are happy and in love. Isn't that what matters?"

I stubbornly refused to respond. I wasn't sure why they'd staged this intervention, but I felt uneasy. Were they here to talk about my screwup with Silas? I looked around the room, seeing genuine concern from each person, so I held up my hands. "Just for the record, I'd like everyone to know I haven't broken any of those rules."

Harper sighed. "The rules were stupid to begin with. You didn't honestly think you could control who people fell in love with, did you?"

"Of course not," I said over the tightening of my throat.

Harper lowered her voice. "Then why do you think you can control who *you* fall in love with?"

I crossed my arms over my chest. "What are you talking about?"

"Sweetie, you're in love with Silas."

"That's ridiculous," I protested, even as my cheeks heated. How much did everyone know? I'd told Harper a bit but hadn't confided in anyone else.

"Is it?" Harper asked, her brow raised.

The rest of the room had fallen silent. Somehow, they'd managed to finish stringing the twinkly lights on the ceiling and turned them on. Someone flicked off the overhead lights, giving the office a nice glow.

I really wanted the champagne, but I didn't think it was the right time for it. Harper wanted something from me, but I wasn't sure what it was.

"For the first time in years, you took off two Sundays in a row."

Prickles of awareness flew down my spine. Was she right about me being in love? "Is that all you've got?"

"You went home for family dinner for the first time in years when Silas was there."

"That doesn't mean anything," I insisted.

"You know what he means to you, even if you won't share it with anyone else. Inside, you know the truth."

I flushed hotter, my skin feeling uncomfortable. I wanted to escape from the truth of her words and the knowing stares of everyone in this room.

Harper shook the paper in the air. "These rules don't mean anything, not when we meet the man that means something to us. You'll break any rule to get what you want."

Did I want Silas? I missed him. It felt like my heart had been shredded into a billion tiny pieces since he walked out the other day. What if he didn't want me? I was difficult. My own father didn't get me. Why would Silas?

But I knew he did. He was the only person who saw all of me and seemed to like me more for it. Could *he* be in love with *me*?

The questions rolled around in my head, making my head spin.

Harper lowered her hand that held the piece of paper that had started everything. "I think if you sit in stillness for just a minute, and stop avoiding the truth for a second, you'll know."

I'd never looked forward to spending time with any man before Silas. I certainly wouldn't have skipped work for anyone else. I'd never felt like I did in his arms. Like I was beautiful and cherished and loved.

"I like him, but love—" I winced.

Harper tipped her head to the side. "Do you want to see him with anyone else?"

The pictures of the women he'd had on his arm in media photos flitted through my head. The mere thought of him with another woman irritated me.

"Can you imagine being with anyone else?" Lily prompted from the corner of the room, where she was struggling with a single strand of lights that refused to turn on.

Even when I thought we were over, I had no intentions of finding anyone else. He felt like the one to me.

Harper's lips twitched. "Are you figuring it out yet?"

"Even if I think he's the one for me, it doesn't mean he feels the same way," I finally admitted, easing the tightness in my chest.

Harper lifted a champagne glass. "First, girls' night, then we tackle Silas." Harper put her arm around my shoulders. "What do you say? Are you ready to set these rules on fire?"

"Why are we doing this again?" I asked, feeling trepidation about letting go of those rules.

Lily moved to stand next to Harper. "To show that we don't live by these rules—or any, for that matter. We fall in love with who we do, regardless of our backgrounds, experiences, and what's expected by everyone else in our lives."

"If you want to date your brother's best friend, who can tell you what to do?" Aria added.

"Or your best friend's brother," Harper smirked, her arm

tightening around me, and anchoring me in the moment. "It only matters what you think. It's your life."

"We only get one precious life. So, what are you going to do with it?" Lily asked with a brow raised.

She raised an interesting point. I wanted to be successful in business, and supported financially, but wasn't there something even more exciting than that? What if there was more to life? What if Silas was my future?

I let Harper lead me outside where we had a picnic table and, apparently, a new addition of a fire pit, where a small fire was already burning. As we stood around the fire, Harper and Lily on either side of me, I asked the question that had been simmering in my gut. "What if Silas doesn't feel the same?"

Harper gave me a sympathetic look. "We can't control other people. If Silas has a problem with your brothers, then that's on him."

The thought of letting go of the control I'd held on to so tightly was scary, but the possibility of a future with Silas was flickering in the distance too.

Harper handed me the piece of paper, the one I thought would protect me and everyone around me from heartache. "Now, are you ready to burn this?"

I sighed, knowing I needed to address everyone who'd been so sweet to come here tonight and attempt to talk some sense into me. "Work has always been the most important thing in the world to me, but Silas helped me see that there's more for me out there. That I can work less and make more. That I can relax, and my work only gets better." Then I paused for a minute and rested my free hand on my churning stomach. "I think I love him, but I'm not sure he feels the same way about me."

"All that matters is that we're true to ourselves. If he's the man I think he is, then he loves you, too. Are you going to do the honors?"

Aria stepped closer to us. "It should be you. They're your rules, after all."

I read over the rules one more time, wondering what I was thinking when I wrote them. "When I wrote these, I thought I could control everything around me. The tighter I held on to things, the easier everything would be. But I was wrong. All I did was hurt everyone in the process." Aria was worried she'd lose her job when I discovered that she'd slept with Finn at the wedding venues while they were supposed to be working. Harper didn't think I'd be friends with her once I found out she was in love with my brother. "But these arbitrary rules don't mean anything. Not when love is involved."

Lily handed out the glasses of champagne, and everyone held theirs in the air.

I raised my voice and the silly piece of paper in my hand. "To Happily Ever Afters. To not living by any set of rules. And to setting our own." Then I smiled, a sliver of hope sliding down my spine. "As long as they make us blissfully happy."

"Hear hear!" Harper cheered as I dropped the piece of paper into the fire.

As we watched it burn, I said, "No one can tell us how to live. We have to follow our own intuitions."

"What's your intuition telling you?" Harper stepped closer to ask.

"That I messed up." I felt miserable admitting it out loud.

"Which part did you screw up?"

"In not trusting all of you to be my friends." When I watched everyone's faces in the light of the fire, there was nothing but understanding, and it buoyed me for the next few things I had to say. "In thinking I needed to prove something to my parents by working all the time. In telling Silas to leave."

"I think it's fully in your power to fix all of that," Lily said softly.

"But how?" I asked, looking around at the women who'd stood by my side. I hadn't truly considered them friends until now.

Harper shoved a glass of champagne into my hand, and I

downed it in one gulp. "It'll come to you just like your brilliant business ideas."

"I brought chairs," Lily said, opening the back of her VW van and pulling out a bunch of camping chairs. We sat around the fire, sipping the champagne.

"I'm sorry I haven't trusted you with everything going on in the business. I thought on some level that women were in competition with each other. It was stupid and shortsighted," I said to everyone.

"Especially when we can support each other," Ireland chided.

"That's what I always told you, but I didn't practice it myself. I kept my vision of the business to myself and drafted those awful rules, thinking I could control everything."

"We want to be there for you," Ireland said.

I chewed my lip, and when Harper nodded, I opened my mouth to share what I'd been hiding from everyone. "I decided to start a course for other wedding planners, and I'm writing a book about my experiences as a business owner and wedding planner. I have no idea if anything will come of it, but I have a good feeling. I've never written anything so fast before."

Lily reached over to touch my arm. "That's amazing."

"I think people will love that," Abby gushed.

Listening to everyone ask questions and talk about it made me think it was a good thing. That something amazing would come from it.

"I searched online and didn't find anything like it. There's nothing tailored to wedding planners," Harper said.

"Most people selling digital courses pair it with a nonfiction book, so hopefully, I'm on the right track. But I've enjoyed the process of getting everything down on paper. I realized I have so much to share, and I hope it helps someone."

"I think you're going to encourage a lot of people who are afraid to take that risk, to take that first step and start their business," Abby said.

Hope filled my heart. "I'd love to share your stories too. Would you be willing to talk about your experiences?"

"I'd love to help. My flower shop wasn't successful on its own. I struggled to make a profit until I got creative and started a subscription service and renovated my barn to host weddings on my farm. It was a dream come true for me, but it took some time to figure things out," Lily said.

"I was afraid to expand my photography business and to hire any help because I was worried I'd overextend myself. I wasn't just supporting myself, but Hunter too," Abby added.

We went around the circle, and everyone shared their struggles in business. It was so nice to hear that we shared similar experiences.

"Your stories are so inspiring," I said to them, excited to include their experiences too. I wondered if my business book could expand to all female business owners and then the course could be centered on wedding planners.

Abby pulled out a bag of marshmallows, and we scrounged for sticks to roast them. We drank more of the champagne Harper brought, laughing and having a good time.

I was happy to finally have been part of this friend group. For so long, I set myself apart from everyone. But there was still something missing. Whenever I thought about Silas, my heart sank, and my stomach twisted.

I knew I should talk to him, but I was afraid it was too late. That when I told him to leave, it signaled the end for us. But then, I'd never been in a relationship where my heart was at stake. I'd never been this invested before, and I wasn't sure how to move on.

"I have something to share with you guys," Ireland said, the firelight dancing across her face.

Everyone got quiet, sensing she was about to tell us something important.

She held up her hand, and it took me a few seconds to realize she was showing off the large diamond on her ring finger. Her boyfriend, James, must have proposed. They'd met on an online dating app and realized they'd grown up in the same social circles but had never met. Lily squealed and lunged at her for a hug.

There was a flurry of congratulations and hugs. When it was my turn to hug Ireland, I felt a sense of loss. If I was more open with my feelings, would I be in a good place with Silas? Was I shutting down the possibility of a future with us?

When the group quieted again, Abby asked, "You've only been dating a short time. Was it love at first sight?"

Something flashed across Ireland's face before she smiled. "He's perfect for me. He comes from a good family, and he believes in love and relationships."

A look of concern passed over Lily's face. "Do you love him?"

Ireland smiled wide, but it didn't quite reach her eyes. "So much. I can't believe that this is my life. That I'm engaged and getting married."

"And here I felt bad for moving out of our apartment and into your brother's house," Aria teased.

I regretted not being closer to Ireland because something about her story seemed off. She said she was in love, and she seemed happy. But something was missing.

I leaned forward. "I have to know... Are we planning your wedding?"

Ireland squealed. "Of course! I'd love to have a Christmas wedding."

"You want to have it at the Christmas tree farm?" I asked, my heart sinking.

"Is that even possible?" Ireland raised her hopeful gaze to mine.

"I was going to suggest you talk to Emmett again about the possibility of us working with them. Maybe if you tell him it's for your wedding, he'll be willing to do it as a test of sorts. Maybe we can show them that we can hold the wedding with minimal disruption to their tree business."

"Is that possible?" Lily asked, her voice laced with concern.

"We'll do our best to minimize the damage by creating a new

parking lot only for the wedding party and keeping our event away from the barn shop and the cut-tree lot."

"You really think I have the best chance of convincing him?" Ireland asked.

"You're the bride. Who could say no to you?" I asked her, but I wasn't so sure. I swear Emmett's gaze had lingered on her when we had met with them previously, which meant he wasn't going to be happy she was engaged to someone else. But then again, every time I saw him, he was grumpy. Maybe that was just his personality.

"At the very least, Lori will want to help."

"Even if we can only hold one wedding on the Monroes' farm, you'll get the wedding of your dreams," I said to her.

Harper shot me a look. "You'd be content with one wedding there?"

Everyone laughed, knowing that wasn't true.

"It's not a secret I want the Monroe farm for our weddings, and I'm going to do everything I can to get it for us. I think Ireland's engagement is our best chance to prove to the Monroes that we won't disrupt their business. We'll shine a spotlight on their brand and bring in even more customers."

Ireland shifted in her chair, looking slightly uncomfortable.

"But only if you're okay with my plan, Ireland. I don't want you to do anything you don't feel comfortable with."

Ireland's gaze steeled. "I want to help, and I do want to get married at the farm."

"I think it's the best way to convince Emmett to allow us to hold weddings there." It felt like the next right action, and I always followed my intuition.

"What do I need to do to convince *you* to talk to *me*?" The male voice startled everyone.

Silas stood behind Abby and Ireland, across the fire from me.

"What are you doing here?" I asked, my voice shaky. It was almost like I'd conjured him here. Was he real or just a figment of my imagination?

"You aren't answering your phone, and Harper said you were having an office meeting." He looked around the circle at us drinking champagne and eating marshmallows. "This looks like something more."

I stood and slowly made my way to him, that glimmer of hope I'd felt earlier growing bigger. "I'm trying something new."

He arched a brow. "Oh yeah? By strong-arming the Monroes into hosting your weddings?"

I smiled. "I always get what I want. Sound familiar?"

"Do you have everything you want?" he asked when I reached him. We stood facing each other but not touching.

I shook my head. "Not at all."

Everyone was quiet, only the crackle of the fire making any noise. "What are you doing here, Silas?"

"I need to talk to you." Silas looked exhausted, like he'd been up all night.

"I want to talk to you too," I said softly, fighting with my desire to jump into his arms before I knew what he was here to say.

"Then why aren't you answering your phone?"

"Honestly, I don't even know where my phone is. But I needed time, and then I was working on my book. It was just flowing for me, and it allowed me to put off what I needed to do with you." I gestured at the women behind us. "But now, Ireland's engaged, and I have all these wonderful friends. Everything is working out for me. Or at least, it seems that way on the outside." I chewed my lip, knowing this was my chasm to fix. "But when I told you to leave the last night, you took a piece of me with you."

His gaze was trained on me, and it was like everyone else faded away. "What piece was that?"

My heart thudded in my ears. I couldn't believe I was about to declare my feelings in front of everyone, including him, but I needed to do this. I kept my gaze steady on his. "*Il mio cuore.* My heart."

Silas took a step closer to me. "What are you saying?"

I threw my hands in the air, deciding to let go and tell him everything that had been on my mind the last twenty-four hours. "*Mi fai impazzire ma ti voglio bene.* You drive me crazy, but I'm in love with you. You challenge me, you encourage me, and you are the best thing that's ever happened to me. You made me see that I could be and do things differently. That I could work less and make more. That with relaxation and time off work comes the best inspiration of my life. You've shown me what it's like to love someone. *Ti amo.* I love you, Silas Sharpe, and I'm so sorry I resisted you all these years. I've wasted so much time."

Twenty-Two

SILAS

Gia was saying everything I needed to hear. I thought I was going to have to convince her, to make her see the feelings she fought so hard to hide. But instead, she was sharing her feelings with me in front of everyone.

Her eyes shiny, Gia asked, "Are you going to say something?"

I stepped closer to her, needing to be near her, wanting to touch her. I slid my fingers through her hair, then cupped the back of her head. "I love you, Gia. I've never loved anyone like I love you. You're it for me."

"Wow," someone said behind us, but I blocked it out.

"And if that's too much for you, you're going to have to get used to it because I'm not changing how I feel or tempering it until you get used to it. I'm all in with you, Gia."

A small smile spread over Gia's face. "I'm all in too. I realized I'd been hiding from myself for years. I've been holding myself back from relationships, too scared to get close to anyone. I thought it was a weakness, but I was wrong. Love is my greatest strength."

It was hard to believe she was saying all the things I wanted to hear and more. Gia Giovanni was in love with me. "And we didn't waste any time, baby. This is the story of our journey, and we're going to look back on it with love."

"I love you," Gia said softly, as if she couldn't stop herself from saying it.

"I love you," I said as I lowered my head and kissed her.

Cheers erupted around us and brought us back to the moment, where the entire staff of Happily Ever Afters was watching our exchange.

When I finally lifted my head, Gia's expression was soft. Her eyes were full of love for me. "I can't believe you came."

"Harper said you were here, and I couldn't wait any longer for you to come to me."

Gia smiled sheepishly. "I would have. I just had to take care of a few things here first."

"We had to burn the rules," Harper said from her spot at the fire.

I lifted my head to look around the circle, noticing for the first time most of the women were a little glossy-eyed. "Have you been celebrating?"

Gia smiled. "I created a set of rules, and they no longer applied to us, so we burned them."

"Do I want to know what these rules are?" I asked Gia, pulling her close to me.

"*Don't sleep with Gia's brothers* was one of them," Harper said.

I grinned. "Well, that one was broken. Was there one about me?"

Gia grabbed my hand. "We should get out of here."

"You don't want to finish your meeting?" I asked, even as I acknowledged it was the least professional meeting I'd ever seen.

"Nope. We're all done here. Clean up, ladies," Gia said as she dragged me around the building to my car.

We stopped at the passenger-side door, facing each other. "Are you sure? I kind of interrupted a thing, and I don't want to intrude."

Gia's hands rested on my biceps. "You already did, and you

were very welcome, but now we need to go home. I want to show you how much I love you."

Distracted by the way her hands were running over my body, I stopped her wrist with my hand. "You're going to tell me about the rules."

Her cheeks heated. "Maybe."

"You will." I was almost positive there was one about me, and I wanted to know what it was. I waited for her to get inside the car and then drove the short distance to her house.

"I want to go to your house, but it's too far away," Gia said.

"We have to talk about that. How is this going to work?" I wasn't naïve enough to think we'd solved everything with a declaration of love.

Gia opened the door and climbed out. "We'll figure it out."

"Is it that easy?" I asked, following her up the walk to her house.

"Uh-huh." She fumbled with the key, so I took it from her and slid it inside the lock. "Have you been drinking too?"

"Just one glass. I wanted to talk to you after the meeting. I was planning on going to you."

"I couldn't wait any longer." A thrill shot through me as I shut the door behind us and pressed her against it.

Her lips curled up. "Me either. I'm so glad you showed up."

I pinned her wrists to the door on either side of her head and nibbled on her neck. She gasped and tipped her head to the side to give me more access.

I lifted my head slightly so I could tug on her earlobe. "Now, about those rules..."

She trembled as I pressed my body against hers. "What about them?"

"I want you to tell me what was in them. What was so embarrassing that you had to burn them?" I sucked on her earlobe.

Gia whimpered. "They weren't embarrassing."

"Then why burn them?" I insisted as I ground my cock against her.

She bit her lip and gazed up at me. "They didn't serve me anymore."

"Don't sleep with your brothers. What was the rest?" I prompted her.

"Don't sleep with the wedding party. Don't sleep with your coworkers—vendors, musicians, that kind of thing."

"Why do I have a feeling you're not telling me the truth?" I asked, lifting myself away so I could see her face. "Why do I have a feeling there's a rule about me, and you don't want to tell me?"

When she remained silent, I said, "I think I can convince you once I have you spread out on your bed, leaving you naked and wanting."

I grabbed her wrist and tugged her to her bedroom, with her laughing. I grinned as we came to a stop in front of the bed. "I want you naked and legs spread on the bed."

"You're bossy tonight," Gia said as she hurried to undress.

"You like it," I said, already loosening my tie and unbuttoning my shirt.

"You're hot like this."

"I'm hot all the time."

She climbed onto the bed, her weight on her elbows as she raised a brow and spread her legs.

"Fuck. That's hot."

She arched a brow. "You said you had some convincing to do."

I placed one knee on the bed and slid my fingers between her folds. "You're already wet."

I moved over her, placing one hand next to her head, keeping my cock away from her pussy, and sucked one nipple into my mouth. She arched against me, and I struggled to keep my distance. I wanted to tease her, to keep her wanting more.

She tugged on the hair at the base of my neck. "Silas."

"You know what I want."

"And I'll tell you if you put your mouth on me."

"That's not how this is going to go." I was going to drive her crazy, and she was going to tell me what I wanted to know before my mouth touched her clit.

I took my time caressing her breasts, tweaking her nipples and sucking them until they were hard.

Whimpers fell from her mouth as her hips gyrated against me.

"Tell me," I said as I moved between her legs, blowing a breath across her pussy.

Her thighs trembled as she went on her elbows to see me. "I want you, Silas."

I raised a brow as she chewed her lip. "I had a rule against sleeping with my brothers' best friend—"

"That's not all of it." I knew there was more.

Her gaze slid off my face. "And my enemy."

I gripped her thighs. "Is that how you see me, as your enemy?"

She shook her head. "Not anymore."

"Does your enemy love you like this?" I asked as I lowered my head and sucked her clit hard.

She fell back to the bed. "Nooo."

"Or like this?" I asked as I used two fingers to slide inside her, pumping like I would with my cock in a minute. I wanted to drive her to the edge.

She merely shook her head, so lost in the buildup she couldn't form any words.

When her muscles tightened, I removed my fingers and kissed my way up her body. "I want you to come on my cock."

"Yes, yes, yes," she said as I kissed her, lining my cock up with her entrance.

I wanted to take my time, but I couldn't. Now that we'd declared our feelings for each other, I had this driving need to make her mine.

I thrust inside in one fluid motion, both of us taking a second to adjust. With her hands on the base of my spine, she urged me to move.

We whispered words of love to each other, lost in the pleasure. I couldn't think. I couldn't slow down. All I could do was feel.

This woman was it for me, and I wouldn't let anything or anyone come between us. Never again.

I'd stand by her side and support her in any way that she needed. I'd never take away from her light or overshadow her.

When we tumbled over the edge, we did it together, in each other's arms. When I finally recovered, I rolled to my side, taking her with me.

There were no words for what just happened. It was an expression of love, of a commitment to this woman.

I held her tightly against me.

Her fingers played with the hair on my chest. "What about everything else?"

I propped my head onto my bent elbow. "You mean, how you live in Annapolis and my resort is an hour away?"

"Yeah, that." Her expression was pensive.

"We make it work. Some days we'll need to be in person at our respective jobs, and others, we can work remotely. You still have that couple you're working with at my resort, and that might turn into a regular thing."

She smacked my chest lightly. "You can't hire me as your wedding planner just because we're seeing each other."

"You know that's not what that is. You're simply the best, and that's what I hire. But it wouldn't be an employer-employee relationship. It would be a partnership. Our lawyers can draw up a contract. Not only are you the only one for the position, but it keeps you close to me."

"What about Hannah?"

"She'll still work for me but won't do the higher-end clients."

"Won't she be upset?" Gia's expression was uncertain.

"I have a feeling she's going out on her own soon anyway. I can see the emails she's sending through the company server."

"Wow, and you haven't already fired her?"

"I've kept a close eye on the situation. I'm not one to stand in the way of someone opening a business. As long as she doesn't screw me over in the process."

"Spoken like a true businessman."

"Our relationship might be unconventional, but that's us. We're busy people with our respective businesses. But I wouldn't have it any other way."

"I love that aspect of us."

It was something I didn't even know I was looking for, someone who could challenge me in every way.

She fell silent for a few seconds.

I finally said, "I talked to Leo."

"About us?"

"I explained what happened, and he understood."

"You're his best friend. Doesn't he feel betrayed?"

I was positive she was remembering how she felt when Evie revealed that Harper was dating Leo. "Not when I said I was in love with you. He said Harper predicted we'd hook up."

Gia lifted to her elbow so she could see my face. "Hook up? She didn't think it would be anything more?"

"She thought we'd hook up and it wouldn't work out. That we were too similar to each other. I think she was talking about how we always fought with each other."

"Yeah, but that's because we were resisting the pull."

"No one is like us. Our story doesn't follow anyone else's."

Gia sighed. "I like that."

"I freaking love that about us. We're unique."

"What about Matteo and Carlo?" Gia asked, sounding nervous for the first time.

As strong as she was, she didn't want her brothers to be upset with her. "Leo said he'd talk to them. I'll still reach out to them too."

"Wow. Leo must be telling the truth. He really is okay with us seeing each other."

I chuckled, content to have Gia in my arms. "I doubt he wants to see me kissing you. But he's open to the idea of us."

Gia let out a breath, and I wondered if she was worried about what her family would think.

"I talked to your father too," I said, and she stiffened under my touch.

Her brow furrowed. "Why would you do that?"

"I didn't like how he talked to you at dinner the other night."

Gia frowned. "What did you say to him?"

"That I didn't like the dynamic between you two, and something needed to change." When Gia remained silent, I continued. "He said he's proud of you. That he means to treat you differently but falls into old patterns when you're around."

Gia sighed and looked torn, as if she wasn't sure what to believe.

"I think he doesn't know how to act around you. You're so different than what he expected, and he'd like for you to work by his side, but he respects that you don't."

Gia bit her lower lip. "I don't know."

"Will you talk to him and give him a chance to explain it to you?" I asked her, hoping she would be open to the idea. I didn't like her being at odds with her parents.

"Do you think it will do any good?" she asked tentatively.

"It can't hurt."

She snorted and plopped onto her back on the bed. "We'll just argue."

"If that's your attitude going into it. But what if you were open to seeing what he had to say?" I said as I propped myself up on an elbow.

She smiled up at me. "I'll try."

I kissed her, my love for her encompassing everything. "I love you."

She wrapped her arms around me. "I love you too."

Twenty-Three

GIA

After we made up, I spent most nights with Silas. We couldn't seem to get enough of each other and, on some level, needed to be close. Since we'd declared our love for each other, I felt freer. Like I could do anything.

Thankfully, Matteo and Carlo took Leo's lead and were okay with my relationship with Silas. I suspected they might have threatened retaliation if Silas ever hurt me, but he wouldn't admit it to me.

Today, we were meeting with the Monroe family to discuss the possibility of Ireland holding her wedding there. I was prepared to campaign hard for her. I knew she wanted to get married and have a holiday wedding, and I wanted the Monroes to see that a partnership would be advantageous to both of us.

My plan was to go in there and act as if the wedding was going to happen. I wouldn't let them make any excuses or put us off anymore. This was their last chance to work with us. I wouldn't make any more offers.

I hadn't discussed my plans with Silas because I was confident my approach would work, and if it didn't, I was ready to walk away. There was nothing more effective in business than when the other person knew you were willing to leave the deal on the table.

I drove to the farm and parked next to Ireland's car, outside the red barn that doubled as a shop for the holiday season. The rolling fields of trees in various stages of growth, in their even and orderly lines, solidified my desire to secure the venue for Ireland.

I got out of my car and went over to Ireland, who'd already gotten out.

"Do you think this is going to work?" Ireland asked nervously.

"If it doesn't, then I'm going to walk away. It's important that they know that. There's nothing more important during negotiations than your willingness to walk away."

She licked her lips. "But I thought you really wanted this partnership?"

"At this point, I'm feeling like they're not ever going to go through with it. No matter what Lori told us in the beginning, her sons run this place. It's their decision that matters, and I don't think Emmett will change his mind."

Ireland blew out a breath. "Yeah, he's stubborn and completely against holding weddings on the farm."

"Today, we'll go in there and act like the wedding is going to happen, but if they say no, that's it. I'm done."

"Is that a bluff?"

"Nope. I'm done with the Monroes after this conversation. I reached out to several other Christmas tree farms, and a few are interested in working with us. They're farther away, but I'd be willing to talk to them."

Ireland nodded. "We have options. Got it."

For me, it wasn't just about Ireland's wedding. I wanted to make her dream come true, but not being underestimated in this business deal was more important for me. I didn't give in, especially when this had gone on as long as it had.

"Let's do it," I said.

At Lori's request, we went inside the barn, where Emmett, his brothers, and Lori waited by the counter. This was the first time we'd seen his brothers.

"Thank you for coming," Lori said, making her way to us for hugs.

I heard a snort, and I was positive it was Emmett.

Lori stepped back. "These are my sons. You've already met Emmett. This is Talon, Heath, Sebastian, and Knox."

I shook each one's hands. All five of them were larger men, with barrel chests and scruff on their face. "It's nice to meet you."

"You said you have a proposition for us," Lori prompted me.

"Is there somewhere we can sit? A meeting room perhaps?"

"I have a craft room in the back. It's big enough for everyone." We followed her to the dark room. She flipped on the lights. There was a large table in the middle and wall-to-wall cupboards on the walls.

"Emmett made these. He's good with his hands."

Emmett stiffened.

Ireland's cheeks flushed, and I barely restrained the twitch of my lips at Lori's unwitting innuendo.

We sat around the table, Ireland and me on one side, and the Monroes lined up on the other. Emmett remained standing.

"Sit down. I don't want to crane my neck to talk to you. I'm sure these ladies don't either," Lori admonished him.

Emmett crossed his beefy arms over his chest. "I don't much care what they think."

Lori lowered her voice and spoke in a tone that could only be described as a mother who shouldn't be messed with. "You will sit while we are talking. It's the polite thing to do."

Emmett finally sat in the chair at the end of the table, which was telling for me. As the eldest, he was the one who'd make the final decision.

"Do you work the farm year-round?" I asked them, curious if the holiday season was their sole moneymaker.

"Sebastian is an accountant and our bookkeeper. Emmett has a furniture business on the side, Knox has a landscaping business, and Talon is an artist of sorts; he makes things out of metal."

"Are you the one who makes the metal trees that are displayed in the shop?" I asked Talon.

"I do those because my mother wants me to provide something to the store, but I usually create lighting and other decorative items for the home. They have an industrial feel."

"I'd love to see them sometime." I wondered if there was something we could use for weddings in Lily's barn.

"Heath bartends in the off-season, and a few of their cousins work here during the busy season too."

"The business isn't sustaining the family year-round?" I asked, needing a better view of what I was working with.

"That's none of your business," Emmett interjected.

"It's okay, Emmett. We make a good living those few months, but with all of us working here, we need more. That's why they have side businesses. I think there are ways we could increase our income, and that's why we agreed to meet with you today."

Irritation flitted over Emmett's face. "Say whatever it is you have to say."

His gruffness didn't get to me. Yet Silas never failed to set me off in conversations. With a professional expression and tone, I said, "Ireland's getting married, and she would love to have the wedding on your farm. It's her dream."

Emmett arched a brow, his entire body stiff as he looked at Ireland. "You're engaged?"

Ireland smiled and lifted the sparkling diamond on her finger. It was huge, probably a testament to her fiancé's bank account. Ireland came from money, and her fiancé came from the same social circle. I had a feeling once they were married, she'd quit working for me. She probably wouldn't need the income, and working as an event planner was beneath her social status.

Emmett shifted in his seat. "You want to get married on my farm?"

I had a feeling that Emmett was attracted to Ireland, and his reaction only confirmed that suspicion.

Ireland was thoughtful for a few seconds. "It's my dream to

get married on a Christmas tree farm. I think it would be romantic."

I believed her when she said she wanted to get married on a Christmas tree farm. I wasn't so sure her fiancé would agree with the venue. But my job was to secure the farm for future Happily Ever Afters weddings, not inquire as to Ireland's relationship with her fiancé.

Emmett leaned his elbows on the table. "Weddings are a one-day party. Marriages are forever."

Her cheeks flushed. "What are you saying?"

Emmett waved a hand in her direction. "Brides don't understand what they're getting into. They get so caught up in the one-day party, they forget they are pledging themselves to someone for life."

Ireland leaned forward and asked shrewdly, "Are you talking from personal experience?"

Emmett flinched at her comment, and Lori looked uncomfortable.

I'd bet anything that Emmett had been jilted by an ex. Was he left at the altar? What would that do to a person? Was that why he was reluctant to allow weddings on his property?

Desperate to get this back on track, I continued as if Emmett hadn't revealed anything. "I'm proposing that Ireland's wedding be held here as a trial. We can have it early in the season, maybe Thanksgiving weekend."

"That's one of the busiest weekends of the season," Emmett bit out.

"Is there a quiet weekend we can hold it in December?" I asked sweetly, already knowing the answer.

Talon shook his head. "It only gets busier."

"That's why I'm proposing Thanksgiving weekend. It will be holiday themed for Ireland, but it allows you to have most of the season without any weddings, if that's what you choose. Then you can decide if it's worth it to hold more. It doesn't make sense to say no until we give it a shot. We have ways to reduce parking issues and crowds." I slid my proposal across the table to Emmett. It was a power move, one acknowledging that I knew he was the one making this decision, not his mother or even his brothers.

"You're used to getting what you want," Emmett said.

"And if I don't, I walk away. This is the final offer. You won't see me on your farm again." My heart was pounding hard, but I kept my expression smooth.

Emmett's gaze flashed to Ireland. "What about you, sweetheart? I thought you *had* to have your wedding here?"

Ireland's eyes widened at the label. "Gia's reached out to other farms. I love your place, but there are always other options. I've even reached out to Longwood Gardens in Pennsylvania."

Lori sucked in a breath. "You would get married at Longwood?"

It was obvious that Lori knew the gravity of Ireland's statement. She had options and the money to back it up.

Ireland hadn't confided in me, and I had a feeling it was James who wanted to get married there. I couldn't even imagine what renting the Dupont Estate would cost at Christmas when it was decorated, and so many people visited to see the lights. "That would be amazing."

Ireland smiled at me. "That's where James wants to hold the wedding."

Emmett slapped the table with his bare hand. "Would you mind leaving the room so we can discuss it as a family?"

I smiled, knowing that we'd done what we intended to. "Of course."

We filed out of the room, and Emmett closed the door behind us.

"Well? What do you think will happen?" Ireland turned to face me.

I smiled triumphantly. "You closed the deal with your talk about Longwood."

Ireland slowly shook her head. "Oh, that wasn't talk. James wants to hold the wedding there."

My forehead wrinkled. "I can't imagine what that would cost—"

Ireland smiled tightly. "Money isn't something we're worried about."

Ireland's take on money was so refreshing. She'd mentioned over the years that money gave you freedom, not happiness. She was grounded despite the size of her trust fund or the way she grew up.

"If money is no object, and you could get married anywhere in the world, is this the location you would want?"

Ireland opened her mouth to answer, but the door to the craft room opened and Emmett walked out.

His jaw was tight, his expression guarded as he handed me the contract. "You've got yourself a deal. But Ireland is my point of contact."

I scanned the document to ensure it had been signed. Looking up from the paperwork, I asked, "Do you want to plan your own wedding?"

Ireland shrugged. "I can do it."

"Well, you have us as your assistants. Whatever you need."

"You want to walk the grounds and pick the location?" Emmett asked, and I wondered what had changed his mind and why he was being so accommodating.

"We've taken a tour before, and there's a map of proposed locations."

A muscle in Emmett's jaw ticked. "I think the bride should walk the grounds again and make her choice."

Ireland was nodding before I could make sense of Emmett's insistence. "Yeah, sure. I'd like that."

I checked my phone. "I have to meet with my dad soon. Can you handle this?"

"Of course," Ireland said, but her smile didn't reach her eyes.

Emmett wanted to deal with her personally, so it didn't make sense for me to stay. "Call me if you need anything," I said to Ireland.

I shook Emmett's hand. "You won't regret this."

"I already do," he mumbled as I walked away.

I was thrilled that Ireland got what she wanted, and hopefully, it was the start of a profitable business relationship with the Monroes. I was confident that once Ireland's wedding went smoothly, they'd come around to the idea and see the advantage. It would build and expand their brand, especially if their mother wanted to extend their busy season to other holidays.

I was flying high as I drove toward the original pizzeria in Annapolis. When I got there, Leo said, "Papà and Mamma are in the back."

"Wish me good luck," I said with a self-deprecating smile.

"You won't need it. It will be fine," Leo said with confidence as he resumed filling the condiments at the tables.

I shook my head, not believing that things between me and my father would ever be great, and continued in the direction of the office.

Leo stopped me when he said, "Oh, I wanted to say I'm happy for you."

My forehead wrinkled as I turned to face him. "For what?"

Leo dipped his chin. "For giving Silas a chance. He's a good guy."

I wanted to argue with him for old times' sake, but it felt good to tell him the truth. "He's the best."

"I'm glad you found each other," Leo said sincerely.

"How do Matteo and Carlo feel about it?" I asked, almost afraid of the answer.

"Once they see that you two are happy, they'll be fine," Leo said.

I chuckled without any humor. "I hope so. I don't need any more tension in the family."

He waved his hand toward the back. "Go talk to them. They're waiting for you."

I nodded and made my way to the back. My heart rate kicked

up as I got closer. Would this be one more time when we wouldn't agree? Would Papà tell me he was disappointed in me?

I took a deep breath and knocked on the door, which was slightly ajar. "You wanted to talk?"

Mamma hugged me. "We're so happy to see you."

I looked at Papà to see if that was true.

His expression was pained, and at Mamma's nod, he said, "I'm sorry for the way I've been acting."

My entire body softened. I couldn't believe he'd admitted that he was different with me. "I haven't been the best daughter either."

Papà held up his hand. "Let me finish. I would love for you to work with me. You're brilliant and hardworking. But it was wrong of me to pressure you to come back, to make you think I wasn't proud of you and your business."

"You are?" I asked, a little surprised.

Papà nodded. "I'm so proud of what you've accomplished."

"But you said no one would ever pay for an event planner," I said, feeling more than a little confused.

"I was wrong. You've obviously made a name for yourself, and you've built a successful business."

"Thank you." I couldn't believe he was saying the words I'd been striving to hear for so long. It was funny because I'd stopped believing I needed them, but they still felt good.

"If you wanted to come back and work here, I wouldn't let you," Papà said.

"Why?"

"You have built something special, and I think you should focus on that."

I chewed my lip for a few seconds, wondering how I could express what I was feeling. "I thought you were disappointed in me."

Papà hugged me and said gruffly, "Never. I could never be disappointed in you."

I returned the hug, relaxing in the knowledge that my family was okay with what I was doing. When he stepped away, I asked, "Did you know I'm writing a book?"

"I didn't hear anything about that," Mamma said.

"I want passive income. My business is service based, and no matter how much we try to streamline things with packages, it's a lot of work."

"It's the same with the restaurant."

"That's why I decided to offer a digital course on wedding planning to other planners and write a book outlining my struggles and successes. I have so much information to share; it just made sense. There's not much offered in the wedding planning space."

"I don't understand what you mean by a digital course."

"It's a big thing in the online world," Mamma said. "I've heard about it. People offer courses in their expertise."

I was surprised by her confession. "Nonfiction books are supposed to be easier to sell than fiction and complement a course nicely. Plus, you can self-publish now, and you don't have to go through the hoops of a traditional publishing house, and you can keep a higher profit."

As we talked about my plans, it was clear Papà didn't understand the value of the course, but he understood what it meant to write a book. He seemed proud of me, and I hoped we'd fixed the rift between us.

When I was ready to head out, Papà gruffly said, "You know that boy loves you."

"Boy? You mean Silas?" When Papà nodded, I said, "He's hardly a boy."

"He's a good man. I told him he was lucky to have you."

"Well, of course, he is," Mamma agreed.

"Are you saying you're okay with me seeing him?" I asked them both.

"He's good for you," Papà said.

In the past, I would have bristled at a comment like that, but now, I appreciated it. "I think so too."

"You're open to love now," Mamma said, and it wasn't a question.

"I am." I wasn't afraid to admit it.

"I want you to be happy," Mamma said.

"I am happy, but not because of Silas. He helped me see there was more to life than work. That I could work less and make more."

"I've been trying to tell your father that for years, but he doesn't believe me."

"I like working. My favorite part is talking to the customers, reminiscing about when my children were tagging along behind me," Papà said with affection.

Papà made Giovanni's special. Without my parents, Giovanni's wouldn't be the same.

Epilogue

GIA

I loved mornings on Silas's deck. We drank coffee and looked out over the water. "I can't believe it's John and Emma's wedding day."

"Does this mean I won't see you here as often?" Silas asked.

"I hope this wedding is just the beginning of many."

Silas's expression sobered. "I don't know if it's going to work out."

I tipped my head to the side. "How many couples have requested me?"

"Too many," Silas admitted as he sipped his coffee.

"I think you need me."

He flashed me a smile. "In more ways than one. I need you in my bed and in my house."

I frowned. "But how will I manage the back-and-forth? My business is in Annapolis."

"Your book and digital course have been released, and it's doing well."

I'd reached out to podcasts and taken every interview offered to me. The publicity had helped my book take off. When I released my digital course, it outsold anything I could have imagined. I decided to keep it open for a limited time, which increased demand and urgency. I planned to launch the course twice a year.

I enjoyed teaching, talking to other women in business, and empowering them to keep going. A few inquired about one-on-one meetings, so I took on a few high-priced coaching clients. It was Harper's idea to offer a cheaper monthly membership for those who couldn't afford the one-on-one coaching. It was an amazing opportunity for the wedding planners to ask questions.

These coaching sessions gave me ideas for other courses to offer. I had ideas for more books. As much as I loved wedding planning, these new offerings fed my soul. I felt more satisfied than I had when I was just planning parties.

The online buzz surrounding the book and course had grown larger than I ever could have imagined. It had the added effect of increasing demand for me as a wedding planner. Now I was seen as an expert in my industry. I increased my prices overall to meet the demand and hired a few more wedding planners to handle the weddings in Annapolis.

Silas leaned back in his chair. "You've put my resort on the map."

His resort was mentioned alongside my name in every article or podcast about me and my offerings.

"I should tell you that *Bridal Magazine* will be on-site today to cover the wedding."

I laughed and then stopped when I saw his serious expression. "You're kidding."

"I'm not."

"Why didn't you tell me? I need to get on-site now and make sure everything is ready." I stood, intending to go inside and get ready.

Silas stopped me with a hand on my wrist. "Babe, everything is covered. Ireland will be here today to assist you. I already talked to her about her keeping an eye on things this morning."

I sat back down, my mind still racing. "You can't expect me to sit around the house when a magazine is covering *my* wedding."

"It's not *your* wedding," Silas said easily.

I waved a hand. "You know what I mean—the one I planned. My reputation is on the line."

"It's not," Silas said firmly. "You've done an amazing job planning everything, and you have a team you can trust to ensure it goes as planned."

I looked out over the water, wanting to enjoy this morning with Silas. I didn't want the stress of John and Emma's wedding, or the fact a magazine was on-site, to infiltrate our bubble.

Silas took my hand, interlacing his fingers with mine. "I have a proposal for you."

"You want me to handle more high-end weddings at your resort?" I asked, anticipating what he was going to say.

He turned my chair so that we were facing each other and held both of my hands.

"What's going on?" His somber expression scared me. Would he propose that we go back to how things were before?

Then he pushed back his chair and dropped to one knee.

My heart galloped in my chest. "Silas?"

Silas took my left hand in both of his. "You came into my life and changed everything—how I viewed life and business and, most importantly, my thoughts on love. I never thought about settling down or spending Saturday mornings with a special someone. But you changed all of that."

I blinked back the tears. "What are you saying?"

"I love you, Gia. I want to spend every Saturday just like this. Will you spend the rest of your life with me, drinking coffee and enjoying the breeze over the water?"

"I'd love to," I said, my heart thumping hard in my chest.

"Will you marry me and be my wife? Will you be my soft place to land at the end of every night?"

I nodded through the blur of tears. "Yes. I'll marry you."

Happiness surged through me as he rested his forehead against mine. "I love you so much. I didn't know what I was going to do if you said no."

"Why would you think that?" I slid off the chair to straddle his lap.

He gave me a look. "Did you forget the part of the proposal where I talked about you challenging me at every turn?"

I laughed, practically giddy with happiness. "I don't remember that."

"I must have forgotten it because I was so nervous you'd say no."

I cupped his jaw with my hands. "I could never say no to you."

He grabbed my wrists. "I want to live here. I want to raise a family in this house. I know your business is elsewhere, but I think we can make this work."

"I've been thinking about expanding the wedding planning business to this area and offering the Annapolis area to Aria or Ireland to be the head wedding planner. Aria wants more responsibility, but I'm not sure which one is right for the position.

"I'm so proud of you."

"Because I finally listened to you and delegated more?" The reason I felt so comfortable doing this now was because of the success of the book and the course. I could finally relax, knowing my business made a consistent profit, and I had plans to increase it.

"We give each other advice and lift each other up." He pulled out a velvet box from his pocket.

"I almost forgot about this."

I was so surprised by the proposal that I hadn't thought about the formalities, like the ring and the wedding.

He slid the yellow diamond onto my ring finger.

"It's gorgeous."

"I wanted something unique and valuable, just like you."

"It's perfect," I murmured as I admired the way it shined in the morning sun.

"You're perfect." Then he kissed me, and I rocked my core against his hardening length. But it was slow and sensual, as if we weren't in a rush to get anywhere. I wanted to enjoy this moment forever.

When he finally pulled back with short kisses, he asked, "Have you thought about *where* we'd get married?"

I frowned because I'd never thought about my wedding. I'd spent so much time planning other people's that I had no idea what I'd want. He shifted me in his arms and lifted me so that we were sitting in one chair.

I rested my head on his shoulder, admiring the view I'd never get enough of. The water. The sun glinting off the surface. Silas's chest under my cheek. "I don't know."

Silas lifted my chin with his finger. "Gia Giovanni, wedding planner extraordinaire, has no idea where she'd hold her wedding?"

"That's right. Getting married wasn't something I thought about."

He kissed me softly, and when he pulled back, I took in the large deck and the flat yard leading to the water. "I love this place. The privacy. The view."

"Would you want to get married here?"

"It could be just our families and friends. Small and private. But I could see it now: twinkly lights strung through the trees, tables and chairs cleared away for a dance floor under the stars. It could be perfect."

He kissed me again. "It is perfect because it's what you want."

"What about you? Don't you have any ideas or thoughts about where you'd want it?"

"This property is my sanctuary, and I can't imagine a better place for us to get married. I wondered if you wanted a big wedding, maybe even a spread in a bridal magazine. I'm positive media outlets will want to cover it."

I shuddered at the thought. "I don't want that attention on me, or the pressure to have a splashy wedding. I want something simple yet elegant. I want something that's us."

And we were this place.

"I'd close down the resort for you."

"You would?" I asked, a little surprised he'd do that.

"Whatever you want."

"Maybe we could close it down for our families, and we could have the rehearsal dinner there."

"I want to give you whatever you want."

"I just want to be with you and love you forever." I wanted an everlasting kind of love, and I had a feeling this thing with Silas would stand the test of time.

"That's the easy part." Then he kissed me until the sun was shining high in the sky.

Bonus Epilogue

SILAS

The trees that lined my driveway were wrapped in white ribbons, and the front porch was covered in flowers. My home was usually a haven from the rest of the world, but today, the grounds were covered with people in various stages of wedding preparation.

Across the cab, my brother, Sebastian, gave me a look. "Are you ready for this?"

"I've been waiting forever for this day." Gia wanted the perfect day, even if it was low-key compared to the other weddings she'd planned. But that didn't mean it was any less elegant. She'd been involved in the planning of every last detail.

As soon as Sebastian pulled his truck up to the porch, Aria opened the door and waved a hand at me. "Come on. Come on. You can't see the bride."

I raised a brow. "She was in my bed this morning."

Aria rolled her eyes and grabbed my hand, tugging me out of the truck. "You can't see her in her dress. You know what I mean. Let's go."

"I'd prefer to see her out of her dress."

"Grooms are impossible. I don't know why I have to deal with them," Aria said teasingly.

"I'll see you at the altar," Sebastian called as I shut the door.

"If all of your brothers are as hot as him, the reception should be interesting," Aria murmured.

"You don't have any more single wedding planners."

"Oh, Gia just hired two more to apprentice with us. I don't think they're dating anyone. At least they haven't mentioned boyfriends, but who knows?

I raised a brow. "I hadn't realized they'd already started working."

"It's like you don't know your fiancée at all. If Gia says she's going to do something, then it's done. That girl has no chill."

"That's just one of the things I love about her." I added a smirk so I wouldn't sound like a lovesick fool, even though that's exactly what I was.

"You two are adorable."

"I wouldn't say that. You're going to ruin my street cred," I grumbled good-naturedly.

Aria pulled the door open to my house. "You did that all by yourself when you crashed our bonfire with your declarations of love and forever. Now Gia's getting ready upstairs, so I'm taking you to the basement."

"It's weird to be escorted around my own house."

"It's one day, and then we'll clean up everything while you're on your honeymoon. By the time you get back, it will be exactly as it was before."

"Mmm. I'm looking forward to that." In truth, I was beyond excited for the wedding itself, and to celebrate at the reception afterward. I didn't want to rush through anything. I wanted to savor every moment of the day I finally made Gia Giovanni my wife.

Downstairs, my brothers, Liam and Wells, stood behind the bar with their white shirts unbuttoned at the top.

Gia's brothers hovered on the other side.

Wells volunteered to play his violin for the ceremony, and Liam and Sebastian would stand beside me. I couldn't be prouder to have them stand up with me.

After finding out about me and Gia, her brothers seemed to have accepted me. I think it helped that I'd proposed. They just wanted to know that I was all in with their sister, and not using her. My love for her was obvious, and that seemed to satisfy them. They just wanted their sister to be happy.

"You ready to become a husband?" Leo asked.

"More than ready. I would have married her the day after the bonfire. We could have eloped, but she wanted to get married here with her friends and family, and I'd do anything to make her happy."

"You're whipped," Liam said.

"And proud of it," I said as they handed me a shot glass. "I'll do one, but that's it. I want to be fully aware of every moment."

"Who knew you were such a sap?" Wells said affectionately.

Sebastian jogged down the steps to join us. "Who knew you'd be the first of us to settle down?"

I placed a hand over my heart. "I'm just more in touch with my emotions."

Seb just raised his brows at me because we both knew that wasn't true. It was Gia who brought out this side of me, and I wasn't afraid for everyone to know how I felt about her.

We raised our glasses and waited for Leo to speak. "To adding another brother to our family."

I nodded, ecstatic that I would soon be officially part of the Giovanni family. "I appreciate it."

Mateo clinked my glass. "Take care of my sister."

"You know I will," I said seriously.

We threw back the dark liquor, the Jäger burning my throat.

Carlo threw his arm around my shoulders. "You know this means you can give us your business advice for free, right?"

I shook my head. "I always gave you advice for free."

Everyone laughed, and when Ireland came down the stairs, we sobered. "It's time."

Everyone scrambled to button their shirts and throw on their jackets. Lily walked around with the boutonnieres, pinning them on our lapels.

"I hope you didn't drink too much," Lily said.

"Just one," Sebastian told her with a wink.

"Don't flirt with the wedding planners or the bridal party," Ireland admonished him.

Sebastian shrugged. "What fun are weddings without hooking up?"

"You're here to celebrate our love, not hook up with anyone," I said to him.

Sebastian threw his tie at me. "I still can't believe Gia would agree to put up with the likes of you forever."

Ireland groaned. "Get it together. We have five minutes for you to be in your places so we can get started. Wells, you're ready. Why don't you warm up?"

"You got it." Then to me, he said, "Good luck. I'm proud of you."

Ireland waited to escort him upstairs.

"You're proud of me?" I asked, a little confused.

"For realizing when you had something great and holding on tight. We should all be that lucky."

"To realize what you have that's maybe right in front of you?" I asked him, trying to understand.

Wells nodded.

"It took me years to figure that out."

"All that matters is that you did," Liam said.

"Thank you for being here, for always supporting me and giving me shit."

Everyone laughed and slapped my back. After that, it was a whirlwind of fixing ties, pinning boutonnieres, and throwing out advice that may or may not have been helpful. I was having a hard time paying attention because I was focused on the moment when Gia would walk down the aisle toward me. Nothing else mattered.

The next thing I knew, I was being ushered to the arbor Harrison custom made for us. It was larger than any I'd seen before, with branches intertwined with real flowers and greenery. I took a steady breath and looked out over the water.

Ireland told me to keep my back to the crowd until it was time to steady my nerves. I hadn't expected to feel so nervous. I think it was because this moment felt so huge to me. I was declaring myself to another person to love and cherish forever. It was a huge responsibility, but I was ready for it.

The music started, and I turned like we'd practiced the night before. My vision was a little blurry as the bridesmaids came down the aisle. Although they'd planned the wedding, the wedding planners were in it too.

That's why Gia had hired a couple of new people to make sure things ran smoothly today. She wanted to relax and enjoy the day.

The last bridesmaid was Harper, and then there was a pause before everyone stood, and Gia walked down the aisle with her father. I only had eyes for her.

She was gorgeous, with her hair pulled back and a veil that hung down her back. Her dress was fitted at the waist but full at the bottom. All the other details were lost to me. She held a large bouquet of red roses. The color was stunning next to the white dress and her beautiful face.

When she reached me, Mr. G. placed her hand in mine, and I promised to take care of her forever. He nodded and said, "See that you do."

And then her fingers were interlaced with mine, and we turned to face each other, with the preacher to my right. He started speaking to the guests, but I couldn't hear a word he was saying.

Gia squeezed my hands and whispered, "I love you."

"I love you too."

Her eyes shone with love and emotion. "I can't believe we're here."

"I can. I think on some level I always knew." I lowered my forehead to hers, soaking in the moment. The preacher's words washed over us, and the hush of the crowd settled in my chest. This was our moment, and I'd never forget any part of it.

I lifted my head, and we listened to the preacher, following his prompts, and recited the vows we'd prepared together. The crowd laughed when we talked about loving each other despite any disagreements.

I blocked it all out because nothing mattered except her gaze on me and her hands in mine.

When we were declared husband and wife, we headed down the aisle, and I couldn't resist holding our joined hands in the air. This union with Gia didn't come easy, but I wouldn't have had it any other way. Our journey was long and unique, but it was ours.

We posed for pictures, and as soon as Abby said we were done, I hauled Gia into a nearby closet.

"What are we doing here?" she asked when I closed the door behind us.

"Going back to where it all began." I backed her up against the wall.

"What are you—"

I knelt on the floor in front of her and gathered her skirts. "We only have a few minutes. Can you be quiet?"

"Absolutely," she said, her voice a little breathless.

Her fingers tangled in my hair as the other hand held up her skirts for me. It wouldn't be easy, but nothing with Gia was.

I loved the garters I found under her skirt, and the tiny strip of white lace that was easy to push aside. I licked and sucked and devoured her with my mouth and fingers. She couldn't stifle her cries, but hopefully, no one heard us. The music was loud, and everyone had drinks and appetizers.

When she went over, her body shuddering in my arms, I knew our lives wouldn't be predictable or boring. Gia would always challenge me and push me to be a better man, and I wouldn't have it any other way.

When she was dressed and I stood in front of her, she asked, "What are we doing?"

"Taking a moment to just be us before we have to go out there."

She looked up at me. "I think this might be my favorite part of the day."

I grinned. "How can you know that when we haven't even shown up to our reception yet?"

"These moments when I'm alone with you are the best. Every time I think I can't love you more, I do. You somehow made the biggest day of our lives more meaningful."

I dipped my chin. "Just to be sure, you're talking about me dragging you into a closet—again."

She smiled mischievously. "It's always an adventure with you."

"Should we get on our boat and sail away now?" I'd planned on sailing to our private cove, making love, and sleeping until we needed to be at the airport to go on our honeymoon tomorrow. I wanted to revisit everything that made our initial coming together so special, starting with this moment.

She patted my chest. "We only have a few more hours to go, and we spent so much time planning the perfect party. We should enjoy it."

"Spoken like a true wedding planner." I kissed her. "I'll give you a few more hours, but then you're mine."

She grinned. "Forever."

I hope you loved Gia and Silas's story! Ireland and Emmett's romance is next in *Runaway Love*!

Special Edition Bundles

If you prefer to read by trope:

Brother's Best Friend

Childhood Crush

Contractors

Enemies to Lovers

Fake Relationship

First in Series

Forbidden Love

Friends to Lovers

Grumpy Meets Sunshine

Hot Heroes

Office Romance

Second Chance Romance

Single Dad

Single Mom

Single Parent

Sports Romance

If you prefer to read series:

All I Want

Annapolis Harbor

Ever After

Mountain Haven

Second Chance Harbor

If you prefer to read paperbacks:

All I Want Series

Annapolis Harbor

Brother's Best Friend

Childhood Crush

Enemies to Lovers

Grumpy Meets Sunshine

Hot Heroes

Office Romance

Second Chance Harbor

Single Mom

Sports Romance

Books by Lea Coll

The Monroe Brothers

Runaway Love

Finding Sunshine

Trusting Forever

Endless Hope

Ever After Series

Feel My Love

The Way You Are

Love Me Like You Do

Give Me a Reason

Somebody to Love

Everything About You

Mountain Haven Series

Infamous Love

Adventurous Love

Impulsive Love

Tempting Love

Inescapable Love

Forbidden Love

Second Chance Harbor Series

Fighting Chance

One More Chance

Lucky Chance

Download a free novella, when you sign up for her newsletter.

To learn more about her books, please visit her website.

About the Author

Lea Coll is a USA Today Bestselling Author of sweet and sexy happily ever afters. She worked as a trial attorney for over ten years. Now she stays home with her three children, plotting stories while fetching snacks and running them back and forth to activities. She enjoys the freedom of writing romance after years of legal writing.

She currently resides in Maryland with her family.

Check out Lea's books on her shop.

Get a free novella when you sign up for Lea's newsletter.

Made in United States
North Haven, CT
15 October 2023

42770244R00157